LIFE
—— OVER ——
DEATH

GRANT W. FLETCHER

Grant W. Fletcher

Life Over Death

5th Edition – November 2016

ISBN – 13: 978-1499674934

Published by CreateSpace – www.createspace.com

Printed in the United States

Grant W. Fletcher

Nashville, Tennessee

http://grantwfletcher.com/index.html

Cover art designed by Jen McCuiston

Many thanks to all who helped guide this, my first story, to its completion. Transforming thoughts and ideas into a novel for all to read is a frightening experience. There is an exposure that comes with this process opening an author up to criticism and judgment that is not always forgiving. However, telling a story that generates conversation and deeper discussion is far more gratifying than the criticism is painful. When a story creeps into the conscience, sometimes it just can't be confined.

I am under no illusion that this is the next great American Novel. I don't place myself into the ranks of any leading authors of our time and I certainly have much to learn and improve upon with character development, syntax, and overall style. However, I wrote a story nonetheless.

I <u>Hope</u> you enjoy the read!

-grant

Grant W. Fletcher

LIFE
—— OVER ——
DEATH

GRANT W. FLETCHER

Chapter One

"When hope is *not* pinned wriggling onto a shiny image or expectation, it sometimes floats forth and opens."
---Anne Lamott

Marina Kostitsen played the part of a casual tourist as she strolled along Beale Street soaking in the breath and soul of Memphis' legendary blues area. The charade was necessary to avoid the attention she might attract if it appeared she was waiting for someone in particular. Although cleaned up from years past, the look and feel of Beale Street was a bit more neon and touristy than she remembered from her previous visit almost eight years ago. At that time, she was with college girlfriends celebrating the pending nuptials of her former roommate. They were carefree and deeply intoxicated then, marching down the street with tiaras and banners proclaiming the end of the golden single era, for one of them at least. She began to wonder… if she knew then what would be given to her would she have changed anything of the past eight years? This internal debate consumed her, often to the point of exhaustion. Irrefutably, the gift had changed her. But had it really redirected her moral compass? Had it altered the course of her life so drastically that she wouldn't recognize herself had the gift not been given? She had no time for the debate now, but she knew her mind wouldn't let it go. As it had a thousand times over the last nine months, she would return to the endless questioning. *Why couldn't my brain accept the verdict after the first time I presented the closing arguments?* Guilt was the obvious answer. *This debate…this quest for certitude is insatiable!*

She stared at her tall, thirty-one-year-old reflection in the window of a cheap gift shop when she noticed Jerry Caruthers leaving his office building and making a direct bee-line to the parking lot behind BB King's Blues Club. He was probably heading straight to the high school gym to catch the end of the boys' junior varsity basketball practice where he could continue courting his next victim.

Sick fuck! Not today, Mr. Perv, Marina thought to herself. As he crossed Beale Street, Marina turned and paced herself to reach him as he stepped onto the sidewalk. She took a deep breath...sighed...and approached the round man of fifty-two.

"Robert? Is that you? It's been so long but you look just the ...". Marina put her hand firmly on the man's shoulder and gave a slight squeeze.

"I think you have mistaken me for someone else, young lady," Jerry Caruthers stated with agitation and surprise. "I suggest you be sure of your friends before you approach a married man on the street and fondle him in public."

"Oh, I'm sorry. It's just that you look so much like Robert. He's an old family friend and I haven't seen him since he moved to Memphis." Marina inwardly cringed as she released the man's shoulder, disgusted by the invisible slime that surely contaminated her. "I am so sorry. I hope I haven't caused you any embarrassment...in public."

"Not unless this conversation continues," he retorted. "Now if you will excuse me I have a deposition appointment to attend."

Marina stood still as Jerry slithered around her and continued walking briskly south on Beale toward the parking garage. She watched as he walked away, following his progress past A. Schwab and Club 152 before he disappeared around the corner. Pleased with the encounter, she lingered on the sidewalk casually observing the comings and goings of the everyday people on the street. Some leaving work, some grabbing a late lunch, some getting ready for a night of drowning their sorrows to the slow rhythmic tones of the blues, supporting the aura of self-pity or remembrance of better times. As a momentary respite from her all-consuming task, she let her mind slip away to absorb the soul of Beale Street.

How could the blues sound so sad and yet be so healing? If you really understood how the music and lyrics were woven together there was actually more expression of hope than despair. That was the magic of the blues...a genre of music born in a time of great human injustice and suffering yet celebrating the joy of life and the simple pleasures it can offer. Hope.

Sirens in the distance seemed to be a heartfelt rhythmic wail infused into the music swelling out of the open door of a nearby club. She awoke from her thoughts and quickly walked to the south corner where the exit to a parking garage spilled its patrons onto South 2nd Street. The sirens got louder as they approached the intersection where she waited. Traffic was light at two o'clock in the afternoon, so the emergency vehicle easily navigated its way to save the life of some afflicted soul. Standing frozen in anticipation of the unknown, she caught a glimpse of a black Mercedes frantically exiting the garage in an attempt to be the first car to get somewhere. Just as the Mercedes turned onto South 2nd Street without a thought of yielding, the 15-ton fire truck, with sirens wailing, slammed broadside into the Mercedes Benz, its momentum driving the car into a metal light pole. By the time the fire truck came to a stop, the Mercedes looked like a piece of aluminum foil folded into an almost perfect V around the unyielding metal pole. The interior space between the driver-side door and the passenger door was probably less than 24 inches and housed the lifeless remains of the perverted 245-pound 5'6" Jerry Caruthers.

"No more sick games with children, you prick...it's time to meet Hope," Marina whispered quietly to herself.

Chapter Two

Running along the broken sidewalk provided the best release from the daily grind. It allowed time for the mind to wander and the soul to refresh. The sidewalk that had long needed replacement ran half a mile along Stillmeadow Elementary School then bent around Cruzan Street for another mile and a half before intersecting Hampton road. The first two miles of the run were the best for Tom —an energizing jaunt of dodging holes and cracks that he fantasized as canyons in a Gulliver's Travels-type world. Between the cracks were islands of safety that demanded precise but unregulated paces as he hopped from one safe haven to the next. He lurched and swayed like a giant lumbering across a land riddled with peril from unknown and barely seen creatures that loomed from the dark places of a fantasy world. An outsider observing Tom's swerving, jumping stride would think something was wrong with this human behavior. For Tom, the stretch between the school and the Hampton Road intersection was a game where he circumnavigated the globe, providing a brief escape into an alternate universe to counter the boredom of running. At Hampton Road, the concrete sidewalk was new and the fantasyland disappeared into a steady pace of expansion joints with little care of stepping on a crack. The final mile along Hampton road brought him back to the school where real life came barreling back into focus. At this point in the run, he would look, observe, and appreciate his south Nashville neighborhood. He loved the mix of houses – old small compact houses sidled up to sprawling, single-story ranch houses perfectly centered on large one-acre and larger plots. It was an old neighborhood, hence the large lot size, with just enough new, two-story replacement houses to keep the scenery interesting. It was one of the few areas in the main hub of

Nashville to successfully maintain its integrity. Too many areas had suffered from a lack of building restrictions and had been inundated with a flurry of cheap, new houses replacing old, small teardowns. Some had even split lots in half and built two cheap monstrosities to replace one quaint, established home. His neighborhood had restricted splitting lots and multi-dwellings, which left a comfortable, neighborhood feel but with individual privacy. It was easy to run here. As he walked the remaining half-mile to his house, he began transitioning his mind back to his family, work, and the world that makes up everyone's reality. This twice-weekly routine was the norm for Tom since he turned 40 and gave him time to let his mind wander to places it usually was not allowed to venture.

The stroll back to the house was occupied thinking of a CNN segment he saw the previous day polling average Americans about what they believed hope really was. What constituted hope and where could hope be found? Answers from the chum bucket of polled respondents ranged from 'hope in a better future for the next generation' to 'hope for the winning lottery ticket.' As a sampling of the populace polled, the reporter interviewed a handful of "people on the street" so they could elaborate on their definition of hope and how it could be found. One woman's response stuck with Tom and generated an internal argument about his belief and understanding of hope:

> "Hope is the fleeting idea that comes and goes within a person's mind that something good will come of a bad situation. Hope can appear without warning, usually in extreme circumstances, or be contrived to deny the possibility of a bad outcome. It makes you wonder if it's an innate desire for good things to happen or a selfish need for your own improvement in life. Just as suddenly as it appears, it disappears…explained as fate or circumstance when the situation is resolved…for good or bad. True hope is not religious. It's a human instinct. A defense against circumstances that may be beyond our control."

While acknowledging some truth to the woman's response, Tom believed that all hope came from the Christian divine—God. It was God and Christianity that provided hope even in the most dismal situations. Hope was the basis of faith. Was it really true that so many people brushed off the resolution of a situation where hope had intervened as nothing more than circumstance? Had our predominantly Christian society in America really become that cynical of the possibility of divine intervention? The answers to these two questions came easily to Tom—definitely yes and yes. He had come to terms long ago with the attitude held by so many to equate good or bad fortune with luck or the lack thereof. Maybe his strict Christian upbringing had closed his eyes to the possibility that hope was something that could live and be validated in the hearts of non-believers. Thoughts like this troubled Tom and invoked religious doubts that left him feeling guilty about his own faith. It was a subject he was unwilling to question. He had been trained to accept the presence of God on earth without question. Blind faith. It had served him well so far, but recently, doubts associated with the presence of the divine had crept into his psyche as he watched more and more tragedy unfold in the world. Where is our God? Where is *my* God? Is He still active in the world at play?

Reaching for the cold door handle of his cozy home, Tom pushed away the questions, unwilling to search deeper for an answer. It was not his job to find an answer. It was his job to just believe.

Walking into the kitchen that badly needed updating, he surveyed his family as they readied for the day. Laura, his wife, was packing lunches while the kids finished their breakfast at the square kitchen table neatly designed for a family of four.

"How was your run, honey?"

"Solved all the world's problems in three miles!"

"I thought you were an 'architecter' not the President of the United States?" chimed in his six-year-old daughter, Anna.

"I am and if we could find a President that could solve the world's problems then he would be a true miracle sent straight from Heaven" replied Tom.

"But I thought that <u>was</u> the President's job" asked a confused Anna.

With the confidence of an adult, Brady, who had recently turned 10 said, "The President's job is to get elected as many times as possible by telling everyone what's wrong with his enemies."

Laura, always the teacher even of a subject way above a six-year-old's head, stated, "Your father is an ar-chi-tect," drawing the word out to correct her daughter's mispronunciation, "and designs buildings for people to live and work in. The President's job is to make sure all the American people are free, safe, and live by the rules that other parts of the government set up. He doesn't solve the problems of other countries…at least not usually."

"So says Mrs. Roddin the educator," Tom poked at his wife. He and Laura had been married for 13 years and so far had maneuvered through the typical strains of any marriage in 21st century. They had settled into a comfortable partnership where respect was earned with each new trial and love grew stronger with each passing victory in life. They certainly weren't perfect, but their life together represented a union that was designed to last. She taught middle school social studies at one of the metro public schools and devoted an inordinate amount of time to preparing creative lessons designed to drag out every last bit of interest from emerging tweens on a subject that was inherently boring to that age group. Her success had garnered three straight "Teacher of the Year" awards from the High Ridge Middle School and she was nominated as state Teacher of the Year for two of those three years. Although losing out to a math teacher both times, her statewide recognition brought a level of satisfaction that made her late hours of lesson planning well worth the sacrifices.

Turning to the kids, Tom asked enthusiastically, "So what are we going to learn today in school?"

"How to write in cursive. We're working on s, t, and v today," stated Brady without any of Tom's enthusiasm.

"We're still trying to color inside the lines and play the recorder," said Anna.

"OK then, let's write cursive like an ancient scribe and color like Monet." Tom was still trying to get the kids excited about learning despite their bored tones.

"What does *money* have to do with coloring?" questioned Anna.

"That's what you learn in third grade!" said Tom, closing the conversation.

After more encouraging banter and putting the finishing touches on the lunch boxes, Tom kissed the kids, groped his wife with all the love and affection two adults were allowed to show in the presence of their children, and escorted them to the door for a day full of adventure and learning. He walked to the bedroom, turned on the shower, and cranked up the volume on the TVs as part of his morning ritual of CNN in the bathroom and Fox News in the bedroom while getting dressed.

While transitioning between CNN and Fox, Tom glanced at the bed and noticed a note card. A playful smile panned across his face as he anticipated the wording of the sensual note from his wife about what he hoped was an invitation for an upcoming tryst.

"I'll bet she's suggesting locking the kids in the washing machine tub for an hour while we have our way with each other!"

He finished dressing, grabbed the note, and headed out the door for his 15-minute drive to work. Settling in at his desk, he checked his email, sent instructions to a junior architect on the

Galston project, and weighed his schedule for the day to see if attending Brady's basketball practice was in the cards for this afternoon. Around 9:30 a.m. he sat back in his chair and thought about the date—November 11, 2011.

"Hmmm. 11/11/11. Ominous or hopeful...what would the mystery woman from CNN say about that?"

Remembering the note, he reached in his coat pocket and removed the card. As he looked at the print and presentation, he realized it was not his wife's handwriting, but rather some sort of fancy script. Like calligraphy but old style. Was this an invitation to a party or a new manner of keeping things exciting between them?

"Surely that nickel-ass of a wife of mine didn't pay to have a sensual message printed on a card?"

A baffled look replaced his natural half-smile expression as he read the card.

You, Mr. Roddin, have been given the ultimate choice of free will, but not for yourself...only for others. You have been given the chance to create 10 miracles in exchange for 10 deaths. You must decide who gets which. Hearts are easily tested, but purity keeps them from being corrupt. More to come...

Hope

Chapter Three

Marina drove the three hours from Memphis to Nashville in her rental car thinking through the meeting she was about to have with an unknown and possibly unwilling man. She wasn't dreading the meeting but was full of anxiety about how she would handle the multitude of scenarios that could arise. For the nine months since she had received the gift of hope, Marina had wondered if this meeting would even be assigned to her. She knew it probably would but at the same time, the place, person, and date of the meeting was a total mystery until 48 hours ago. How convenient that the location was close to her most recent planned encounter. As she thought about the best approach for convincing the man to accept the proposal that lay out before him, she remembered her own encounter nine months earlier with Aarzu.

Marina had spent an hour and a half with Aarzu when he introduced himself to her on February 24, 2011. Ninety minutes of a rollercoaster ride of emotions. Shock, denial, confusion, anger, understanding, fear and ultimately a deep love for the 13-year-old boy who sat across from her. He possessed the calm wisdom of an ancient soul. Yet there he was, a young, handsome Palestinian boy explaining a mystery to her beyond most people's comprehension and belief. Just as she was about to mentally anoint him some sort of modern-day prophet, he would giggle at a question or even one of his answers as if they were talking about which girl in his grade was the cutest. The jumping back and forth between mystery and reality made the conversation surreal, almost forgettable. Yet even now, almost nine months later, she remembered every word of their conversation. More importantly, she remembered her own calmness and clarity when he finally stood up and said, "I was promised some homemade ice cream by my uncle and I think it's ready now. It was very nice to meet you. Like my own instructor...and probably like my instructor's instructor...ha, and I guess like me...you have a good heart. Corrupt hearts don't get to make these kinds of choices." And then he was off.

Marina never spoke with Aarzu again. She stayed at the café table by the window for another hour processing all that had been said between them. The more she processed, the more she understood the implications of the gift. The more she respected the ancient boy.

As she drove, her anxiety led her back to the question that continually shrouded her actions in doubt. It was a debate she had become all too familiar with since that strange day in February. *Would she have done things differently over the short course of her adulthood if she knew what gift would be given her?* Marina knew she was generally a good person. She believed the human spirit was designed to be gracious and giving. It was designed to help others and provide Hope for those in desperate need of a good story. But the influences of society and the greed it perpetuated made her question the current state of human evolution. How could the good deeds of so many be overwhelmingly concealed by the manipulation and self-serving actions of people who somehow dominated our social landscape? How could the validation of Hope be so tightly tucked away in society's consciousness, hidden away like an attic trunk that rarely got opened to appreciate its musty contents? We were peppered daily by a barrage of news about the famous, powerful, rich—people who believed they were a higher race in life and deserve all the excesses, especially if it was more than what their neighbors had. And yet, these were the people we aspired to be. They only inspired false Hope. A Hope that we too deserved to live like them and be a dominant figure in the world's social landscape while totally ignoring the more common elements of Hope...like believing we could overcome a disease. Believing children deserved not to be victimized. Believing that dignity could come at the end of life when the mind was unwilling to compromise with senility. Where were the stories that should dominate the news and be the foundation of a moral framework relating to people's actions that validated Hope for others? They seemed to be lost. What happened to "and the meek shall inherit the earth?"

"Well, good luck with that!" she said to the empty car. I guess meekness will be an Internet commodity sold to the highest bidder as soon as the earth is up for auction. The meek will be standing around saying "Can we just take the moon and leave all you idiots here on earth? " *No...I don't think I would have done things differently over the years even with the knowledge I have now. Even when I am done, I will still search my small universe to champion people who give a shit about other people by validating their Hope in better things to come.* Hope had not necessarily been redefined for Marina since February, but rather it had been clarified for her. It required action, sometimes by strangers, to improve the lot of someone deserving. Validation. People needed to begin believing again that, no matter how dire their situation, no matter how vile their victimization, circumstances could change for the better. Hope could be validated by actions that gave everyone an equal share of worthiness for the value of their life. It didn't mean everyone should be equal. That was unrealistic. Class division was a natural human tendency and one that should and would survive to the end of mankind. Without a division of classes, humans would be unproductive, ignorant, and quickly nonexistent. An equal share of worthiness meant everyone deserved to be a part of the human society. Don't abandon Hope just because your social standing was lower than someone else's. We all deserved some dignity to go along with our lot in life. Providing that dignity, the worthiness, was what Marina intended to carry forward after her journey with the gift was completed.

She suddenly realized it had happened again...she had justified her actions of the last nine months by quelling the internal argument that kept questioning her moral bearing...her true north. Finding a quick end to the argument was becoming easier as the gift neared its ending point for her. The debates in the early stages were wrought with good and evil more equally wrangling for control. After her first few choices she thought

12

for sure the darkness would prevail. But as time passed, the goodness of her journey…of her choices…began to make more sense.

As she crossed the Tennessee River, 60 miles west of her destination in Nashville, her anxiety shifted. The doubt surrounding her choices had been quelled…for now. The new anxiety was rooted in whether she would be able to convey the justification for the gift to the man she was about to meet. Convincing herself was one thing. Convincing a potentially reluctant stranger was a serious challenge—one she desperately needed to script in her mind.

Chapter Four

Tom was finishing up a working lunch in the conference room with his project team when he remembered the note and decided to call his wife during school recess. He was leading a team of junior architects on a strip mall project and they had been discussing plans, schedules, and assignments all morning and into lunch. They had wrapped things up and he only had one more firm commitment for the day, which meant he might make Brady's basketball practice after all. He texted Laura to see if recess was still on and if she had time for a quick call.

"Yes but over soon. Not called recess...7th grade has graduated to 'break'. Call me".

He touched her name on his phone and within seconds a soft, sweet, sexy voice was saying, "Hello matador. What's your pleasure?"

"How about one hour of uninterrupted, uninhibited playtime with my favorite mistress?" he purred.

"Well, check with your wife to see about your free time and maybe she'll approve of a rendezvous with your mistress" Laura mused.

"She said that's fine and I am free to tryst away...she likes you, ya know."

"Does she now? Well, maybe I can break away Thursday September 14th 2021 when the kids are more independent and scattering to the four winds. I should have the bubble gum out of my hair by then and maybe enough energy to last an entire hour! By the way, will you be able to make it to Brady's practice today?"

"I thought we were still negotiating a date? One that might actually take place this century?"

"Mistresses don't negotiate. They just state the conditions and you're free to participate if you like."

"I think I need a new mistress. I have one appointment at 2:00, so I should be over there by 3:30. Brady and I will be home around 5:00. Are you taking Anna to Target for her initial Christmas list development?"

"Yep. She grabbed a notecard from my stationary box this morning to write everything down. Plain paper is just not good enough for Santa."

"Oh, and did someone else get into the stationary box this morning?" he jokingly prompted her hoping to reveal the mystery behind her cryptic note.

"What do you mean?" she said flatly.

"I found a note card on the bed this morning. I was hoping it was one of your 'invitation' notes, hence the mistress negotiations."

"Not me. Anna must have dropped one by accident while she was picking out the cleanest, whitest card for the list."

"Then who wrote…" A clamor of activity filled the earpiece in Tom's phone as the 7th graders returned from break. Laura gave some quick settling instructions to the kids and returned her attention to Tom.

"Back to work. I'll see about improving that 2021 date. Anna and I will pick up dinner on the way home and see you boys around 5:30. Chinese ok?"

"Sounds great. Pick up enough for my mistress too…I may bring her home to meet the fam. Love you."

"You too, dear. I'll have a strong latte at Target so maybe I can stay up past the kids bedtime tonight," she whispered into the phone.

Tom was even more baffled by the note now. He took it out and re-read the message. The more he examined it, the more it looked like pen ink instead of printed ink. But who in the world had that kind of perfect handwriting? After reading the message a third time, he could only guess that it was some type of printing example that was stuck in the middle of the stationary box to remind the consumer what could be done with the notecards. *A strange message for advertising...and how did they get my name*? He tucked it away making a mental note to show it to Laura tonight. Maybe the stationary company needed a call so they could explain the meaning behind their odd advertising scheme. This wasn't the best tag line for a stationary company...or any company for that matter.

For the next 40 minutes or so, Tom prepared as best he could for his 2:00 appointment. There wasn't much to work with since the client had provided very little detail over the phone about the potential project. All he knew was that they had some interest in designing a stand-alone 65,000-square-foot spa or retreat center in Phoenix. They had seen his firm's work on a similar project in Scottsdale and wanted to talk through some ideas. It was odd that they were insistent on meeting alone with him even though the Scottsdale project was done by Barry Johnston, another senior architect and a full partner in the firm. Barry had been with the firm for 15 years and had become a bit stale in Tom's mind. He wasn't the nicest of guys and, as of late, seemed to ride on the coattails of more equipped coworkers, but he had connections that brought in a lot of high-end clients. More times than not, the junior architects performed all the magic on Barry's projects, yet he always took full credit for the designs and rarely shared any gratitude for their progressive approach to creating wonderful buildings and facades. The behind-the-scenes joke with the junior architects was that working on a Barry Johnston project meant that you would never make senior level. You couldn't even use his projects as an example in your own portfolio because he monitored and edited every junior level architect's profile to ensure they didn't take credit for any of 'his' designs. He had run off more than a few really promising folks in the firm purely out of fear that someone would discover his ego was much larger than his capabilities. Maybe this new client had heard of Barry's pretense and therefore had specifically requested someone other than him. No matter. Tom had put together the normal new client presentation material and had chatted with the lead junior architect from the Scottsdale project to gather information about any nuances with Arizona rules, available building materials, and general contractor experiences. He loved new projects, especially stand-alone structures. He had been working strip mall design and renovation for nearly the entire year and welcomed a chance to change the pace and stretch out again.

At precisely 1:58, Marge called his line to tell him his 2:00 had arrived.

"Come on down…you're the next contestant on the Price is Right", he told Marge.

With a slight laugh and a loving 'you're a dork' tone, Marge replied, "I'll bring her right over."

Tom rose from his desk and walked toward his office door right about the time Marge presented the new client.

"Ms. Kostitsen, did I say that right? Meet Tom Roddin. Tom, Ms. Kostitsen."

Taken aback by his instant recognition of the client, he managed to stammer, "It's a pleasure to meet you, Ms. Kostitsen. Please have a seat. Is there anything we can get you? Coffee, water, soft drink?"

"No thank you. I appreciate you seeing me on such short notice and with so little information."

"Thanks, Marge. Your reward for the introduction will be in next year's check," he joked. Turning to Marina he said, "We try to take care of Marge since she has to put up with all our architectural oddities on a daily basis."

"Make sure he stays focused on you for the entire meeting," Marge retorted. "He tends to daydream about ways to make life miserable for me if he is not engaged. Let me know if you need saving Ms. Kostitsen."

Appreciating the good-natured bantering between boss and plebe, Marina replied, "I think I'll be able to pique his interest long enough to spare you any misery...at least for today. But keep your phone handy in case I need to press the panic button."

Tom was going to like this project. Hopefully he could close the deal and this was not just a courtesy visit for a third-party bid to justify their first choice.

Tom sat down in a chair next to his prospective client and said, "What can we do for you Ms. Kostitsen? "

"Please, call me Marina."

"I understand you are interested in designing a structure for a spa or retreat facility, Marina. How did you hear about our small firm here in Nashville all the way out in Phoenix?"

"Well..." a bit embarrassed Marina fumbled for the opening words despite her preparation for the encounter. "I'm afraid I've come here under somewhat false pretenses. I wanted to talk to you about Hope".

"Hope?" Tom wasn't ready to admit his recognition of the woman.

"Yes Hope. I believe we have something in common that I need to share with you."

"And what is that?"

"You and I, and presumably others as well, have been given a gift related to Hope. Do you believe in Hope, Tom?"

"You're the woman from CNN. The poll...about what hope means and where it can be found."

"You saw that." It wasn't as much a question as it was a statement.

Tom's mind began to reel. The interview, the note, the strangeness of her presence at his office suddenly made him dizzy, like the moment you realize you've had one too many glasses of wine. Awkwardly, he stuttered, "Your response was...well...very real...and cynical...but in a way that showed true understanding of human nature. It really grabbed my attention and disrupted the normal 'escape-from-reality' thoughts on my run this morning. It sounded as if you didn't think hope was something our current society could appreciate or deserved to experience."

"Quite the opposite. I think Hope is essential in our lives, especially in our current society. I just think Hope has been demoted to fantasy in the eyes of too many people. True Hope has been diluted by fantasy hope, making Hope, in general less miraculous."

"Come again?"

"People have been brainwashed into hoping for the wrong things, which dilutes the validation of real Hope. Hope that can actually make people feel better about their lot in life."

"Isn't hope part of a person's faith that keeps people believing in a better outcome when faced with desperate circumstances?" Tom challenged.

"Absolutely. Depending on one's faith, Hope is all about positive outcomes. But it's more than that. I believe Hope is a moral driver in mankind's actions. With true Hope comes miracles. With miracles comes a desire to be better fathers, daughters, mothers, neighbors, co-workers...you name it. It gives society a reason to believe that good things will come from good actions. It validates a person's legitimacy in life no matter their social standing."

"I'm having trouble making the connection between miracles and the desire to be good. People will do whatever they have to in order to be part of a 'miracle'. Hell, they'll try to buy miracles. Like putting themselves in reality TV shows in the hope that their 15 minutes of fame lasts a lifetime. It's a miracle!" Tom mockingly shouted with hands in the air.

"I'm talking about true miracles. Miracles of life...and miracles of death," Marina said softly.

The last statement pushed his already bursting curiosity over the edge as he tied the relationship of the note to their conversation. Miracles...that was the fifth time she had used that word and now she was using it in the context of life AND death. A surreal feeling engulfed his whole body and mind. *Am I daydreaming?* he thought to himself. Who is this woman that made an appointment with an architect for no architectural reason and is talking to me about hope? Did she write the note? Is this a joke from the staff?

Marina absorbed his stare in complete silence for what must have been 30 or 40 seconds. She could see the struggle in his mind...his confusion with the relevancy between her presence and his note. Next would come the anger. Then it would be her turn to provide the clarity and acceptance he needed to begin his own journey. Aarzu had handled their encounter with such perfection and grace that she wondered if it was easier to accept instructions from a child as opposed to a strange adult. *Give him a moment and let him release his anger before he can move on to understanding*, she instructed herself.

"Who are you and why are you here? Is this some kind of joke or test?" Tom tried to stay calm despite his building agitation.

"Not at all. It's about the gift of Hope", she said with a steady, sympathetic voice. "I know about the note."

Unable to hide his agitation, Tom said, "What note?"

"The gift of Hope note. It's ok…I received one too."

Unsure of whether to acknowledge the note or call her crazy and escort her out of the building, he said, "And what is the gift of hope note?"

"It's what my instructor called it. Let me tell you a brief story. The day after receiving my note I met a 13-year-old Muslim boy from Palestine named Aarzu. He approached me one day in a coffee house and said 'I'm here as your instructor'. Having no clue what this polite young man was talking about, I quickly told him I wasn't interested in buying any instructions. He giggled, and said 'No, it's free. It's about your note…your gift of Hope'. Like you, Tom, I nearly fell out of my seat from shock since I had told no one about the note. In a very matter-of-fact manner—typical of adults—I denied any knowledge of the note and asked him what he really wanted and who he was. After another childish giggle and a little roll of his eyes, he told me how he had received his note 18 months before. His instructor, ironically enough, was an older Israeli man who was nearly killed on his trip to the West Bank to meet Aarzu. 'The man gave me instructions on the gift of Hope, the rules or guidelines, and then disappeared never to be heard from again,' said Aarzu. 'Now it is my time to share the instructions with you,' he told me. Confused, I listened as this young boy explained the gift of Hope to me with an understanding of life that was way beyond his years. He was like a Gandhi or the Dalai Lama or something, but wrapped in this boyish, pimple-faced body. He delivered his instructions in an unbiased stream of clear statements. I was totally floored by what was happening to me. Once my confusion, anger, and fear subsided, I was actually able to ask some real questions about the…process…and what it all meant. An hour and a half after he introduced himself to me, he left. That was February 24th of this year."

"What did your note say?" Tom asked hesitantly.

"Same as yours, I presume. 10 miracles for 10 deaths."

Shocked at the reality of her knowledge, Tom was still battling the thought that this was some sort of joke. "And you have been given this...power?"

"Power, no. Gift, yes. It's a gift to make choices that confirm Hope."

"Killing people is not a gift, it is a sin according to my beliefs."

"Mine too even though I am totally agnostic. But this is different. We can choose a death that creates a good outcome. A death may bring comfort. It may give Hope to other people who knew and potentially suffered under the deceased. It can provide Hope."

"That is murder...in the first degree," said Tom defiantly.

"It depends on your moral boundary. Could you relieve a person from life if it meant saving many other people?"

"I can see the possible good but murder is still a sin."

"I believe the pure heart sees sin as letting evil continue unchecked. Could you turn a blind eye to someone hurting or even killing children?"

"No, but I could turn them over to the authorities."

"Yes, you could. And then maybe, just maybe that person would get convicted after making the child expose themselves to the courts, the media, their peers. For certain situations I see the gift as a way to save hurt for the victims and, more importantly, a means to keep it from happening to another...and another...and so on. It's not simple and it certainly has led to some soul searching for me. Just because I am agnostic does not mean I haven't struggled with the moral boundary that is crossed with taking a human life."

"Aren't you kind of playing God?" asked Tom.

"No. I see it as making a choice that God or *something* has asked you to make. Again, as Aarzu said, only people with pure hearts are given the gift of Hope. I believe that and have learned to trust that my own heart is pure."

"What if God or *something* makes a mistake and gives the gift to someone who is not so pure?"

"You should know from your own faith that God doesn't make mistakes. He sees into the heart far deeper than we see into our own heart and soul. I know He didn't make a mistake with Aarzu and I am confident He hasn't made one with me either."

"For a non-believer you sure make a lot of references to God," Tom said in a somewhat challenging manner.

"It's easier when presenting the justification to you...a devout Christian man. I have my doubts about the God you refer to, but *something* is giving us this gift."

Tom shrugged off her rebuttal and realized his comment was unfair. "What is your count...or your number of...how many sentences have you carried out?" stumbled Tom, still trying to absorb her justification for murder.

With a slight grin despite the serious nature of the subject, Marina replied, "7/9."

"7/9? What's that?"

"7 over 9. You have 10 over 10 total or, as Aarzu called it, life over death. It's like a fraction—life is the numerator, death is the denominator. I am 7 over 9."

"You've been busy this year", Tom said a little too sarcastically.

"It's been almost nine months, but it feels like the gift has been with me for a thousand years. Not as a burden, but more as enlightenment."

"How do you do it? Do you stab, shoot, or strangle your denominator victims?"

"No, nothing like that. Once you've made up your mind about either 'victim' as you incorrectly call them, it's all taken care of by a slight squeeze on their shoulder. You must make physical contact with the recipient and apparently only on the shoulder in order to pass on the...'sentence'."

"Do they fall down dead right there on the spot like after Spock administers the Vulcan grip?"

Marina chuckled lightly. "No, the denominators are relieved of their duties in a variety of ways...auto accidents, heart attacks, crime victims, whatever suits the environment or the nature of their own moral crime."

"Do you witness their death?"

"Yes. It usually takes place within 15 to 30 minutes of your contact. Aarzu said the witnessing of the denominator, as we are calling it, was essential to ensure we don't randomly fill our quota without thoroughly understanding the reason for our choice. I didn't fully get his meaning until after number 3. Watching a person die helps validate your choice in some strange way. It very much makes you carefully consider why you made a particular choice and what choice to make for other recipients."

"Isn't this a bit narcissistic...to believe that we have been chosen by God or *something* to act like a God or *something* and play the grim reaper for people you don't know? What's the mythological story of the person who thought he was a god and flew into the sun? It's not right for me or you or any human for that matter to have the divine power of choice for another human."

"Bad example. That was the story of Icarus and it's not the same. He was just a boy who disobeyed his father. But, putting it in mythological terms, none of those characters had the power of miracles. They only had the ambition for absolute power. The gift of Hope has the power of miracles – both in life and in death. If you turn your faith toward morality, I think you'll find that your pure heart will be able to justify death as a means of Hope."

At this point Tom was calmer but the magnitude of the conversation still took a toll on his mind. He struggled with the burden of this task and was angry that he had been presumably given the gift of Hope. "Can I refuse the gift? I mean respectfully decline to play the game and fulfill my quota?"

"Funny. I asked Aarzu the same thing. I honestly don't know, but like Aarzu told me, once you see the clarity of the gift, you won't want to refuse it."

"When did the clarity come to you?"

"About 30 seconds after Aarzu left me. His parting words put everything we had talked about in perspective for me."

"And what were the parting words of wisdom from this little Gandhi?"

With a smile built from a fond memory she said, "He was going to be treated to homemade ice cream by his uncle."

"And that's what did it for you?"

"Not really. That's what woke me from my dream state and put everything into perspective. It was his other wisdom, or rather philosophy, that provided clarity for me. Well, the clarity didn't come until after the ice cream statement, but his other words of wisdom planted the seeds that sprouted when I tested the reality of the gift. Here we were, talking about something so deep, so mysterious, so unrealistic, yet when he made the ice cream statement, he placed the reality of our life right there in front of me. No child could have made up the story or known about my note. It was surreal and real at the same time. I realized this was no joke and that the gift was now a part of my own life. Seeing how at peace he was with the gift and the choices he had made really had an impact on me. He told me of two of his 'under' recipient choices, as he liked to refer to the denominators, and I was amazed that a boy of 13 had the depth of understanding to turn death into a miracle. That was his goal...for all his unders to be miracles in an immediate way. For their deaths to be beneficial, not only to them but to someone close to them that was deserving. I was embarrassed that it took a 13-year-old to explain something deeply philosophical and religious to me that I had never considered. I had always looked at death as tragic. He presented death in the form of Hope. It certainly has made my own 'under' choices more palatable."

"So he has turned it into 20 miracles in a sense."

"Yes...he has." Marina seemed distant for a moment in some thought then quickly returned to the conversation. "Anyway. One of the things he said that helped clear my confusion was that miracles validate Hope. And the more people believe in Hope the more goodness will grow and spread and be recognized in this world. He felt it was about time that good should be larger than evil. Therefore it was up to us to create more Hope. That is really the purpose of the gift."

"So our gift is an exercise to make hope more fashionable in our crazy world. Why not proselytize or sell hope on Amazon? I thought that's what the church and evangelists were here for?" said Tom, again a bit too sarcastically.

"Yes and we see how well that's worked for us over the past 2000 years. No, these are unrecognized choices not associated with any particular religion, emperor, sect, race, or region. They are choices that maintain the mystery of where the miracles come from or why the miracles take place. There is no 'aha I did that' or bargaining for salvation. It is ordinary good people—you, me, Aarzu, the Israeli—making choices based on what we see down here in daily life. They're simply pure."

"So, you're telling me I actually have the ability to save and/or kill 20 people just by squeezing their shoulders?"

"Yes. Overwhelming isn't it? But very real, Tom. It's a series of choices that can change the lives of many, including you, by validating Hope for them."

"Does anyone besides me, you, and Aarzu know about your gift?"

Ah…that was the question Marina had been waiting for. She had asked the same thing of Aarzu but only after her confusion and anger had waned and she actually had started accepting the reality and value of the gift. It was a question that showed Tom was falling into the belief of the gift…the confusion was parting and the anger was waning. "No, he recommended keeping it a secret and I agree with him more and more each day."

"Why? I would like to tell my wife and share this burden with someone else to make sure I make the right choices."

"I don't believe you should tell anyone. No matter how pure the heart is your choices can get complicated when you deal with outside influences and other opinions. No matter how close you are to your wife and her heart, there will always be doubt and mistrust that you didn't do what she wanted. Then you lose the pureness of the choice. Sounds backwards, but in this case, with a committee there is always a stronger possibility of corruption."

"I don't like keeping secrets from my wife."

"Do you share with your wife all your conversations with God?"

"No."

"Place it in the same category. This is between you and your God and the growth of Hope."

"I thought you were agnostic and didn't believe in a God or anything spiritual?"

Marina smiled, paused and said, "Being agnostic doesn't mean you have no spirituality or soul. It means you do not associate it with any formalized God or Allah. I didn't have very strong spiritual beliefs in my life before the gift. I still don't as it relates to organized religion. But this gift comes from somewhere or *something*. Trust me when I say that I am infinitely more in tune with my spirituality today than I was nine months ago."

"Do you know who your next recipients are?" asked Tom with a little more understanding.

"I have a few candidates I'm researching, but nothing final yet."

"If I accept this…I mean if I find my clarity, can I call you for advice or even comfort?"

"No. This will probably be the last time we see each other unless there is a random encounter. You have 24 months to complete the fraction. And before you ask, I have no idea what happens if you don't reach your quota by then. Aarzu and his instructor spent a lot of time thinking about this and apparently they believe something will happen to fill the quota…a bus wreck, a bomb, a fire, or something else to keep us from copping out on the denominators and just giving out numerator miracles. This makes the unders random, which seems unfair to me. So, I don't plan on finding out. I see this as a gift, not a burden. A gift far too precious to waste because of fear or cowardice."

Tom recognized her challenge with those words. "What was Aarzu's over/under when he contacted you?"

28

"He was 6 over 9." Marina said.

"Wow…a 13 year old boy…6/9."

"Yes. He thinks the instruction encounters are purposely spread out so the instructor is almost finished when he/she makes an encounter with another 'gifter'. This keeps us from getting together and pooling all our miracles into a large bowl and making group decisions affecting larger numbers. That would be called genocide. No, it's all about individual, isolated, pure choices."

"Marina…"

"Yes Tom."

"How did you know that you had the capability to make the RIGHT choices? I mean choose the right people? Did you ever feel like you made a mistake?"

"There have been times when I wondered whether my choices were selfish. But I always came back to what Aarzu told me… if you are certain that your choice validates Hope for at least two people, then your choice was worth the gift. In the words of my little Muslim messiah, 'Like my own instructor …and probably like my instructor's instructor…and I guess like me…you have a good heart. Corrupt hearts don't get to make these kinds of choices.' Trust in your own goodness Tom. And trust that Hope is worth saving."

They talked for a few more minutes and Tom asked other questions about her personal life just to come more in tune with her pure heart. He asked her about her first 'sentence' and whether it was a numerator or a denominator. Marina told him that she…based on Aarzu's philosophy…wanted to start with a numerator and end with a numerator. But they both felt it was important to keep the denominator ratio ahead of the numerators after the first choice. That way a slew of denominators at the end wouldn't leave the gifter feeling morbid. Did she really feel like she was validating hope with

29

her choices, he had asked. Her reply was an immediate "Absolutely." Marina delivered her answers and advice with a steely calmness that put Tom more at ease as the conversation maneuvered over different topics.

She wondered what his first choice would be and if doubts would creep into his soul in the early stages of his journey as they had for her. He had to trust his heart. She had told him that, but it was up to him to learn how to believe it. Eventually Marina got up from the chair and took a long slow breath to reinvigorate her muscles. They had been sitting undisturbed for an hour and 45 minutes and she felt she had conveyed all that should be conveyed. Tom had come around but the true moment of clarity and acceptance had not yet pierced his mind. He was still sitting in the chair deep in thought, mesmerized by the challenge of the gift not noticing that she had stood up.

Marina quite playfully announced, "Well, I'm going to Brentwood for some brisket tacos at a place that has been bragged about all the way in Phoenix."

Tom, startled out of his daydream, rose from his chair and said, "Ok. Well, um…"

Marina broke in to save the awkward moment. "I am sorry about the false pretense on the project. You can tell your partners that I was just fishing for a unrealistically low bid to straighten up my first-choice architect who was trying to charge too much."

"Don't worry about it. I'll come up with something clever to get them off the scent." Tom paused for a moment looking directly into Marina's eyes. They looked relieved. Peaceful even. Very content with her soul and inner self. "Thank you. Aarzu taught you well in the art of instructing. I guess I have some serious thinking to do."

Before he could say another thing, Marina smiled, turned, and confidently strolled out of his office toward the front lobby. He never laid eyes on Marina Kostitsen again.

Tom closed his door and sat at his desk for a moment to take it all in. The manner in which she went from this deep mystical conversation to the thought of food was…awkward…no, just matter of fact…or…then suddenly it dawned on him what she meant about the moment of clarity. It wasn't full understanding but rather acceptance that this really could be a challenge that his faith had prepared him for. Moments before he was in a bit of a dream. Now he was sitting at his desk with work and life staring directly at him. The dichotomy made him realize that somewhere in the middle was a place he would dwell for the next 24 months…maybe even for a lifetime depending the gift's after-effects. Tom was a man who did not handle change well. Change and surprises in general equated to anxiety for his logical personality. Despite his acknowledgement that having a wife and family meant dealing with unknown circumstances in life, his reaction to surprises was a flaw that was all too obvious to Laura. Less so for the kids at their young age, but with each passing year they became more aware of which parent to approach first when something broke, went wrong, or created a stressful situation. The gift would test his innate desire to control life with planned expectations. However, Marina's presentation of the instructions left him strangely at ease, at least for the moment. Clarity, for her and now for him had come in the form of food. A simple real-life desire for something normal, but exceptionally indulgent in the midst of a bizarre metaphysical discussion. Homemade ice cream with an uncle or a famous brisket taco. She had him.

Chapter Five

Tom left the office around four and headed to Brady's school to catch the end of practice. He didn't speak to anyone and sat by himself on the bleachers thinking through a thousand scenarios that could happen in the next 24 months. *This couldn't be a joke*, he thought to himself. It was too strange, too deep to have any punch line. The note, the appearance of the woman from CNN, her knowledge of the note, and of course the story of Aarzu. No one would put that much planning into a prank or a test. It must be real. As he pondered, he looked around at the other parents and wondered if any of them were worthy of either a miracle or death. Death...*how in the world will I decide on my denominators*. Despite the obvious desire to talk to someone about the whole encounter, he understood the advice Marina had given him about the need for secrecy. Even his wife...his wonderfully caring-for-everything-living wife put the pureness of the decisions at risk. He could certainly poll her for advice about deserving people in her life, but letting her in on the secret could complicate matters more than they already would be. No, the gift of Hope would stay with him alone...at least for the time being.

Tom and Brady headed home after practice and, despite the strangeness of his day, the Roddins had a fairly normal evening. After the kids went to bed he and Laura found some time to talk about the mundane happenings of their workdays. The conversation somehow drifted to their life together and what they had accomplished with the kids, their professions, and their own relationship. Things were very good between them. They were very different people but they balanced those differences through work and family. There was no denying that the kids always came first, but they still managed to find time for themselves to continue working through their differences and strengthening their bond. Laura must have had a double espresso at Target because even after the chatting, she was still ready and willing to be a wife. As always, these times with Laura made him feel like the luckiest man alive. Laura was a sharp, good-natured, good-looking woman of 41 with a lean figure and confident air about her that was far from cocky. Laura was comfortable. That was the way Tom had described her to many people—comfortable. Obviously very attractive, but comfortable in her own skin, comfortable around all types of people, and comfortable with her state of mind. She wasn't preachy, she was rarely judgmental, and she had a way about her that made others comfortable in her presence. She had her flaws, but they were few compared to her good features. Tom on the other hand was 5'11" rather gangly at 165 pounds with a mop of dark brown hair piled up on his head. He was attractive but not 'good looking'. Although coordinated, he wasn't really an athlete. In fact, at first glance, he often got labeled as a nerd. But he had an endearing quality about him that made everyone love him. Fortunately for Tom, that made him much more attractive to Laura and she often claimed to want her nerdy husband just the way he was rather than some shallow underwear model who would just frustrate her. He was grateful for the lie and counted his lucky stars that Laura had looked past his homeliness and fallen in love with his insides.

Tom awoke the next day with a combined feeling of anxiety and excitement and was eager to begin exploring options for the gift. For the moment, he pushed aside his doubt and decided to accept the gift in the same manner that he accepted his faith. Blindly. Don't question it, just practice it. Make a choice and see what happens. When he arrived at work, he attacked his responsibilities providing encouragement to his staff on the progress of their projects. Tom was a person who got things done. Procrastination was something he just didn't understand. If you have a list of things to do, waiting didn't make them go away. So, you might as well get up, prioritize the list, and work them out. Laura and his friends called it anal-retentive. He called it productive. In his mind their procrastination was laziness. Unfortunately, that thought had caused many an argument in their marriage. Too many times, Tom would stare at a kitchen full of dirty dishes in an attempt to wait out Laura and see who would cave first. Laura was a pro! She could stare at dirty dishes, unfolded laundry, or toys scattered across the house all week. When it finally got unbearable, she went on a cleaning frenzy and got it all done at once. Tom wouldn't last an hour. He cleaned things as they got dirty. If you use a bowl, put it in the dishwasher. If you get a blanket out, fold it back up when you're done. His philosophy was to take care of a mess— or task for that matter—when it was in front of you. That way, it didn't build up into something so large that it seemed insurmountable. Make a list, check off the items and move on to the next day where a new list will materialize out of thin air.

True to his nature, by lunch he had cleaned up the morning's tasks and put in motion the afternoon's activities. Eating a sandwich at his desk, he stole away some time to create a list. What would be the criteria for his choices? Would he search out bad people for the denominators or would he search for people in pain and suffering who needed relief? But if they needed relief then why not give them the miracle and make them well or rich or give them a cure for whatever caused the ailment? That would use up his numerators quickly, he thought. *No, I have to accept the fact of death and find an Aarzu-way to make death a validator of hope. How to do that...who to do that to?* These were not going to be simple decisions, but he had to start somewhere. He was certain that more ideas, more clarity would come once the process really began. *Let's start with a miracle!*

Chapter Six

Tom wanted to have fun with the first miracle. Despite the seriousness of the gift, he wanted his first experiment to be one that made someone happy in a life-changing way. He knew he would eventually attempt to heal someone from a sickness, but that would have to come later. He'd go for simple first…just in case the gift was not actually real. He thought for a while about whether it would be a random person or someone he knew. Random may not prove to be worthy. Validating hope for a moron wouldn't necessarily further the cause. But, making a choice for someone he knew might risk exposure of the gift. No, he needed to do research so the miracles were bestowed upon worthy individuals, random or known, in a way that didn't lead to suspicion.

He recalled Laura telling him about her students and their home lives. She was so wonderful at giving even the most unresponsive students some form of self-worth despite their being embedded in a cultural existence that almost guaranteed failure in life. Laura had told him about a set of twins she was teaching who were well below the poverty line. Their father was completely absent, possibly even unknown, and the mother, despite her best efforts to clean up, had fallen in and out of drug use and depression. She was a decent Mom for parts of the year but just couldn't kick her bad habits for good. Laura loved the twins and said that despite their situation they were smart and enthusiastic about learning, but worried that this desire would not last into high school if the mother continued waffling between sobriety and addiction. That would surely send the kids right into the path of repeating history. Breaking out of a family cycle of poverty and drugs was not a high percentage bet. When it did happen it was…a miracle. Maybe Tom could provide her with strength to end her addiction once and for all and find enough stability to finish the job of raising her kids. He made a note to ask Laura their names. *This was going to be good! This is going to feel good.*

He finished the day taking care of project work and reassuring his teams on their progress. In between, he managed time to consider who would be his first denominator and what type of death-miracles he could create. He jotted down some initial ideas and decided that the denominators—he had to come up with a better term for this—couldn't be children or young adults. That just didn't seem fair. Any child or young adult still presumably had time to turn themselves around. He couldn't face the risk that he might take life away from someone who potentially had a full and productive life ahead of them. For now that would be one ground rule for the denominators. *Denominators. Denominators...what can I call them? What did Aarzu call them? Unders. Hmmm...how about ...blessed. Bless-ed. Blesseds. Nope, what if I find some mean son of a gun that deserves death to spare someone else misery? Blessed would be too good for that type of denominator.*

He thought for a moment, and came to the conclusion that 'unders' was probably the right term. It was fairly neutral...not good or evil...just...well, neutral. That could apply to any type of choice. *Smart little messiah! I wish I could meet Aarzu.* He liked using the term miracle for the numerators, or should he just call them 'overs' to keep the neutral feel of both? Did it really matter what he called them since he would not be discussing this with anyone else? Not really. But what about if and when he had to give instructions to another gifter? This thought brought an unexpected wave of anxiety to his mind. Would he be able to convince someone about the reality of the gift? Who in the world would it be? As a matter of fact, how did Marina know to contact him—Tom Roddin—for her encounter? He had completely forgotten to ask this question that now seemed so obvious.

"I guess I'll find out when the time arrives. Maybe another note?" he said out loud to no one but himself. According to their conversation it was probably a long way off, so he put it out of his mind for now. *I will call them 'over' and 'under' for now. I like that better than numerator and denominator.*

That night as Tom and Laura were catching up on each other's day, Laura mentioned the twins without any prompting. She said the mother had just returned to a city-run rehab center and the twins were living temporarily with a family of a friend of theirs at school. Once again, the kids were embarrassed about their situation and tried to keep their family secret quiet. But, as is the case in middle school, word got out and some of the meaner students made fun of them for their plight. This always set them back a bit in their schoolwork and made them rather reclusive socially. "Hopefully, the mother will come out clean and stay clean this time," Laura said. "They are so smart and kind. I just worry one of these episodes will push them over the edge and they'll fall into the same pattern and waste their lives away. The rehab clinic counselors told Miley's parents…you remember Miley—the twins' best friend…that if the mother was going to finally kick the habit, they would see it in her private sessions. They said there's a moment in private counseling when the addict finally breaks apart and realizes the path of destruction they have left in their wake and who it has affected. Although this happens often with addicts, it's their actions in the days following that moment that really determine the success or failure rate of permanent recovery. When they finally accept responsibility for the hurt they have caused AND the counselors see subtle signs—the commitment, the hope, the clarity of long-term consequences—then the chance of successful recovery is enormously increased. They told Miley's parents that despite this woman's good heart and love for her children, they haven't seen those positive signs during her previous rehab stints. She has always had a feeling that she could control her habit without abandoning it."

"Have they seen those signs this time?" asked Tom.

"She's only been reinstated for two days, so no. I hope she can find the strength and self-worth to make it stick. These kids are so sweet and forgiving. They really love their mother despite the pain she has caused them."

"What are their names again?"

"Terri and Lila Ruffin. The mom's name is…Candace, I think. Candace Ruffin. She is a nice lady, medium build, attractive, just a bit worn out from poverty and drugs. I can imagine at one time she was quite the looker. It's funny, because she strikes me as someone who, if given a chance early on, might have become successful in life. She looks like she could have fit into any office building providing value to a company. Ah, such a shame. I really hope she can pull out of this."

Chapter Seven

Candace sat on the edge of her bed with a garbage can between her legs. The nausea had her throwing up most of the morning and she shook from the lack of dope in her bloodstream. She thought about two nights ago when she had her last fix and the warm sensation of relief that always started in her hair and eventually spread evenly down to her actual toenails. The feeling was euphoric…for about 10 minutes. Then the demons crept into her head and took away the comfort. It was at this moment that she regretted her habit and tried to counter the demons convincing her that another dose would make them go away. She would give in, take another dose, and repeat the cycle. Only this time the euphoria only lasted about 6 minutes and then the demons would return with even more vengeance. She knew the cycle would eventually kill her or she would kill herself to be rid of these creatures. But the 10 minutes of pleasure was worth the pain. Another wave of vomiting brought her back to reality putting on hold the possibility of a near-term hit. Not until she could get out of here. Based on her last few treatment attempts, she knew her current condition would eventually subside in about four days. She would attend the sessions, both group and private, pretend to make peace with things, and then return home with her kids. Poor Terri and Lila. They didn't deserve this shit but they couldn't understand the pain their mother had gone through in her life. She needed the escape. She deserved the escape. She just needed to control it better so her dosings coincided with times when the kids were gone for a night or weekend at a friend's house. That way she could still love her kids and still love her doses. It was doable. Just hold on for a few more days and dream about that first dose with her new cleaned up blood.

Her first high after a stint in rehab was always the best and made her current misery worthwhile.

The next day Candace sat in the common area watching Days of Our Lives with a few other "inmates." She had made it through the morning group session, barely, before heading back to the trash can for lunch. She felt a bit more stable now although she couldn't get warm in the open room or in her bed. She sat there shivering under a wool throw blanket when an attendant stuck her head in the room and called her name. She automatically stood up and turned towards the door with programmed movements thinking it was time for more meds. When she neared the door, the nurse said, "You have a visitor."

"A visitor? I didn't think I was allowed any visitors during my first week? Who is it?"

"He says he's from your children's' school and needs to ask you a quick question about getting more clothes for the kids from your house. We made an exception this one time since you have been here before and know the process. You've only got five minutes."

"Damn. I might throw up on his shoes just for bothering me."

"Come on Candace, think about your kids. They need some clothes, so now is not the time to be selfish."

Candace walked into the visitor room and saw a man in a suit standing there looking out the window. He definitely didn't look familiar but she didn't get to many school functions. Even if she was sober, the embarrassment of everyone knowing about her problem usually kept her away. Was he a teacher? Not one of her kids' teachers. She knew what most of them looked like either from the rare parent teacher conferences or from the kids' yearbooks. She always made it a point to check out the kids' teachers to see what they looked like. She was usually pretty good at judging people even if just from a photograph. She didn't know if it was a talent or just luck, but her first impression of a person was almost always right on the mark. *No matter...sounds like he wants to get into my house.*

Tom turned from the window and saw Candace in all her recovery glory. No makeup, completely washed-out-skin tone from her withdrawal vomiting, loose pajama pants and an old ripped sweatshirt. The wool blanket was still wrapped around her. She was quite a sight, but Tom immediately recognized what Laura had seen. She had a natural beauty hidden inside somewhere. Not gorgeous, not plain, but just attractive enough to warrant a second look if she passed you on the street.

"Hi, I'm Tom Roddin. My wife teaches at High Ridge Middle School where your kids are enrolled. I just wanted to stop by and see if you needed anything for your stay?"

"Why the hell are you here? And who the fuck are you to care about what I need?"

"I know you have a lot of potential as a parent and your children have a good life in front of them. You have the strength and courage to beat this. You just need to believe in hope. The hope that your children have in you. They believe you can come out of this a new person."

"I don't need any preaching to. I can manage this in my own way and I don't need any help from a stranger. Are you here as part of Church group? 'Cause if you are, you're wasting your time."

"No, Candace. I am not here from a church or any other organization." Tom moved cautiously toward the woman and put his hand on her shoulder and gave it a slight squeeze. "I am here to show you that hope is real and worth believing in. Trust in the process and know that you will get better even if you don't think you're ready."

Tom released her shoulder and took a step back. Candace stood still, looking at him intently. She was not afraid, yet she was a bit unsettled. Normally this was the kind of crap that she blew off as psychoanalyst bullshit from her counselors. But for a moment she felt that his words actually had some weight to them. After she recovered she said in a soft non-defensive voice, "You talk of hope like it's a magic potion. It's easy for you since your life is probably normal. Hope in my life gets drowned out by reality."

"Believing in hope is the hard part. Letting hope cure you doesn't require any effort. Just belief. That's all I'm asking. If not for yourself, then for your children. They believe. So show them hope works." Tom smiled politely and walked out of the visitation room.

In his car, Tom let out a long deep breath and sat blankly before turning the ignition. He'd been a nervous wreck going into the encounter, afraid his message would be received as arrogant or pretentious. He had planned ahead for the meeting and wondered if he would even get a chance to physically touch Candace. More than anything, he was afraid the gift was not real and that he would preach hope to this woman only to have her fail in her rehab and forever crush the belief in hope for her children. If this didn't work, if he did it wrong, or if the gift wasn't real, he could send Candace and her beautiful twins on the downward spiral that so many similar families encountered as they repeated history over and over again with each generation. Now that it was finished, he felt some relief. He still had no proof this was going to work, but nonetheless he was calmed by the process. He had done the right thing. Even if the gift was a ruse, maybe he had given her the courage to believe in herself so she could find the strength to create her own miracle. That was enough for him. Over #1 was completed...kind of. He still needed to see the outcome. He hoped the next few days would provide him confirmation of the gift. But more importantly, he hoped the next few days would find two children thankful that their hope was validated. *Maybe, just maybe, we created a miracle.*

Chapter Eight

Candace finished dinner and got ready for her private counseling session that routinely closed out her day at the center. She had been unusually quiet throughout the afternoon and evening after her meeting with the stranger from her children's school. Actually he wasn't even from the school. What did he say...he was the husband of a teacher at the school? Why would he come to visit her? What interest did he have in her or Terri and Lila? Despite the mystery surrounding his visit, Candace spent most of the time thinking about his words. Hope. He wanted her to believe in hope so the kids would see that it works. *What works? Hope?* Despite her skepticism his words had an effect. She actually wondered for the first time in years whether she could live without her doses and the comfort they provided. *Could I really achieve the same level of comfort just from being a mom?*

During the session with the counselor, Candace asked lots of questions about life after rehab. Questions about how to integrate herself wholly back into society as a sober person. Questions the counselor had never heard her ask before. The session lasted almost two hours and Candace, exhausted, went to bed with a purpose she hadn't felt in years, maybe ever, actually...not since she was in middle school when her own dreams of a productive life turned to despair. Ironically, the same age as her children now. *My God, they are almost the same age as me when my life got all fucked up.* It was abuse by her father and abandonment by her mother that prevented Candace from fighting the pending disaster of her future. *I can't repeat that for Teri and Lila. I have to do this for them, and maybe I can find some peace for myself in the process. Hope. I will help them believe in it*, she whispered to herself as she laid her head on the pillow.

A week and three days after her meeting with the 'husband', Candace sat with Terri and Lila in the center's visitor room listening to them talk about their activities at school. Candace was engaged with their conversation in a way she hadn't been in years. Although she had always enjoyed a good relationship with her daughters, she was always thinking in the back of her mind about the next opportunity to get a fix. That thought had always consumed her and made her engagement with the kids temporary, almost fake as the impatience and anxiety of a her next free moment created distance between them. Sitting here now, listening to their excitement about the smallest things in their lives, the haunting thoughts of addiction were nowhere in sight. Never before had she felt the freedom from her demons ring so true and feel so permanent. After lots of giggling and sharing of secrets, the three of them looked at each other in a brief, awkward moment of silence. Candace smiled at them, "I want to make a promise to you two. Never again will you girls have to worry about your mother being here for you. And I mean your sober mother. The life I created for you has not been perfect and you deserve better. I'm here now to give you that better. I'm feeling…well…feeling peaceful—a deep down peaceful feeling within myself. Something has given me strength to carry us down a new path. I found hope in a very dark place, hope that I haven't felt since I was your age, and it's taking care of me. I am so excited about sharing our new lives together. I love you both dearly and I will never forget that again."

"Mom, you know we love you. We just want you to be happy and healthy again. We're going to help you," said Lila.

"Yep, we're going to clean our room more often and help take care of the apartment. We'll try not to stress you out anymore," Terri butted in.

"Girls, none of this and I mean NONE of this is your fault. You are two of the most precious children a mother could ask for. My stress and addiction was caused by me and me alone. You played no part. If anything, you girls kept me from getting worse. Without you, I would have been abusing drugs every single day, which might have killed me. The time we did spend together kept me alive. Your hope and belief in me made this recovery possible. Don't ever lose faith in hope and what hope can do for your own lives."

<u>Chapter Nine</u>

Tom spent the week engrossed in work and in research for other 'under' and 'over' recipients. Despite his burning curiosity about Candace's progress, he resisted the urge to ask Laura. He almost called the treatment center a few days after their meeting but decided his inquiries might be questioned. He certainly didn't want to bring attention to his and Candace's 'relationship.' It was already a bit risky that he had gone to the center using his real name and given the woman a chance to see him. It could be awkward explaining to someone, including his wife, that he had gone to the center to see her. Surely, the outcome of his choice would reveal itself without him having to risk exposure. He would have to wait.

As he researched other choices, he couldn't help but let his sense of humor infuse his serious thoughts. Jokingly, he considered using an over choice on a Tennessee Titan wide receiver's knee that had been blown out the week before in a home game against the Colts. Tom was at the game, as always, and had seen the injury occur in a live setting. Despite being 20 rows up from the field, he and his buddies knew it was likely a season-ending injury. His mind immediately went to the gift. *Miraculously fixing his knee would certainly improve their chances of making the playoffs.* But the gift was not meant for torn cartilage. It was meant for meaningful life changes. *But boy, a good playoff run was long overdue.*

More pressing and concerning were thoughts of his first under and who it should be. After mulling through a variety of scenarios, he decided he would relieve someone who was old and probably ready to die anyway. This seemed safe enough for his conscience to determine if he could actually swallow a 'miracle' of this nature. He often wondered if he could remain

46

immune from the effects of the gift's power. He was afraid the gift would falsely feed his ego to the point of making him feel superior to everyone else. It hadn't happened yet, but his fear of it kept him second-guessing everything he did now. His work decisions, his home decisions, everything seemed to be weighed against whether a feeling of superiority was influencing his choices. At times this internal argument led to high anxiety. Other times, his assessment of the recent decisions he had made in his normal life were put into clear perspective and he realized that those decisions were the same ones the nerdy Tom would have made. Nothing had changed. Of course, as of now, nothing *had* really changed. He still had no validation that the gift was real. The anxiety was completely unfounded…at least until the gift was proven to him.

"Mr. Roddin?"

Tom was startled out of his thoughts by Lisa Harrington standing in his office doorway. "Hi Lisa. Come on in. What's up?"

"I'm sorry to bother you but I have a problem…or err…a question."

"Sure. I'll be glad to help if I can."

"Well…" Lisa hesitantly began, "…The Springfield project, the one in Birmingham, we've finished the design and are presenting all the final artifacts to the client early next week. I was just wondering…well…I have really put my heart and soul into this project over the last eight months. And…"

"Spit it out Lisa. You know I'll be honest with you."

"Mr. Johnston said that he'll handle the final presentations with the client. That he didn't need me to be present at the meeting."

"Barry said that? That you didn't need to be at the meeting?"

"Yes. I told him that I would let him present all the material and I would only engage if they had specific questions about the changes we've incorporated since our last review with them. But he said that wouldn't be necessary since the design is now final. I just …well…I don't know if anyone else in the firm can have a say in the matter or if it's just dead in the water given his…position in the firm."

"I assume your discussion didn't stop after the first mention of his solo flight concept?" Tom knew Lisa would not give in so easily, even to Barry whom he knew she loathed. She would have argued for hours with Barry to get him to see the value in her presence there. The fact that she was coming to Tom for advice on the matter meant that Barry had not budged an inch from his opening argument. *Dammit Barry. Why do you keep doing this?* Here was another brilliant junior architect he was going to run off because of his ego. Tom and the other senior architects always took the lead project architect and sometimes the entire team when they presented final designs. It was their moment to shine and get some satisfaction out of the effort they had put in.

"Yes. I argued my point until he finally told me to leave his office or risk being taken off the construction phase of the project. I need the experience for that phase to complete my profile before…" Lisa suddenly hesitated and left the sentence linger.

"Before you submit your resume and profile to a firm that will actually let you grow into a full-time architect?"

"Mr. Roddin, you know I love it here. It's just…room for growth when working under Mr. Johnston is not…there just isn't any."

"I hear you Lisa. This is not the way things are supposed to be done. It's gotten worse lately and I've talked to the other partners about it, although that actually puts my own career at risk since I am not a partner myself. Let me talk to Rodney and see if he can persuade Barry to let you attend the meeting. You deserve credit for this project and I will certainly make that clear to Rodney. In the meantime, if you send your resume or profile to another firm before letting me try to do something about Barry, I will personally call the other firm and tell them that you are an alien from another planet with diseases we cannot even pronounce. Agreed?"

With a smile, Lisa replied warmly, "Agreed. I am so sorry to bring you into this mess but I didn't know where else to go. You know that all the plebes in this firm are hoping you get elevated to partner this year so you can begin taking over the firm when Rodney retires. You're our favorite. You have this great balance between teaching and letting us stretch our own wings."

"I am happily married young lady so stop trying to flatter me," he joked. "When is the meeting?"

"Thursday December 1."

"Ok. I'll talk to Rodney this afternoon and get back to you before the week is out. Keep preparing as if you're going, but I may only be able to swing your presence there. Having you present the final design might not be achievable."

"That's fine. I have a great working relationship with the client's worker bees and they trust my ability to find compromise with the contractor as brick and mortar starts to take a physical shape. I think the underlings know who did all the work. It's just Mr. Simon, our client's CEO, who will think Barry deserves all the credit if he presents alone."

"Ok. I am sorry this is even an issue, Lisa. Give us a chance to change the culture on his projects. You have a very bright future and I personally would like to see it blossom here."

"Thanks, Mr. Roddin."

Chapter Ten

Tom walked down the main hallway to Rodney's office and took a deep breath. Seeking out the owner of the firm for another awkward conversation about a partner was not on his list of fun things to do. But Tom had always been a peacemaker and his inherent trait to stick up for others was a cross he seemed obligated to bear.

"Hey, Rodney!"

"Hi Tom. What can I do you for?" Rodney Turnage had launched his company in 1976 as a small, two-person architectural firm. Although not huge, the firm had become a reputable business in middle Tennessee and had found leverage with several large projects outside the area and in other parts of the country, in large part due to the contacts Rodney had made in college. He was approaching 70 and beginning to show signs of wanting to let go of the daily grind of running a business. He hadn't chosen a successor yet but all signs pointed to Barry. He had been a partner for 15 years, brought in after Rodney's original partner died from cancer. Barry provided a solid address book and brought in a lot of business, but his architectural skills had become a bit stale. He relied on junior architects to do just about everything except take the clients to expensive lunches and play marquee golf courses around the country. Barry's waning architectural skills were only overshadowed by his total lack of personal skills, which would make him a questionable manager of the firm. Nobody liked the guy and people hid in closets and behind water coolers to avoid being assigned to one of his projects. Tom was unsure whether Rodney really saw this flaw. He had only worked there for nine years and was awaiting a decision by Rodney, Barry, and Allen Clark—the other partner—on whether he would be invited into the partnership group. He liked Rodney but didn't know him well enough to openly trash the presumed heir-apparent. So, the few conversations he had had with Rodney about Barry had been very carefully planned. Tom had decided a few months before that he could not be afraid to let Rodney know what was going on in the trenches for fear of not being advanced. If Rodney was going to let Barry take over the firm, then this was probably not the place for him long term. So, Tom would use today's discussion to set the stage for a more serious discussion that was sure to come after the first of the year.

"I was wondering if you could talk to Barry about his meeting on the Springfield project next week. Seems he is going to take the final designs down there and do the presentation himself...without bringing the team or even the lead junior architect with him." Tom was more matter of fact about the suggestion than he had planned, but couldn't figure out another way to present the dilemma. *Might as well set the stage with all the props in place.*

"How do you know he's planning on flying solo?" asked Rodney.

"Well, there is some concern that he might not have all the details about the contingency revisions that may be needed as construction gets underway."

"And why can't he be made aware of these contingency plans—he should be close enough to the project to present these if they are outlined clearly for him?"

"True, but I believe he's not as close to the project itself as he is to the client's CEO. So, the team that did most of the work should be there to lay out the transition and integration plans from design to construction."

"I see. So, I'll ask again, how do you know he is planning on flying solo on this?"

"A concern was expressed to me by the team," Tom said flatly, not wanting to expose Lisa as the culprit.

"Sit down for a minute Tom." Rodney gestured towards a chair and closed his office door before settling in on the couch. "Tom, you have been here for nine years and possess a lot of talent. You're creative, meticulous, and excellent with your clients. More importantly, you're very well liked and trusted by the entire staff. It's obvious they respect your opinion and enjoy working with you because you give them room to be creative, make mistakes, correct them, and learn from them. Don't think I haven't noticed that the staff typically comes to you with problems and looks to you to resolve them. And here you are again approaching me about a situation where you're trying to do the right thing. Do right by them. Are you telling me that one of my partners is a prick to his team and that this is unfair?"

A bit taken aback, Tom stammered, "Well...with all due respect sir, yes. The team has worked very hard and deserves to be involved in the next phase not to mention get credit for their work and creativity."

Rodney smiled with a slight chuckle and said, "Good. Good for you Tom. I realize we haven't had much time to talk recently about your position in the firm but that will soon change. Tom, I plan on making you a partner but I have to set some things in order first to make sure your acceptance is...well...let's say whole. I think it's great that you are standing up for the staff. They need and deserve that. Without them we certainly would not be in business and I recognize their value even if Barry does not. Allen and I have had a lot of conversations regarding that issue and we have a plan to resolve it. If Barry didn't have the Rolodex he did, he would have been gone long ago. But he does bring in a lot of business so we can't throw him away just because he's a prick. So, we'll continue being a cushion between him and the staff to keep them from hanging him upside down by his bloody toenails."

Tom smiled just enough to show his appreciation but not enough to be disrespectful. "I understand. I am glad you recognize the team's worth. We have some really talented young folks here that I believe are part of our future success."

"I agree. I'll talk to Barry and make sure he understands that Lisa and at least one of her team members will need to attend the meeting."

"Thanks Rodney. And if you can phrase it in a way that doesn't look like the team went around his back, that would be great."

"I understand. Be patient with me for a few more months, Tom, and we'll make things work for your future here."

"I certainly will."

During the drive home Tom was amused by what had transpired that afternoon. He basically went in to tell the owner of the firm that one of the partners was a complete asshole, and he came out with assurances that he would be made partner soon. Not a bad day at the office.

While making dinner that night, he and Laura talked about his conversation with Rodney. The kids were sitting in front of the box getting brain-drained, so they dissected the conversation going back and forth about how Rodney meant to remedy the office environment.

"Do you think they'll fire Barry?" she asked.

"I don't think Rodney is willing to give up Barry's Rolodex. I think they're trying to figure out how to let him down easy about adding me as a partner and the possibility that he won't be taking over the firm."

"Do you really think they might be grooming you for that position?"

"I don't know. I do get along well with everyone on the staff, but I've only been there nine years."

"What about Allen? Why doesn't he want to take over the firm? He and Rodney have been friends and worked together for years."

"I think Allen's told Rodney he doesn't want the responsibility. He just wants to be an architect. That way he can work as long as he wants without the pressure of running a business. He can gradually choose fewer projects and be freely engrossed in the ones he really finds interesting. That puts him on a less stressful path to retirement," Tom said.

"Wow. That would be really big. You know you deserve this, Tom. You're a great architect and an even better man. You have a good, pure heart and the staff would love working for you."

Tom hesitated a minute when he heard his wife use the word pure about his heart. He instantly flashed back to what Aarzu had told Marina and what she had in turn told him—'...you have a good heart. Corrupt hearts don't get to make these kinds of choices.'

"Oh..." Laura suddenly said. "Do you remember me telling you about the twins at school? I talked to Miley's mom today—they were the ones that took the twins in while their mother was in rehab. She said the mom, what was her name, Candace...she said Candace is getting out of rehab at the end of this week and that her counselors say she has really shown signs of recovery that have never been there before. They said she's like a new person. Not like before because they always knew somehow that she was faking her recovery just to get out of rehab. No, this time she's really taken it all to heart and has made a whole new commitment to her kids and herself. They've never seen such a drastic and sudden change in a patient before. One of them actually went so far as to call it a miracle."

54

Tom stopped cutting his onion and tried to subdue the wave of emotion that came over him. He hid it well from Laura but inside, the reality of the gift, its validation nearly made him black out. "Wow. That's great. Maybe there is hope for the twins after all." Hope. Tom decided that with confirmation of the reality of the gift, that hope was really Hope. Hope with a capital H. His head swam. *Oh my God. This is really happening.*

Chapter Eleven

Valenia Hernandez lay silently on the bloody sheets with her eyes wide open and her mind numb. All she could focus on was the sound of laughing as it faded down the hallway of the apartment complex. When complete silence engulfed the room, she allowed herself to breathe activating the pain in her face, arms, and private entrances to her body. She had felt this type of pain before, but never by the hands of so many at once. The first time was almost a year ago. She had been raped two other times since then, always by the same punk, 'Angel the Man' with his knife tattoo dripping from his left eye. This time he felt the need to share her with his friends.

Valenia's cousin, Raul, had gotten mixed up in a local gang in Nashville and was trying to recover his street cred after rumors soared that he had barked to the police about the gang's activities. A snitch was usually killed immediately under these circumstances, but because the police were watching the leading members closely, they decide to take their vengeance on Raul's 'sweet piece of ass' 15-year old cousin. Angel was the new leader of the gang and had probably raped hundreds of other women—girls actually. But he was also feared and protected vehemently by the other members of the gang. Raul would eventually pay the price for trying to get in, then out of a gang, but for now, Valenia was the only victim. She gathered her courage and lifted herself upright off the sheets planting her feet on the floor. Slowly, she tested her strength and hobbled to the bathroom to vomit. She had to clean herself before her mother came home from work or things might get worse. If her mother knew her little girl had been raped, she would most certainly call the police. *God love the woman but she wouldn't understand the long-term consequences.* Within hours the whole apartment complex, maybe even the whole Latino community in southeast Nashville would know about it. Angel might get arrested, might even spend a little time in jail, but she and her mother would most likely be killed or even worse, live. The beatings, the rapes, the constant harassment would be their nightmare and shame forever. The gang never forgot and although the players might change their revenge was passed down like an heirloom. So, Valenia bathed, washed the sheets, and hid her secret in a place reserved for pain that should never be experienced. She hid it with the hope that one day...some day she could be free of the threat and learn how to heal. *One day.*

<u>Chapter Twelve</u>

Tom walked into the Oak Chase retirement home, bypassed the front desk and headed straight toward the bank of elevators. He entered the cramped lift with a couple in their late forties and rode to the third floor, which housed the more serious dementia patients. It was November twenty-second and the common area was decorated with turkeys and pumpkins announcing Thanksgiving. A menu on the common-room table identified the dishes to be served for Thursday dinner that included all the usual suspects. This was more for the visiting families than the patients, so loved ones would feel less guilty about not providing a feast during a holiday that was famous for family gatherings. Tom sat on the couch and observed. Several patients were walking around rather oblivious to the fact that they were essentially prisoners to this floor of the facility. One man was fully exposed through his robe and appeared to be readying himself to pee in the radiator at end of the hallway. Another was busy washing his underwear and t-shirt in the huge fish tank at the other end of the common area. Very politely, an attendant walked over to Mr. Robinson and told him that this was not a washing machine. "Let's get your clothes and put them in the hamper in your room and they'll be cleaned on Friday—wash day." After some defiance Mr. Robinson finally walked away leaving his laundry in the tank muttering something about poor hygiene in the 'apartment complex.'

Tom quickly realized the caretakers on this floor didn't get paid enough to deal with patients who had no memory. Occasionally family members would come in or out of a room, excited to show their loved ones they still cared or totally distraught at the distance the disease of dementia put between them. The pain of feeling useless coupled with the frustration of not being able to comfort someone you loved who didn't recognize you must be agonizing. Twenty minutes into his observation, Tom heard a patient yell at unrecognized family members. "Cassy. Cassy, get these strangers out of my house. You know I don't like strangers coming in here trying to sell me shit! They are going to steal my belongings and eat up my jello."

After thirty minutes, Tom went to the elevator and asked the nurse to key in the code that allowed the sane people to leave the prison floor. He went to the dining hall, now empty except for a few family members who were talking privately, got himself a cup of coffee, and sat down at an empty table contemplating what he might have done if his own parents were still alive and in this state of decline. His parents had died just three months apart, his father from a sudden massive heart attack and his mother from a mysterious aneurysm that Tom always wondered if she had dialed up herself because she didn't want to live without her husband. Fortunately for him, he was never faced with the decision to put his parents in a home or have to witness their mental demise. If he had, he wondered if he would be comforted by their death.

Not long after he sat down, a couple came in and occupied the table next to his. The woman was distraught and the man was trying to comfort her with reassuring statements about being able to let go. He had seen the couple on the third floor as they exited the elevator and headed down the left wing to a room.

"He's getting worse. Far worse than he was just a few weeks ago," the woman said. "How in the world could he not recognize us? We're his children. He cared for us for over 45 years and now he can't remember us. This is not right. We need to bring him home so he can be reminded every day of who he is and who we are."

"Joan, you know we can't do that. He needs constant care that we can't provide. These people are trained to care for people in his condition. Bringing him to one of our houses is not going to make him remember. It's not going to cure his disease," the brother said.

"I know…but it's just so painful to see him like this. He has no quality of life."

"Sounds like he looks forward to Monday's beef stroganoff," he caringly joked to lighten the mood.

"Jesus. His life has been reduced to forgetting everything he's accomplished in his life to craving a crappy meal on Mondays. I just hope he's not lonely. I hope he doesn't have those moments of clarity when we aren't there and wonders if we've abandoned him."

"The nurse says that in his good moments he talks about Mom. But those are getting less and less frequent. I feel the same way but we have to believe in our decision. As hard as it is to swallow, he's better off here than with either one of us."

"I just hope it goes away soon. I can't stand to see him degrade this way," said Joan.

"What goes away soon? The disease? It's not going to get better. It's just going to get worse."

"I meant him. I hope he goes away soon. I don't mean Dad, I mean the man who is in that room who doesn't know who he is. Now that I've seen this end of things, it would be easier if he had passed on suddenly like Mom did. God, I can't believe those words actually came out of my mouth."

"I understand what you meant…or mean. It would be much easier to accept his death than sit here watching his demise. If he were sane and could see what he has become, he would hate us for not finding Dr. Kevorkian for him."

"They're taking good care of him aren't they? Strange…he can remember his nurse's name but can't recognize his own blood. Please shoot me if we find out in our twilight years that this is hereditary."

"No way. I'll be going crazy first just so I won't have to deal with your demands."

"I love you, John. You have always been the calm, rational voice of the family."

"That's why I get more of the inheritance than you," he joked. "Come on. Let's go. We can talk more Thursday at our house. What time are you guys coming over?"

"Probably around 11. Robert and the kids want to come by to see Dad first thing Thursday morning and wish him a Happy Turkey Day. I just hope he doesn't frighten the girls with any outbursts."

The brother and sister left the table and walked to the lobby having paid no attention to Tom who was listening intently to their conversation. He wondered if the desire to see their dad pass peacefully would be comforting to them. Especially during the holiday season. People often wished for things only to feel betrayed by their desires after they become a reality. The woman had expressed the emotion correctly when she questioned her father's feelings of loneliness and abandonment. Were his moments of clarity full of doubt and anger about the perceived lack of love from his children? If only he could see their pain and the struggle they went through each day trying to live with their decision to place him in a home. Their pain was a true expression of the love they had for their father. He may have forgotten them, but they certainly had not forgotten him. *His passing would certainly keep the recent memories from overshadowing a whole lifetime of love this man probably gave them.* Tom had not come today to actually make a choice. His intent was to observe the patients to determine if this was a worthy setting for an under. After listening to the brother and sister's conversation and thinking through his own desires if his parents were in a similar situation, he decided to act. For some reason, in that moment, he felt confident the choice would be easy. He couldn't do it today, he was already running late to pick up Brady from practice. It would have to wait until after the holidays. He was ready. *Let's validate their Hope.*

The Monday after Thanksgiving, Tom returned to Oak Chase and again took the elevator to the third floor. His confidence had wavered over the long weekend and he was counting on his courage returning once he walked into the facility. Instead, anxiety and doubt washed over him as he exited the elevator. He remembered that the brother and sister had entered the last room on the left in the main hallway to the right of the common area. He prayed the patients didn't frequently change rooms, thus turning his first under into a case of mistaken identity. As he approached the door, he felt a wave of nausea overcome his midsection. Could he really do this? Did he have the authority to make these kinds of choices for someone else? He was turning away from the door when a nurse came out of the man's room and almost bumped into Tom standing in the hallway.

"Hi there. Are you here to see Mr. Goddard?"

"Yes. Is this a good time?" Tom was surprised at his answer.

"As good as any I suppose. He just finished his lunch and is gearing up for his afternoon soaps. He thinks one of the characters on One Life to Live is his daughter. But he only makes it through about five minutes before he falls asleep. Are you a family member? I don't think I've seen you here before."

"No. I'm a friend of the family. I just wanted to say hello quickly. Really just a courtesy call."

"Well, don't be offended if he thinks you're President Johnson or some other character from history. He seems to remember them better than he does his own family and friends."

"Can I ask you something? Did Joan, his daughter, and the kids come by on Thanksgiving?"

"Yes, they did. He wasn't in one of his better states. He thought they were Girl Scouts trying to sell him cookies. He pretty much kicked them out when they told him that cookies aren't sold until the spring. Poor girls were pretty freaked out by the whole thing. They left pretty soon after they got here."

"Yeah. I can imagine it's hard to take when it is a blood relative. Well, I'll just be a minute and hopefully he won't ask me to repeat Johnson's inaugural speech from 1968."

"You'd better get in there in a hurry. He'll be asleep before you have a chance to say goodbye. Then I'll be in there to pry his hands off that cup of coffee so he doesn't spill it all over himself in his sleep."

Tom entered the room and saw Mr. Goddard sitting in his recliner intently watching the TV. He pushed a slight glance toward Tom and then immediately returned his gaze to the TV. "Are you here to check my prostate again?" Mr. Goddard yelled without looking at him.

"No sir. I am just here to say hello and see how you're doing."

"Well, I'm trying to watch my daughter on television if you and the other agents would stop interrupting me. I told you once already that I have no affiliation with the communist party. I'm American and have no interest in the pinkos on the other side of the world."

"Well, we're glad to hear that, sir. They're really causing some disruption here in the U.S. and we're doing our best to keep their idealistic crap out of the minds of our younger generation." Tom placed his hand on the man's shoulder, then hesitated. Could he really do this? Finally, he gave Mr. Goddard's shoulder a slight squeeze. "We really appreciate your patriotism and will do everything we can to keep America safe."

"Safe from what?" the man said.

"Safe from communism," Tom replied.

Mr. Goddard gave Tom a puzzling look. "Not sure who you are young man, but I am trying to watch my daughter on TV. If you need to draw blood then let's get it over with."

"No need sir. Have a good afternoon."

Tom walked back down the hallway and asked to be coded into the elevator. When he arrived in the lobby, he couldn't decide whether to stay and witness the result or just leave. Marina had told him that the unders usually get addressed within 30 minutes and that she and Aarzu felt it was important to witness the passing. Since this was his first under, he felt he should trust their judgment. After 20 uncomfortable minutes on the lobby couch, he noticed two EMTs coming through a set of double doors with an empty gurney. The wave of nausea came back again and nearly left him crippled. Gathering all his composure, he followed the men into the elevator and rode it to the third floor. They immediately turned toward the right hallway and casually worked their way to Mr. Goddard's room without causing alarm to the other patients. The nurse was there giving instructions as the EMTs entered the room.

"No, he didn't yell or cry or even crap himself like most heart attack patients do. I came in and he was slumped in the chair with his eyes wide open. No pulse, no breathing…nothing. Couldn't have looked any more peaceful, to tell you the truth," the nurse said.

One of the EMTs gave a kind smile and said, "Well, see what you can do to keep the other patients in their rooms when we bring him out. We don't want to start a riot up here about how we kill people we don't like."

"Most of them are napping for the afternoon, but I'll round up the others. I hate to see him go. He was a nice man when he first came in. His problems came on fast though. He was fortunate to leave so quickly and let go of his suffering. God bless him."

<u>Chapter Thirteen</u>

Tom's first under left him disheartened. He helped Laura get the kids off to school and went back to bed attempting to sleep through his depression. Laura recognized these moments of depression and often played the part of cheerleader to shake him from slipping in too deeply. With Laura and kids gone for the day, Tom decided to call in sick and wallow in his misery...the magnitude of his decision for Mr. Goddard weighing heavily on his soul. Although he felt he had saved the man and certainly his family some painful moments, he couldn't shake the fact that he was ultimately responsible for his death. He caused the man to die...he made the choice for him. The power associated with the gift left him questioning his own moral fiber. *Am I really equipped to make decisions like this? Can I justify that man's death by assuming he is better off or that his family is better off? How in the world would you know without seeing how his life would have played out?* Tom wondered if Mr. Goddard would have stabilized and lived peacefully in the home remembering some days and not others. Maybe there would be a cure for dementia tomorrow that could have saved him. Maybe the family would blame themselves for accelerating his death by putting him in the home. God, the questions they must have...the what-ifs.

The next day, Tom returned to work but the analysis of his actions was still running through his head. Thankfully, Lisa interrupted his dark thoughts.

"Mr. Roddin, I just wanted to thank you for whatever you did regarding the meeting this week. Mr. Johnston informed me that I will be attending the meeting on the Springfield job and to bring along two more team members associated with the construction drawings."

"That's great Lisa. I didn't do much but I'm glad he had a change of heart," replied Tom.

"I'm not sure it was a change of heart. His tone sounded like it was more of an order. He didn't seem thrilled with the idea and told us to only talk if spoken to directly. But I'll take it."

"Well, now that you're in, take the opportunity to show your knowledge of the next phase that we'll do together with the contractor. He can't stop you in the meeting without embarrassing himself, so go for it."

"I will. Thanks again and sorry for bringing you into this mess." Her tone was sincere and had an edge of excitement that was certainly missing in their last meeting.

"Let me know how it goes and good luck. I'm sure you'll do fine."

Lisa disappeared and Tom struggled to concentrate on the work in front of him. His thoughts were so divided between the responsibilities of the gift and his real life as an architect that neither one was progressing. The sudden ringing of his phone brought relief and respite from the struggle going on in his head about which aspect of his life was more important.

"Hello, this is Tom."

"Hello Tom. This is Marina."

After a pause Tom spoke into the mouthpiece with a quiet suspicion. "I didn't think I would see or hear from you again."

"I thought it was best to leave that impression, although I knew we would probably speak one more time. I just wanted to provide you some reassurance about the choices you've made."

"And how do you know I have made any choices?"

"I don't for sure and I certainly don't know what those choices were. But, I have been instructed…well…prompted to call you. So, I assume that at least one choice or more has been made."

"Who...prompted you to call me?"

"Relax. You are not being watched, at least not by anything earthly. I received another note today saying it was time to comfort you. Aarzu did me the same courtesy, evidently prompted by a note, at a time when I was struggling with the ability to justify using the gift. So, I can only assume that *something* knows of your progress and that you could use some comforting."

Tom was unnerved by the timing of the call. "Well, either we're both the victims of some sick game or God is paying attention and actually knows what He's doing."

"Someone or something surely knows what they're doing. Have you made any choices yet?"

"I have and yes I am struggling with my first under. I am not sure that making this choice for someone else is...well, fair, or justified. There are too many unknown circumstances that could make our choices wrong. Oh, I can tell myself I saved them from suffering, or that they are in a better place, but ultimately, how do I really know? How can I decide this for them?"

"I had the same struggles...presumably we all have had the same struggles, all of those who have been given the gift of Hope for as long as it has been going on. And who knows how long that's been? Maybe it started with the person before the Israeli. Maybe it's been going on since the caveman days. We can decide because someone, something has chosen us, put their trust in us to choose. It was hard for me at first because my beliefs are not deeply rooted in a Christian God. The Divine for me was something less tangible, less singular than a God or an Allah. So the idea that something singular chose me as worthy of the gift was not something I got my head around easily. Aarzu told me to trust in the Divine's choice of us, no matter how we each defined the Divine. But ultimately, I can justify the choices by looking closely at the reality of our modern day world. In reality, your first under was probably not going to improve. In reality, the loved ones will miss the person, but are probably relieved too that the suffering is over. In reality, this person has probably given everything he's got to offer society…it was his time."

Tom listened to Marina reveal her spirituality and choked back his desire to explain the gift in terms of a religious manifestation that his upbringing forced him to believe was pure Christianity. He would bury his Christian alignment to the gift for now, unwilling to explore other spiritual explanations. The religious doubt exposed from such exploration frightened him. "But what about the possibility of mistakes? They can't be taken back."

"Tom, the world is full of mistakes. But in our case I don't believe any of our choices can be considered mistakes. We are choosing based on our hearts…our pure hearts…making pure choices. People die and live needlessly all the time in our existence. We are just making a few small choices in the larger scheme of things. We're making choices to help other people based on our judgments. *Something* obviously likes us doing this and trusts us to make these decisions based on our human eyes living in the world today. There is no punishment or judgment that comes with it. Essentially, no consequences as long as the choices are made without hatred, revenge, or greed."

"That's the first time I have heard you use those words as the guidelines for the choices. Did Aarzu tell you that?"

"No, those are my words based on my own moral compass that is founded in my beliefs. Despite what you may think of my 'spirituality' and lack of acceptance of institutionalized Christian doctrine, I have a deep belief in the moral responsibilities that come with being a human."

"Hmmm…pretty religious of you if you'll forgive my improper labeling." Tom said in a soft complimentary tone. "I just can't help second-guessing the choice I made. The guilt is a bit overwhelming."

"Yes it is at first. But trust that you're not being asked to perform all of God's duties. You're just helping Him make choices. Think of it as Him gaining further insight into the human thought process from people He trusts...and likes."

"There you go again...using the word God as if you were a true Christian."

"Ha...I was doing that for your benefit," she chuckled.

"Do you really believe our choices come without consequences? That we are not altering a set plan where one of our 'choices' might actually have been better off if we had just stayed out of it?"

"No. I don't believe there is a *set* plan. I believe our choices help shape an ongoing and ever-changing plan...one that is organic. Under that guise our choices can't be right or wrong...they are just choices. Choices that help Hope shape the plan. Remember, this is all about validating Hope so it can grow within our society. Marianne Edgar Budde, an Episcopal bishop of Washington, DC, once said, 'the whole purpose of faith is to be a source of guidance, strength and perspective in difficult times. To be human is to have a sense of purpose, an awareness that our life is an utterly unique expression of creation and we want to live it with meaning, grace and beauty.' To me, that's where faith and Hope are intertwined. The validation of Hope is what drives many people to live their life with that grace and beauty she is referring to."

"Hope. It certainly is easier to validate Hope by the overs than it is for the unders. But, I think I understand what you mean. If you accept *something's* trust, then there should be no guilt, no second-guessing about what might have been. Kind of goes against my Presbyterian upbringing that fate is part of the Divine plan."

"Well, I don't believe we are all predestined on a set path. I believe we make most of the choices for ourselves, some are made by others, but mostly we get to make them. It gets easier, Tom, even when a choice is made out of anger, which I have done for many of my unders. Not revenge, but anger at their despicable treatment of other humans. Aarzu hinted that most of his under choices were made to relieve suffering and therefore, in turn, were miracles. My under choices have been more about relieving the suffering of others at the hand of what I consider to be bad people. It took a while but I am free of guilt from my choices because of the lives I have saved or cured by eliminating a bad influence in their lives…mostly influences they did not choose to be around or couldn't escape."

"Tell me that I'm not on your naughty list Santa."

"You're safe, Tom," Marina said with a warm laugh.

Marina's choices based on despicable acts that she determined as evil, struck a chord with Tom. Maybe that was the way to avoid the guilt? Mr. Goddard was a nice gentleman who didn't portray evil incarnate. *I should try looking for evil in my other unders.* "Thanks. Your call came at the right time. *Something* does know what they are doing."

"You're welcome. This time I'm telling the truth when I say we won't have contact again unless by sheer chance. After this call of support from Aarzu, I never heard from him again."

"I won't hold my breath, but I understand. You really have comforted me. I think I'm ready to move along with my journey. "

"It is a journey, isn't it…literally and spiritually? Goodbye Tom."

"Goodbye Marina."

When Tom hung up the phone he realized how much Laura would like Marina. They both followed a strict moral code of conduct without using Christianity as its sole foundation.

Maybe there was a lesson to be learned from that irony. Stubbornly, he still hung on to the idea that the giver of the gift was his God.

Chapter Fourteen

The Jefferson County courthouse in Louisville was crowded on a Tuesday morning for general session hearings. There were 13 cases on the docket for the morning session, ranging from minor possession of marijuana to domestic violence cases. Tom was in Louisville to oversee a zoning and permit hearing associated with one of his projects. This support was typical of their services for most clients, where he either presented the design to a committee for approval or was on hand to answer questions about the design and its adherence to local building codes, by-laws, or zoning restrictions. His committee hearing wasn't until later that evening but Tom had the idea that a trip to general sessions court might give him some ideas about the gift of Hope. So, he traveled the day before and positioned himself this morning in the third row of the courtroom to see the alleged perpetrators and also have a field of view of the victims and their families sitting in the courtroom pews with him. He could have performed this same observance in Nashville, but somehow the out-of-town investigation of human flaws was less awkward...less personal. He wasn't ready to take the chance that he might want to investigate a choice for someone he knew in Nashville or was somehow associated with someone he knew. He realized now how the close association with Candace could have been exposed. So for now, he felt his observance of the court proceedings in another town was the safe way to decide if this was an avenue for finding people deserving of a choice as either an over or an under.

The first few cases brought before the judge were pretty routine crimes. One was a college student caught with about four ounces of pot. He was charged with intent to sell and explained to the judge that six of his friends went in on it together just for their own stupid habits. They had no intention of selling their shares and he was simply the single appointee for the transaction. When the full quantity was found in his dorm room before they could divide it up, he took the blame to save his friends from embarrassment. Once he understood that the charge came with intent to sell—a much more serious crime—he sang like a bird about the involvement of others and had cooperated with the local police and the campus administration to identify the seller. He looked like a nice kid who had a bad but rather harmless college habit.

The next three involved a DUI, an alimony dispute, and a worker's green card violation. The fifth case was a domestic violence complaint against a husband by his wife. The man was in his late 30's and looked like a middle-income average guy...fairly handsome, probably well-educated with a steady job...but he had a cocky, uninterested air about him that made Tom suspicious. He'd been arrested the previous week after the police were called to the house. He made bail, and apparently had gone home and beat the shit out of his wife again for calling the police in the first place. When he was arrested Sunday night for the second time in six days, his bail was temporarily denied until he appeared in court for today's proceedings. As the case was presented to the judge, the man constantly glanced toward a woman at the end of Tom's pew. The woman was dressed in a pair of mid-priced slacks, a black tank top covered by a Gap cardigan sweater, and plain low heeled shoes. She was petite, average-looking, and appeared to be his middle-income suburbia wife. She had an obvious cut on her lip and a slight bruise under her left eye that was barely noticeable under expertly applied makeup. It was hard to read her expressions. There were times when Tom thought he noticed fear and other times when he thought she showed sympathy toward her husband. The man's expression was rather flat and he appeared to have a contrived apologetic look on display for the judge. He was not at all daunted by his predicament as his lawyer presented a defense that blamed everything on alcohol and the man's suspicion that his wife was having an affair. His lawyer told the judge that the man, Ryan Miller, was ashamed of his actions, had admitted to his mistakes, and apologized to his wife and their six-year-old daughter. He asked for probation, counseling, and participation in a weekly substance-abuse program so the two could resolve their marriage issues without the added difficulty of jail or restraining orders. The judge didn't seem optimistic about the man's remorse but agreed to the conditions with the added requirement for the man and his wife to appear before the judge in private quarters two weeks from now. Tom wrote Ryan Miller's name on a notepad for good measure, although he doubted that minor marital disputes were worthy of investigating a choice for Hope.

The remaining cases were fairly benign and uninteresting and by 12:30, Tom was sitting in J. Graham's Café at the Brown Hotel enjoying the famous 'Hot Brown' sandwich. Tom had worked several projects in Louisville, mostly on the outskirts of the east side where growth seemed to be most prevalent. He had done a new façade design for a tear-down in the pedestrian-friendly Highlands area. The project required a great deal of creativity where old met new while maintaining the historic feel of an area that had been largely taken over by young liberal professionals. His success in meeting the requirements of the conservative zoning committee while satisfying the hip, artistic style of the property owner's customer base had earned Tom a good reputation within a circle of well-to-doers in the Louisville community, leading to several other projects. Included in this was the design of several mega-houses in the affluent Mockingbird Valley area where southern conservatism still ran true in the blood stream. He loved those projects because clients typically wanted something completely out of the box and were willing to spend tens of thousands on the design to ensure they were not outdone by their neighbors. It was a clean-slate type of project with few limitations and allowed Tom and his team to stretch their imagination.

Tom finished his lunch and headed over to the client's office for a pre-committee prep meeting to go over the design and presentation oddities. His main client was the Houston Group, who represented a cadre of shop owners who would have equity shares in the building. Their shares allowed them to provide feedback on the size and shape of their retail space but not much in the way of overall design. Their presence today was in the nature of a courtesy invite on behalf of the Houston Group to show them the front elevations and building code restrictions. Since the shop owners had no approval authority over the design being presented tonight at the zoning hearing, Tom focused most of his attention on the Houston Group representatives in the room and didn't notice several of the shop owners were not present. He would work with them individually to incorporate the specific needs of each and mediate the space allocation negotiations that would take place once the overall footprint was approved. The group was pleased with the design and the presentation Tom had put together. He promised to return soon, possibly next week if all went well at the hearing, to meet with the individual tenants and address their specific needs for the complex's interior.

The following day Tom was back in his office when Rodney stepped in. "Hi Tom. How did the zoning committee go last night?"

"It went really well. They asked for a few minor changes but didn't require another hearing. They'll check that I incorporated their changes when we present the final construction drawings. I'm heading back there next week to negotiate the space allocation with the shop tenants so the team can finish up the detailed drawings. We should have everything ready for the Houston Group to solicit construction bids in about a month or less."

"That's great. Congratulations on getting through the zoning committee. They must really love you because you are the only one I know of that can fly through on the first go around."

"It's the obsessive-compulsive detailer in me!" Tom said with a self-deprecating laugh. "And the team did a great job with the design."

"No, you have a knack for knowing what they are going to hammer you on and then avoiding it. You seem to be able to draw their attention away from the targets they normally focus on by having something unique in the design. It makes them forget all about their typical concerns."

"Well, thanks Rodney. Let's hope the wool stays over their eyes for the final approval. Hey, thanks for talking to Barry about the Springfield job. Lisa told me she and two of the key construction guys were going to the meeting last week. Did you hear how it went?"

"Everything went fine. The customer was very pleased with the work. However, Barry wasn't very pleased that I forced his hand on the attendance. I think he was a tad suspicious of how I got involved."

"Well, I hope you blamed it on me instead of Lisa," said Tom.

"Neither, I said I ran across the two-week travel itinerary and noticed he was going to Birmingham alone. When I asked him if it was the design-construction merger meeting, he seemed a little embarrassed to admit that he was traveling alone. I reminded him of our policy and gave him subtle encouragement to allow his team to be more front and center."

"Great. Thanks again."

"No problem. I need to do it more often so he doesn't feel that he can run his own show without consequences. It's time to pull in the reins a bit. "

Tom liked where things seemed to be heading with the firm and hoped that Rodney would stick to his promise to keep Barry in line. If he did, hopefully the firm would be able to retain the junior architects and other employees that were crucial to making their projects successful. Tom put his mind back to the job at hand, and after working on the minor changes requested by the Louisville committee and giving instructions to the team on the prep work for the next phase, he took some time to Google Ryan Miller, the defendant in the domestic violence case.

The first page of hits was all for the Buffalo Sabres goaltender—recent stats, a Wikipedia page, and articles relating to a hit another player put on Miller that ended in a suspension and lots of controversy. A link on the second page directed Tom to an article in the Courier-Journal about a Louisville real-estate businessman who had been evicting renters without proper refunds of deposits and rent that had been paid in advance. The article described Mr. Miller as the owner of approximately thirty-two rather low-end rental houses. He had been requiring advance payment of up to six months by the renters and would evict them after approximately four months, keeping their deposit and last two months of rent while flipping over to a new renter with the same requirements. Thus, he was getting two months' additional rent on each house every four months. Then, under a false identity, the man led the evicted families to leave one house and, unsuspectingly, sign the same deal on a different one of his rentals. The availability of low-end housing was incredibly limited so the renters had little choice but to sign the six-month deals, often times getting advances on their salaries or exchanging their car titles for cash just to come up with the six-month up-front money. Losing the two months of rent plus the damage deposit was devastating for many of the victims who now couldn't afford to find another place to live. This had been going on for about two years before someone finally brought it to the attention of the local real-estate board.

The article stated that a review by the board could not find evidence of wrongdoing on Mr. Miller's part as the damage claims against the properties filed with the insurance agency justified the early termination of rental agreements. Apparently the board did not take into consideration the number of times this breach of contract had taken place and therefore did not look at the cumulative data to discover the obvious, consistent trend of four-month evictions. The author basically wrote that the board did not do their investigation very well and that something was rotten in the state of Denmark! This guy was ripping off poor people and probably the insurance company as well. The author wondered if someone on the board was 'in his pocket' too. The bio showed Mr. Miller to be

> "...37-years-old and active in the Louisville real-estate market for 10 years, mostly in the rental house arena. He had two commercial deals—one in 2010 and one in 2008—that had both ended in a feud with the business partners and foreclosure. He is currently involved in a retail development project with the Houston Group in the south-side shopping district. He is married to Janice Docher Miller of Cincinnati."

Tom couldn't believe the irony of what he was reading. This clown was one of the shop owners with an equity stake in Tom's project. The picture in the article confirmed that he was also the same Ryan Miller from the courtroom yesterday. The coincidence was more than Tom could ignore. He started to wonder if his choices were actually choices at all. Were they being presented to him under the guise of circumstance? Were they being laid before him in a manner that made him feel as if he were actually finding the gift recipients on his own? If that was the case, then they really weren't his own choices but rather pre-destined choices he was being led to. *Why not just kill them yourself?* he asked *something. Why bring me along to do your dirty work if you already know who the victims will be?* Tom suddenly felt betrayed, or used. Was the whole idea of going to the courthouse that morning a seed planted in his head by God, just so he could find this Mr. Miller whom God had obviously already chosen as an under? *Why do You need me to carry out the sentence?*

Tom was staring out the window deep in thought and anger when Marge poked her head into the office. "I'm taking off for the day and remember I won't be in tomorrow."

"Oh that's right. How is Jenny? Was today the final checkup?"

"Yes, she got a clean bill of health this morning so we're going to dinner and then shopping all day tomorrow. I hate to tell you I'm wasting a day off shopping but when I put in for the day off we were unsure about the possible results. It was either going to be a day of trauma or day of celebration. Based on this morning's results we're celebrating!"

"No worries at all. Have a great time and tell her I'm truly happy for her. Looks like she made the right choice with the surgery instead of a second, more intense round of chemo."

"Looks like it, but it was a difficult decision. She kind of went against the grain with a couple of her doctors," Marge said with some trepidation.

"How's that?" asked Tom curious to learn about a patient's choice in treatment.

"Two of her doctors wanted her to do the second round of chemo instead of the surgery and implant. It was only Dr. Crocker who told her that the risks were about even either way and that she needed to listen to her body and her heart."

"So *she* ultimately made the decision of which way to go?"

"Yep. We talked about it a lot and weighed the advantages and disadvantages. She struggled with ignoring the advice of two doctors against the advice of one who really didn't give advice on the option…just on the process of her decision."

"Hmmm. That's pretty strong of her…and the belief in herself."

"We decided that they can lead you to the water but it's up to you to decide whether to drink it or not. She felt her body was ready to fight the potential rejection of the implant better than to trust the chemo to fight the disease. 'Trust in the heart and soul' is her new motto!"

"Do they think she's still at risk for the rejection?"

"Possibly, but the most dangerous period is over. If her body was going to reject the implant, it probably would have done so by now. We can only hope that the rejection isn't a delayed reaction. I think the second round of chemo would have killed her, but who really knows."

"Well...good for her. Sounds like Dr. Crocker is the one to seek advice from for my next medical emergency. Have fun and we'll cover the fort tomorrow."

"Thanks Tom. See you on Friday."

Marge unknowingly had a way of putting things into perspective for Tom. The most mundane conversations with her always seemed to have a shred of enlightenment that was appropriate for whatever dilemma Tom was privately struggling with. This time, it was her sister's decision process that gave him some clarity about his anger towards God and the gift. Hope was being validated in meaningful ways every day in the world. Marge's sister was just one example of many. Tom wondered...did it really matter that he was being led to candidates? *Maybe I am being led to a potential choice but ultimately I'm making the final decision. God is leaving it up to me to decide, even if He is helping me find candidates. If I like the person or see a hint of possible good in them, then I don't make the choice.* What was it that Marina said, "...*Something* obviously likes us doing this and trusts us to make these decisions based on our human eyes living in the world today." *Choices made through human eyes living in the world today. Maybe God is unable to replace his divine perspective with the human perspective, so he's allowing the two to mingle. That's where the gifter comes in.* Tom wondered how often we surprise Him with our choices.

<u>Chapter Fifteen</u>

Tom spent Friday night at Brady's basketball game with Laura and Anna where his team won giving them a record of 8-2. Brady wasn't the star player but like his father he did everything with grit. Never giving up despite being one of the shortest players on the team, Brady played with enough focused energy to be a factor in the game and garner praise from coaches and teammates. Tom was definitely watching a younger version of himself when he observed Brady in a competitive environment. Not usually the best one on the court, field, or conference room, but always the one trying harder than the rest. Saturday morning was consumed with winter yard work while the afternoon provided a trip to the mall so he and Laura could finish their Christmas shopping for the kids. With Brady at a friend's house, Tom distracted Anna at the Build-a-Bear store while Laura roamed the remainder of the mall picking up the last few gifts and stocking stuffers. Although the mall was crazy with bitter and frantic shoppers, Tom loved the Christmas Holiday Season. He enjoyed the music, the movies, the decorations, but had to constantly remind himself of the true meaning of the season—Christ's birth. His experience with the gift had begun to open his eyes to a new view of religious meaning. He couldn't ignore the fact that *something* had exposed itself to a young Muslim boy and an agnostic woman. Christ didn't seem to be the only player on the religious field. Christianity was founded in the miracle of Christ's birth and resurrection, setting the course for the faithful to continue believing in miracles. Tom was comfortable with that relational tie to the gift. But it declared murder as a cardinal sin. With the gift, Tom was adhering to the principles of miracles but using a sin to complete them. The logic of the Christian religion as it related to the gift failed Tom with this thought. His wife and

Marina's philosophy of global spirituality was beginning to ring true for Tom and the sound was enticing, pleasing to the ear like seasonal hand bells, but with oddly provocative bitter notes. Their philosophy was exciting to wrap your arms around, almost invigorating as if you were hugging a forbidden stranger. Just when he was ready to free his mind from the bonds of his blind faith, the betrayal of his teachings would intervene and blanket his soul with guilt and shame. The thorny crown seemed to prick just enough to keep him from hugging global spiritual awareness too closely. And so, his struggle with faith continued.

Saturday night was the office Christmas party at Rodney's house. With a few exceptions, everyone was usually very relaxed and the conversations were tilted more toward family and personal lives rather than office talk. While Tom normally avoided long conversations with Barry at these parties, tonight their arrival unintentionally coincided with that of Barry and his wife, Christine.

"Hi Barry...Christine, good to see you," Tom said politely.

"Here for another miserable Christmas party?" replied Barry flatly.

"Stop being such a Grinch, Barry," said Christine. "Some people actually like socializing."

Barry shot an evil glance towards Christine that only Tom recognized. "My apologies Laura for not being excited about seeing the kind folks I work with all week on a Saturday evening. Good to see you again," faked Barry.

"Good to see you too Barry," Laura said with more enthusiasm than she felt. "Christine, how are the kids doing?"

"They're fine. Barry Jr. is in the middle of his sophomore year at Belmont and Robin is about to graduate from Vanderbilt with an internship already lined up with a law firm in

Chattanooga for the summer. She hopes to start Vandy Law School in the fall. How are Brady and Anna?"

Christine and Laura continued chatting up the steps and in the door while Tom and Barry followed behind in awkward silence. Most of the office had already arrived and the staff took notice when Tom and Barry arrived together. A little embarrassed, Tom made it a point throughout the night to let his companions know that they had arrived together by accident and that the two couples had not met earlier for pre-party socializing. Most knew that was the case but didn't hesitate from poking fun at the 'bond' between him and Barry. The evening went well and as always Tom took a sincere interest in the conversations with the staff away from the office. They left the party around 10:00 p.m. and headed home to relieve the babysitter. In the car Laura asked if Tom had a chance to talk with Christine.

"No, I never really did. Why?"

"I was just wondering if you noticed anything about her…about her appearance and her demeanor?"

"No, she seemed nice as always. I like Christine, I just rarely see her. When I do, I'm scared to death I'll blurt out the obvious question and ask her why she is married to such a jerk."

"She was different tonight. Almost like she was trying too hard to appear…happy. She also had a bruise on the side of her face."

"Really?" Tom said with a new curiosity. "I didn't notice."

"She had it covered very discreetly with makeup, but I noticed it. I wanted to ask what happened but then stopped to avoid a potentially awkward response. You don't think he hits her, do you?"

"I don't know. He certainly has a temper and ego, but I don't think she would allow herself to be treated like that."

"I don't think so either, but tonight she was just acting…well…like I said, trying too hard to be happy. If that SOB is hitting her, I may take a rusty knife to his family jewels."

"I am sure there are several folks in the office who would cheer you on."

"Well, she and I talked about going to lunch sometime in the next month to catch up. It would be nice if we could continue our friendship while you and he continue fighting for control of the firm," she mused.

"God, I hope it doesn't come to that!"

Sunday morning Tom was reading the paper with an eye on the weather for the upcoming week. Snow was in the forecast, which meant panic in a southern city. He kept browsing and ran across an article about gang problems in middle Tennessee. Who would have figured that Nashville had so many different gangs. There were the typical elements—Crips, Bloods, Asian gangs, Latino gangs, even a Kurdish gang— all operating on adjacent turfs for drugs and prostitution. The closeness of their boundaries caused constant turf wars and killings had increased significantly over the last two years. They actually had pictures of several of the gang leaders. You would think they would just go arrest the guys if they had their pictures right there for everyone to see. But the article concluded with a whole section on how difficult it was to prosecute gang members without actual proof of their crimes. Tom stared long and hard at the pictures to see if he could find something in their eyes that resembled fear or even remorse for their way of life, but they all seemed ice cold and immune to any human moral code. Their moral code resided inside the gang and only inside the gang. They would live and die for another gang member, but they'd cut the toes off the twelve-year-old sibling of a rival gang member to prove a worthless point of dominance. Crazy.

Chapter Sixteen

Lacy Miller hid under her bed until she heard the door shut. She was armed with a small Disney Princess flashlight and her favorite book, *The Hungry Caterpillar*. At six years old, soon to be seven, she couldn't read all the words but she had long ago committed them to memory. She and her mother had shared the book a thousand times with giggles and laughter over Lacy's insistence that the main character was a callipitar. Her mother had given up trying to convince her daughter that the word was caterpillar...the 't' came before the 'l'. It would be their joke for a lifetime. They had several inside jokes that made an unbreakable bond despite the nightmare that frequently invaded their lives. Even at this young age, Lacy knew she should wait until she had 'read' the book at least two more times before leaving the relative safety of the princess palace under her bed. Her mother needed time to 'fix herself up' before they enjoyed the freedom part of their day.

When she did finally go to her mother, Lacy crawled into her lap and gently snuggled her head into her mother's chest to listen to her heartbeat. After a bit of comforting, she stole a glance at her face to survey the damage. This morning's fight had lasted longer than usual and Lacy was frightened to see the temporary but lasting effects. She could tell her mother had been crying. That was always consistent. But the marks on the face exposed the real details of the argument. Today had definitely been an ugly fight.

"And what would you like to do today?" her mother asked with as much dignity as she could muster.

"Well, my Lady, should we clean the castle or ride to the village and shop?" Ever since her first grade teacher had the kids acting out stories set in the early 1900's when the British aristocracy ruled, Lacy would spill out these statements and call her mother 'my Lady'. It was hysterically funny and always made her mother feel special, even if for a brief moment.

Her tears changing from grief to joy, Lacy's mom gave the girl an engulfing hug. "How about we plan your birthday party and bake some cupcakes just for practice. Ms. Bell said you could have your party in the classroom on your birthday. We'll taste different flavors today and see which ones we like best."

"That sounds grand, my Lady! I'll get the bowls out." Lacy stared deeply into her mother's eyes and kissed her softly on the reddened cheek.

A day in the house with just the two of them was normal. They would play, clean, bake, watch tv, or talk. All of which was relaxed and fun...easy, as Lacy called it. She adored her mother as if they were friends in the same grade, but respected her as an adult when the times were appropriate. They often slept together tangled comfortably in Lacy's little bed. Lacy knew the nights when it was bad for her mother. Those nights she would crawl into bed crying and hold Lacy so tight she thought she might suffocate. But, suffocating in a bear hug from her mother wasn't the worst way to die...she had been threatened before with other options that were far less appealing. Sometimes she would feign sleep when her mother came, other times, she would simply wipe away a tear from her mother's cheek and listen to her heartbeat.

"Momma, what's it called when you...when your body does this?" Lacy squinched her shoulders up into her neck, tensed every muscle in her body, and made a face that crinkled her forehead, raised her eyebrows, and pursed her lips straight denying a frown or a smile.

Her mother immediately recognized the imitation. "Oh, I might call that tensing your body. Tension. You are showing tension from either fear or something you think is gross. Stiffen might be another word. Why do you ask?"

"I just didn't know what to call it. You know when your body reacts to a…to a place you don't like…or even a person."

"Like when the principal comes into your classroom and you're not sure if someone is in trouble?"

"Kinda. Although Ms. Clark's never mean to anyone, even if they did something wrong."

"You can say that your body reacts to the tension in the room when something changes. 'The servants could sense the change in atmosphere every time the Duke entered the large room for afternoon Tea'." Lacy's mother made her best attempt at a British accent to make the example play funny in her daughter's delicate mind.

"See, the Duke changed the atmosphere when he brought his mean thoughts or anger into the room. Everyone could feel the tension rise wondering what he might do or say."

"That makes sense. Tension." Lacy repeated the word with thought.

"Does your body do that often?"

Lacy was a bit shy about her answer. Unable to find the words, she just looked up and gave her mother a sweet smile. The message was conveyed easily enough.

That night Lacy knelt beside her bed to say her prayers. It was always the same prayer, "Dear Lord, thank you for all the wonderful joys in my life. My mother; my friends Graham, Darla, Lisa, Annabelle, and Lindsey; thank You for all my stuffed animals and my palace under the bed; also, Lord, please show me how to help my mother be happy and how to make the feeling of…well…I learned a word today…I don't like the tension in the house when my father is here. Help us be happy without tension. Amen."

Lacy unfolded her hands and opened her eyes. She stayed on her knees a minute longer and asked herself, *I wonder if prayers and birthday wishes are answered by the same person? It couldn't hurt to wish for the same thing you prayed about. That would be two times the chance of it coming true.*

Chapter Seventeen

Tom started the week with an icy commute to work. It had started sleeting early Monday morning and was supposed to get worse with a mix of snow and sleet continuing throughout the day. Normally Tom would work from home to avoid the driving hazards and have some time with Laura and the kids while they were out for the holidays. But he needed the plans for the Houston Group project in Louisville to get ready for his next visit at the end of the week provided the weather calmed down. When he arrived at the office, the peace and quiet lured him into a couple of hours of uninterrupted productivity. He had prepared all the notes and space allocation contingencies for negotiations with the individual tenants when he heard movement down the hall. Walking into the drafting room he found Marvin, one of the newest employees, hunched over a light board making some pencil adjustments to the front elevation of a Barry project. Tom surprised the young man as he was fully engaged in his work with headphones blocking out all potential interferences. Marvin removed the headphones, grabbed his chest to keep his heart from pounding through his skin, and declared, "You scared the shit out me!"

"Sorry about that. I thought I was alone here and heard some noise so I came down. I guess I should have thrown something at you first to get your attention. What are you working on that's so important to come in on a day like this?"

"I'm just making some adjustments to the Sculley front elevation."

"Why are you doing it by hand?"

"Well, if I touch the electronic version I may get fired...so I'm making the adjustments by hand and I'll present the changes to Mr. Johnston for consideration. That way, when he says he doesn't like them I don't have to go back and take them out of the electronic version."

"Can't you just save the revisions as a new file and present that? That wouldn't affect the current version." Tom knew Marvin was smart enough to realize this but the question was really aimed at bringing out the truth of why he was doing it by hand.

"Well of course I could. But...well...this way I have proof that it was actually my idea. I'll hang it on the wall in the team room with my name on it. He will have to ask me to incorporate the changes into the electronic file since he doesn't know the new software version we're using. Actually, I don't think he knows the old version, but anyway...I guess I'm just protecting my ideas from poaching."

"You know, he's going to take credit with the client either way. So you may be doing double the work for the same result." Tom added this statement with a bit of humor to make Marvin realize he understood why the staff had started doing these little tricks to ensure credit was given where credit was due.

"You're probably right, but there is something about protecting our ideas that is now being infused in all our work."

"Well, I am sorry it's gotten to that point with Barry. He's a good architect, a bit old-fashioned, but he shouldn't feel threatened by anyone in the firm. He can stand on his own if he puts in the time and elbow grease."

"I'll take your word for it."

"You hungry? There's a Mexican place down the street that may be the only place open in this weather. I'm buying."

"Sure, but you'll have to drive. My little Honda didn't do too well on the ride over this morning."

"No problem. I've got the old jeep today so we should be good."

Tom and Marvin talked over lunch in the quiet restaurant about the project and the adjustments Marvin was making to the front elevation.

"I think by taking the middle section up a little higher it adds some uniqueness to the front without any increase in construction costs. The top beams need to be higher than they are right now to accommodate the pump station for the sprinkler system which is currently on the ground in the biggest tenant area taking up precious space. It will also make that middle space more attractive for a higher end tenant. It gives them marquis space for a special sign or attractor."

"Sounds like a good idea. How will the construction costs remain level though?" asked Tom.

The front door of the restaurant opened issuing in a cold blast of air that drew attention to the conditions outside. Three young men entered, positioning themselves a few tables away from Tom and Marvin. The restaurant was empty except for one other table where a young couple was enjoying their time out of school. Tom immediately recognized one of the faces as a gang leader from the article he had read the day before. He couldn't remember the guy's name or the gang he was affiliated with but the face was unmistakable. He had a tattoo of a knife under his left eye that apparently represented the weapon used in his first killing. Tom had considered the gift when he was reading the article but never dreamed he would actually see or meet any of the men in the photos. For a few brief minutes after going to bed he had tried to devise a plan to find one of the men—or all of them for that matter—but quickly decided he was out of his element trying to track down gang members. It would be putting himself and his family at too much risk. Yet here he was sitting ten feet away from one the leaders and two of his posse. Once again, *something* was creating the opportunity. Tom started sweating as he racked his brain about how to make casual, physical contact with the men in this quiet, open setting.

"You ok? You look like you've seen a ghost and you're sweating," Marvin observed.

"What? Yeah...these chili peppers are hotter than I expected."

Marvin continued to talk about the savings on the construction costs while Tom worked through a safe approach in his mind. He was scared to death but decided this was an opportunity to provide Hope to some young victim that surely wished these guys would be removed from their life.

"I need to go to the head." Tom struggled to stand as his knees got weak. He walked slowly toward the bathroom, which would bring him right past the gang's table. Just before he reached their table, Tom slipped and propelled himself forward with arms outstretched to catch himself on anything he could grasp. He reached as far as he could and landed a hand on each shoulder of the two posse members who had their backs to him. This steadied him, preventing him from falling face first onto the tile floors just behind their chairs. All three gang bangers immediately jumped up reaching towards their pockets for what were certainly hidden weapons. Tom immediately put his hands in the air with an it-was-an-accident expression, but the bangers kept their threatening posture.

"Sorry about that. The floor is slippery with all the snow and ice being tracked in. I didn't mean to surprise you, but thanks for being there. You saved me from cracking my head on the floor."

"You should think twice about who you fall on. Your head's about to get cracked without the floor getting in the way," said posse guy #2.

"I'm really sorry." Tom swept away from the table heading to the bathroom with bile creeping into his throat. He splashed water on his face and collected himself for the return visit. He had only touched two of the guys and neither was the gang leader. *Shit, how does this work?* Would touching the two affect the whole group? Or do I need to get the third guy also? These are the kind of questions he hadn't thought to ask Marina. How could he have imagined a situation like this to even have thought up the question? *I can't risk another touch with guys like this. They could get violent without batting an eye…especially in a place where there are basically no witnesses. I can't do this to my family. The two posse members will have to do.*

Tom looked in the mirror and took a few deep breaths. He washed his hands and found his resolve return to him. *I have to think this through. They don't know that I know they are vicious bangers. They have no reason to feel threatened by a clumsy old white guy. What would you do if they weren't bangers and you had just slipped… truly by accident? You'd be embarrassed and make a joke. That's what you'd do.*

Tom walked out the bathroom and all three bangers eyed him suspiciously. He smiled a goofy grin and walked toward their table.

"I really am sorry to startle you guys. I need to put some sticky stuff on my shoes and not be so clumsy." As he said this Tom gently touched the shoulder of the gang leader as he passed the table. Not threatening, just a guy being friendly who had no idea who he was dealing with.

The gang leader leaned away from Tom at his touch but the reaction was not as severe as the initial encounter. None of them said a word in response to his attempt at self-deprecating humor, but they didn't seem threatened either. Tom returned to his table relieved that he was able to complete the encounter but anxious to see how Hope would be validated.

"Are you ok?" Marvin whispered. "I thought they were going to kill you. Did you see them reach for their weapons?"

"Yeah I'm fine. I almost busted my ass when I slipped."

Tom tried to continue his work conversation with Marvin as casually as he could to delay their departure from the restaurant. Marvin was surprised when Tom ordered a dessert of ice cream with chocolate syrup on the coldest day of the year so far. Eventually, the bangers finished their meal and paid the check. They exited the restaurant and got in their tricked out Toyota Camry with knife-eye behind the wheel. The snow had been falling all morning covering the sheet of ice hugging the pavement. As the bangers drove toward the street there was a utility boom truck approaching on their left. The truck was pacing slowly down a fairly steep hill when the driver of the Camry ran out of patience and decided to move out. It was obvious the banger had little experience driving in icy conditions and pushed the pedal to the floor thinking he would have enough traction to get ahead of the truck. Instead, the wheels began to spin inching the little car out into the street. The truck tried to brake and swerved to the right to avoid the impact. Careening sideways, the massive truck struck the curb and rolled onto its side. Still sliding, the truck hit a wooden power pole with all its mass and snapped it in half. Just as the bangers felt relief that a major collision had been averted, the top half of the pole came crashing down on the Camry igniting a flurry of sparks. From the door of the restaurant Tom and Marvin watched the accident seemingly in slow motion. As the pole with its transformer and power lines made contact with the vehicle, Tom could see and feel the electricity pulsating through the car. Although no fire erupted, the sparks and smoke of the frying interior quickly consumed its occupants. When Tom and Marvin walked closer to the vehicle they could smell the acrid odor of burning flesh. The wooden T of the pole had shattered the car's sunroof and the transformer with main power lines still attached had entered the hole and literally fried everything inside.

All three men were charred and promptly dismissed of their living duties. Hope had been validated for someone. Whether it was validated for past victims or victims that had yet to be identified—it was validated. Despite his earlier confirmation that the gift was real, Tom was taken aback by the finality of his decision. And it had happened in a matter of minutes...his decision, the actions to execute his choice, and the carrying out of the sentence. All within a surprising and unplanned twenty minutes. This part of the gift was still surreal for him. Even for these three gang bangers who had raped, killed, and threatened dozens of people...dealing out death as justice was still hard for Tom to swallow. But it came with much less guilt than he had experienced with Mr. Goddard. After another hour of talking to the utility workers—all of whom were ok—and the police, Tom and Marvin returned to the office to collect their things and call it a day. Visibly shaken by the whole ordeal, Marvin asked for a ride home so he wouldn't have to risk the same fate driving in a car ill-equipped to deal with the icy, snowy conditions.

<u>Chapter Eighteen</u>

Tom arrived home around 3:30 and told Laura about the bizarre afternoon. She didn't know the guys were gang bangers and that one was the leader of a notoriously violent group. Tom left his knowledge of that out of the story and just said they looked a little rough but had no idea who they were.

"That's awful," said Laura. "How bizarre that the pole and the lines fell right into the car. Are you ok?"

"Yeah, I'm fine. It's strange…maybe there is a mother or father out their grieving, but maybe there is a victim out there celebrating. Who knows why these things happen. I think Marvin was a little shaken up though."

"Probably his first time to see someone die." Laura said. "I'll never forget the accident we saw on our trip to Atlanta that time. Remember? The whole family crushed in their SUV and nothing we could do to help them. Awful. I've always wondered if it would have been better for the little girl to have died in the crash, instead of hanging on for a few weeks in pain knowing the rest of her family was gone. She died in the end anyway. Maybe it would have been better if she had just let go in the car and avoided the pain and knowledge that she had to endure for two weeks."

"Yeah. That would be a tough decision to make."

"What do you mean?"

"Well…I mean…if you had the choice of saving her or letting her go. I realize nobody really has that choice, but if you did, at the time, would you have known that she was going to die anyway and tried to save her the misery?"

"If I had the power of that choice? Looking at the damage to her body, even if she had lived, her life would have been severely altered. She probably would have lost both legs and her brain never would have been right again. I think I could have made the choice to set her free and 'stay' with her family."

Tom looked at his wife and realized that she was probably better equipped for the gift of Hope than he was. She had a firm, decisive logic about her spirituality that would not get the way of her validating Hope for the unders. She wouldn't have questioned or second-guessed her decisions. Morality was the absolute truth of her faith. It outweighed fear of being punished for not following strict religious doctrine. It didn't matter if a minister, a priest, or a rabbi agreed with her. If it fell within her moral boundary to do the right thing, she would do it. Laura had grown up in a more religiously open family where Christianity as the one true religion was up for debate. The divine to her was a consolidation of all faiths, but mostly incorporating human morality. Each had an element of truth to them that when combined gave her an understanding of her role as a human on earth. *She would definitely like Marina Kostitsen.*

She and Tom were very different in their religious views, which was a point of contention between them early in their relationship. Tom eventually accepted their differences knowing that her faith, while a bit untraditional, guided her with the same moral compass and sense of responsibility that was instilled in him. In turn, she agreed to raise the kids in the Presbyterian Church to give them a religious foundation that they could follow, question, or abandon when they were old enough to investigate their own needs for spirituality. With each choice of the gift, Tom was tilting more and more away from his conventional thoughts of Christianity and leaning into Laura's philosophies.

Tom spent the next day at home with Laura and the kids, limiting his work to only a few hours to take advantage of the family time. Although his street had been spared, several other adjacent neighborhoods had been without electricity for more than twenty-four hours. Laura decided to cook two large lasagna casseroles for some friends a few blocks away who were living with candles and a roaring fire to make-do until the electricity was restored. They all bundled up and walked in the snow to deliver the dinner and see if other families needed anything. The journey home included an impromptu snowman-building session and several well-made snow angels.

"Look Daddy. These are the angels that will help sick people get better and bad people go away!" delighted Anna.

"Yes, and you know you're one of those angels too."

"No, not me. They come from heaven but look just like us so we can't tell who they are. That way we always have to be on our best behavior. You never want to be mean to an angel."

"No, you don't. Angels can come in handy when you need them," Tom said. "But you may be an angel and just not know it yet. You never know what God has in store for you."

About the same time the snow angels were taking form, Valenia Hernandez was reading the article in the paper about the strange death of three Latinos in Southeast Nashville. The article attributed the deaths to the ice storm, but the manner of their death was indisputably odd. Electrocution. It couldn't have been more fitting in her eyes. *Death by electrocution...just like the electric chair from a deserving sentence.* Valenia couldn't help but smile as a real tear dripped from her own eye. Hope had proven worthy of trusting for her life.

Chapter Nineteen

The next day Tom decided to check in on his friend Lester Howe to see how well he had managed the snowstorm and make sure he had electricity and food. Lester was a former professional hockey player who was world-renowned as one of the best to ever play the game. How he had settled in Nashville after his career and become friends with Tom was a long story. But friends they were and Tom had worried about him over the last few years as he began showing signs of confusion and forgetfulness. He was eventually diagnosed with Pick's disease, ironically the same disease his wife had died from several years earlier, and his condition was worsening. At eighty-one, he still refused to move to a retirement home where they could help manage his condition, so Tom and a few other close friends in the area did the best they could to keep him safe and secure in his familiar surroundings. While watching his wife deteriorate from the awful disease, Lester made Tom promise that if he ever showed serious signs of degradation similar to her condition, Tom would help him 'not be a burden'. "Find a way to take me out Tom," he had said. Tom just nodded with a smile. He repeated it again making Tom say the words. "I'll try." That was three years ago. Ever since the gift, Tom wondered if his friend was prophetic.

"Hi Lester."

"Well hello there Tom. What brings you over in this nasty weather?" said Lester with a hint of sarcasm. He had grown up in the northeast and was well-accustomed to winter wonderlands. As a matter of fact, he loved the winter months and the cold air that came with them. Winter to Lester conjured up images of frozen ponds and spur-of-the-moment neighborhood hockey games where the kids would run home from school, lace up their Sears and Roebuck skates, and play hockey until the light faded and the dinner bell rang. Lester had always said that winter sports were what made men out of boys. This characteristic of Lester's just added confusion to the story of why he moved to Nashville…a town that saw probably three snowfalls a year, at best, and hovered around an average winter temperature of 46 degrees. Not very conducive to the winter sport theme.

"Just wanted to stop by and make sure you weren't a frozen carcass sitting in your Lazy-Boy. You have electricity and heat?"

"Frozen carcass…ha…I could survive for months in this heat wave you guys call winter down here. Yeah, I'm fine. Lost power for about two hours but that was it. How did you guys make out during the 'storm'?" Lester said keeping his sarcasm flowing.

"We did fine. We actually never lost power but one street over is still out. A big Maple tree came down over the lines so all of Crestwood is out. Should be fixed by this afternoon or tomorrow though. How you doin' otherwise?" Tom always asked a question trying to hint toward Lester's long-term health but he rarely got a bite from him. Lester was a proud, stubborn man and rarely gave a glimpse inside his steel exterior. So, Tom and all of Lester's friends had to play question games coupled with close observation to understand where the old man's mind was straying.

"I'm doing fine. Got a call from an assistant coach the other day from the Penguins asking me about an offensive scheme we used to run in Hartford back in the day. Even though I couldn't remember the scheme, I made something up. Sounded like he bought it."

"Your memory slipping?" asked Tom bluntly but with a bit of humor.

"No. Not really. The scheme was a blur but that doesn't mean anything. We had thousands of them over the years. I could barely remember them the next week much less fifty years later. All in all I'm doing good."

"So it's not time to 'take you out' as you so eloquently directed me?"

"Hell no. Not yet. The marbles are still rolling around and making noise in this beat-up head of mine. I'll let you know when it's time."

The two friends visited a while longer and Tom was relieved to find that Lester still had his wits about him for the most part. Ever since the gift had arrived in Tom's lap he had been nervous about visiting Lester, afraid to see the condition of his mind. Administering an under to someone he knew well was a challenge he didn't think he could overcome. At least for now, he didn't have to face that decision.

Chapter Twenty

A few days later, with all the snow essentially melted, Tom was on his way to Louisville to meet with the tenants of the Houston Project. He was well-prepared for the space negotiations but had some anxiety about meeting Ryan Miller—the shyster. Tom breezed through the first six sessions with little fanfare and the tenants were pleased with the original space allocations and Tom's willingness to make small adjustments as needed. It was almost 3:30 and he had two more to go. Next up was Mr. Miller. He came strolling into the Houston Group's office with a battle-ready look on his face. He was late, arrogant, and looked determined to get something out of this negotiation that would make him feel like he cheated someone out of something. He had plenty of space for his client's electronic shop but, as expected, he tried to negotiate more space for the same price. After an hour and a half going round and round, Ryan Miller stood up and declared that his client was not interested.

"You're going to deny your client a deal because of 65 square feet?" asked Ron Hardy of the Houston Group's team. "The space allocation is exactly what the client desired plus an additional 120 square feet that Mr. Roddin made available for you by moving a few walls around."

"My client isn't satisfied with the per-unit price based on comparison of other retail centers."

"Well, your client didn't have an issue with those prices a month ago when the original lease agreements were signed. Maybe we can call your client and have him provide us with his concerns first-hand." Ron Hardy knew about Ryan Miller's real estate history and was not in favor of having him act as a broker between the electronics company and the developer. All the other tenants were directly representing themselves, as was the norm.

"My client has hired me to negotiate on his behalf and I don't feel he's getting a good deal. He should be compensated for helping use space that you couldn't otherwise lease."

"Actually, the adjacent tenant would gladly take the extra space and is very pleased with the unit price. So if your client is unwilling to move in because we are not giving him 65 extra square feet for free, then we certainly have another interested party," stated Tom. "The choice is yours and I suggest you weigh the fees and deposits that will be incurred by your client if he backs away from the lease agreement at this stage."

Ryan Miller was furious but held his composure for the moment. "I'll have to talk to my client."

"By all means, feel free to call him privately in the next office," stated Ron.

"They won't be willing to make a decision that quickly. We'll get back to you by the end of next week."

"I'm sorry but that won't do. As we discussed before, the contracts need to be finalized tonight so we can move forward with the construction contractor. We can give you a few hours to discuss it with your client, but we will need your signature this evening."

"Well, I won't be able to come back to your office this evening. So it will have to wait unless you are willing to meet me at my house tonight."

Tom jumped right in and offered to go to his house later that night for the signature. Despite wanting to get the deal done, he was intrigued to see Ryan's wife again and check on their state of reconciliation. Ryan Miller left in a huff after giving Tom his home address and the time of 7:30 p.m. for the meeting. The final tenant negotiations went off without a hitch. Tom checked into his hotel and had a drink in the bar while he contemplated a choice for Ryan Miller.

Tom arrived around 7:20 at the Miller residence just east of Louisville in a modest neighborhood. It was a typical two-story house on a half-acre lot in a subdivision where three or four builders were responsible for all the houses. This led to having the same five or six house designs dominate the subdivision and rob it of any real character or uniqueness. Tom always wondered what the attraction was to a subdivision where all the houses looked the same. As an architect, it seemed boring and common. To the average Joe, Tom's opinion seemed snobby. As he walked to the front door, he noticed a balloon tied to the mailbox. Tom rang the doorbell and waited. As the door opened, a surprised woman dressed in yoga pants and a sweater looked at Tom without saying a word.

"Hi. Mrs. Miller? I'm Tom Roddin. I'm here to see Ryan about finalizing some paperwork on a retail lease."

"Ryan's not here right now." She was standing in the doorframe a little in the shadows but gave no indication that she would invite him in.

"He asked me to come by at 7:30 so I could get his signature. I guess I am a few minutes early."

"No. He's probably late."

"I am really sorry to interrupt your night. I normally would let business wait until the daylight hours but we have to get all the tenant signatures in place this evening to meet our agreement with the construction firm. I'll just wait outside if that's ok?"

"No. It's freezing out here. Come on in. Lacy and I were just about to cut some birthday cake." She opened the door and invited him to the foyer. He noticed right away in the new light that she had a light bruise on her right cheek. This definitely wasn't the same bruise that she had covered up so well in court the week before.

"Oh. Whose birthday is it?"

Just then a little girl about the same age as Anna came bouncing around the corner and declared, "It's mine! I am turning seven today."

"Well congratulations and Happy Birthday!" said Tom. "Seven...that's a big day indeed."

Mrs. Miller gave a slight grin when Lacy announced her proud day. You could tell she loved the little girl but there was a sadness that came with the adoring look that hinted at an uncertain future. As Tom followed them into the kitchen he noticed Lacy also had a slight discoloration on her arm. It was barely noticeable but definitely there. The kitchen table had three place settings but only one with a plate full of untouched food. Lacy's father had obviously missed the birthday dinner and was about to miss the cake cutting ceremony as well. Mrs. Miller pulled the burned candles out of the cake and began to cut Lacy the first slice.

"May I please have the blue rose on this side, My Lady?" asked Lacy in a pretend accent.

"Absolutely, dear. Get the ice cream out of the freezer and let's get some big scoops to go along with it."

"Yummy," declared the little girl as she ran to the freezer and pulled open the drawer.

"Mr. Roddin, how about some cake to help us celebrate?"

"Absolutely. But only a small piece, I don't want to spoil my dinner."

Tom sat there eating cake with Lacy and her Mom as Lacy went on and on about the cupcakes they had at school today in her honor. After about 15 minutes, the door leading from the garage opened and Ryan Miller walked in. The deadly look that occupied his face when he entered the room quickly turned to a fake smile when he noticed Tom eating cake with his family. You could instantly feel the tension rise in the room. When he walked toward Lacy to give her a hug, she showed the slightest bit of hesitation and half-heartedly returned a squeeze. Ryan never said anything to Mrs. Miller who was obviously ignoring him.

"Mr. Roddin, right?" he said with an extended hand.

"Yes. Good to see you again. Sorry to have interrupted the big celebration tonight."

"No. That's fine. Her real party isn't until this weekend. Just a quiet family dinner tonight." Ryan quickly glanced at the table with the two empty plates and his untouched meal. "How was the birthday girl's day at school?"

"Fine." Lacy had stopped talking and the excitement of her day and the accompanying celebration had completely left her. She sat quietly mixing her cake and ice cream on the saucer.

Tom realized at once that Ryan Miller was not only an abusive husband but was also a shitty father. He couldn't know for sure that Ryan caused the bruise on Lacy's arm but he understood completely that he dealt out plenty of mental abuse in the form of no love or appreciation for the gift of fatherhood. He was definitely putting on an act in front of the stranger in his house.

"May I be excused?" Lacy asked her Mom.

"Sure thing birthday girl. You can take your cake into the den if you want and finish it there."

"Is that a good idea to let her mess up the den?" Ryan said flatly to his wife.

Mrs. Miller just gave him a cold stare. "I'll let you two take care of business," she managed as she exited the kitchen.

Tom could sense the hatred in her voice but it was a sense of fear that filled the room. He could only imagine the argument that would ensue when he left as she questioned him about what was so important that kept him from having dinner with his little girl on her birthday. Tom had been debating all afternoon whether Ryan Miller would be an under, but so far, his encounter tonight left no doubt that something good would come from letting him meet Hope. They sat down at the kitchen table and pushed aside the three plates as Tom brought out the space allocation portion of the lease agreement.

"I talked with my client and he is not happy about the price but has agreed to sign it to avoid the fees of breaking the original agreement."

"Well, I think they'll be happy with the space," said Tom with complete indifference. "Here is the new square footage you requested and the signature page is here."

"You architects really have a good con going here. You charge all this money to make a sketch and then screw the lease holders at the last minute when it's too late to get out."

"I'm sorry you feel that way but as a person heavy into real estate I would think you would understand how much effort goes into getting things ready to build. I believe we have been more than fair and accommodating with all the tenants in the lease agreement and especially the space allocations."

"You don't have the first clue about how to make money in real estate. Otherwise you would understand why it is so disappointing for me to sign this agreement."

Tom understood completely. Ryan was preparing to cheat his client by getting extra space for free but still charging them for the full allocation. Screw him…this guy was a prick in business and an even worse human to his family. *Get the signature, give him a squeeze, and get the hell out.*

Ryan signed the documents and pushed the papers across the table to Tom. Without hesitation, he collected the papers and arose from his chair. Ryan remained seated and snorted a disrespectful sigh as Tom laid his hand on the man's shoulder. With a slight squeeze, he said, "You should have learned to appreciate your wife and daughter. That way, they might have actually missed you."

Ryan Miller gave Tom a quizzical but aggressive sneer and rose to his feet in a confrontational manner. "What the hell are you talking about? You don't know shit about me or my family. Get the fuck out of my house!"

"Gladly," said Tom. As he walked to the front door he stuck his head into the den to say goodbye to Lacy and Mrs. Miller. "Happy Birthday Lacy and thanks again for sharing your cake!"

Lacy smiled and gave him a polite, "You're welcome."

Tom got into his car, drove two houses down, and parked. He still had a view of the Miller's house but was far enough away not to be seen. He desperately wanted Hope to arrive before any more physical abuse could be administered. "Please make it quick", he whispered to the silent windshield in the car. After twenty minutes, Tom heard a siren singing in the distance. Minutes later, an ambulance arrived at the house and EMTs entered. Tom waited another thirty minutes before he got the confirmation he was anticipating, as the EMTs rolled a gurney out of the house with a sheet covering an entire body. He saw Mrs. Miller in the doorway as they loaded the ambulance with Ryan's body. Her face was expressionless...stoic. Not a tear or shred of grief. Although he was 75 yards away, Tom would swear that he saw relief in her posture. In the living room window looking out through the drapes, seven-year old Lacy was watching the ambulance pull away with the same indifference. Hope had been validated for at least two people tonight. *I am ok with this one.*

Chapter Twenty-One

After last night's encounter, Tom decided he needed to end this trip on a more positive note. Not that he doubted his actions in helping the Miller girls, but he was ready to save a life instead of providing death as a miracle. Tom visited the Kosair Children's Hospital and went to the critical care unit to inquire about the young patients. At the information desk, Tom spoke to the nurses about the ward and the type of comfort they provided for the children. He posed as a consulting representative from Vanderbilt Children's hospital who was doing research on other child care facilities. He was particularly interested in the care provided for children with diseases with low probability of survival. The head nurse quickly stated that no child was deemed beyond recovery and all the patients in the critical ward were focused on positive outcomes no matter the seriousness of the disease's progression.

Tom appreciated the nurse's optimism in an environment where pain and death were harder to deal with due to the age and innocence of the victims.

"I didn't mean to imply that you put any of your patients out to pasture," he said with pure sincerity. "I was just wondering about your communication and care of children who are facing very risky surgeries or treatments."

"It's difficult," said one of the nurses. "We always tell them the truth about the risks provided the family is willing to let them hear it. These children have an amazing ability to see the bright side of things despite their obvious fear. They are truly little angels with an innate will to dream of a normal future."

"We have an eight-year-old boy going in for his sixth surgery in ten months. This surgery is really the last effort to cure a neurological disorder that has crippled him for most of his memory. He is so strong…he told me earlier that this is the one! He's completely convinced that this is the surgery that will give his life normalcy. He's too innocent to comprehend the risks with a surgery that is completely experimental. But he's put his life in the hands of hope."

"Hope is the right place to put it," said Tom. "He sounds like an incredibly strong young man."

"He is. It's difficult…we all become so involved with these kids. When one is lost it's like losing a family member."

"And when one is saved it is a victory for all," said Tom. "Would it be possible to visit with the boy…just for a minute?"

"No offense Mr…?"

"Roddin. Tom Roddin."

"No offense Mr. Roddin, but have you coordinated through the administration department?"

"Not yet. I'm afraid we are in the early stages of deciding which hospitals to partner with. I was in town for other business and came by just to see the facilities and get a feel for the atmosphere. It's completely unofficial…like a preliminary site survey. I completely understand if you'd rather wait for the proper protocols to be in place."

The nurse hesitated for a slight moment while presumably gauging Tom's character. Satisfied, she said, "I'd have to ask his parents. Will you be interviewing him?"

"No. No, I just want to see his state of mind and wish him well. I'll only stay a moment. Vanderbilt has always judged its care on the patient's state of mind before and after risky treatment. Comfort is the true sign of success and failure from my research perspective."

"Let me see what they think."

The nurse disappeared into a room down the hall as the other nurses went about their duties. The head nurse looked toward Tom and said, "Our care here is very personal for each patient. I assume the same is true at Vanderbilt and we would love an opportunity to come visit your hospital to exchange some ideas and see your methods."

"I'll talk to the administrator and have them contact you. I believe we both could learn a lot from each other. We certainly have a common goal."

The nurse returned to the desk a few minutes later. "They said it's fine if it's brief. He's a bit tired but otherwise doing ok considering what he faces tomorrow," said the nurse.

"How invasive is the surgery?"

"It's pretty serious. They're going in at the lower back portion of the skull and working the probes and lasers into the upper middle part of the brain. The actual incision is very small but the path they take around the nerve bundle and around the brain is very risky."

"Has anyone survived this surgery…with any success?" asked Tom.

"It's only been performed three times. Two died on the table and one lived for about six weeks, but most of that was on life support. The problem is they haven't found a safe path through the brain tissue to get to the affected area without messing up other functional areas. But they feel they've made progress since then."

"Realistically, what do you think are his chances?"

The nurse hesitated for a moment, about to lose her composure. As tears welled up in her eyes, she said, "He is such a sweet boy and has been through so much. More than anyone should go through in a lifetime. This is really a last ditch effort for them. I hate to even say that, but why not have hope and try?"

111

Tom looked at the nurse and with a comforting smile said, "You all provide so much for these kids under the worst of circumstances. You are as much heroes and healers as the doctors and patients themselves. I have a good feeling about this one."

As Tom walked into Tommy Dechard's room, he saw a figure in the bed that barely resembled a human being. He was wired up to tubes, probes, and monitors and was stick thin from his life-long battle with the disease. Despite the disguise, Tommy gave Tom a huge grin when he walked in.

"Hi Tommy. I'm Tom Roddin. I just wanted to stop in quickly to say hello."

"Hi there. We have the same first name," said Tommy with delight.

"Yes we do. It's a good name isn't it?"

Tom introduced himself to Tommy's parents telling them that he would only be a minute and just wanted to see if Tommy was comfortable.

"You feeling ok today, Tommy?"

"Alright except for this one tube that keeps itching my arm." Tommy pointed to the tube in his left arm that was supplying antibiotics in preparation for tomorrow's surgery.

"Well that tube might be the tickle tube to keep you smiling."

"Well, it's more a bother than a tickle. I'd rather be tickled under my arms to get a good giggle."

"Well I'm sure that can be arranged! I understand you have a big day tomorrow. I think you are going to be fine. Strong, brave young men always come out on top."

"Well, I'm not excited about another surgery but I think this is the one to make me better."

112

"I think so too Tommy." Tom leaned over the young boy and gently squeezed his shoulder. "You're going to do fine. Hope is on your side."

"Thanks. I'll let you know how it turns out."

Tom took his leave and left the family to prepare for tomorrow's trials. He only wished he could comfort the parents today so they wouldn't have to suffer through the next 24 hours waiting for the miracle.

<u>Chapter Twenty-Two</u>

"Well, you know I don't want to intrude but if you ever need anything you know you can call me," said Laura as she and Christine Johnston were finishing their lunch at the Puffy Muffin.

"I know. Thank you for listening. I don't want you and Tom to get the wrong impression. Barry really has his sweet moments. It's just that lately our relationship has been a bit strained. He's kind of shut down recently and doesn't seem interested in talking through some surprises we've had. I'm sure he feels the distance between us but he's unable or unwilling to do anything to rebuild the bridge. I want you to know...I am not afraid of him...physically that is...I am more afraid *for* him."

"In what way?"

"He's never had the gentle, teaching personality that Tom so genuinely possesses, but he's always appreciated the work that others have done to help on his projects. He just can't show it well...not to me and not to co-workers. I worry that his current state is causing irreparable tension in the office with the junior staff as well as the partners. He senses the hatred from the staff and now the partners obviously recognize the issues. I worry he may be losing his ability to adapt to a new work environment where young kids are coming in and doing some amazing things. Being an architect is his only real passion...his only hobby, and he is letting it slip it away through sheer stubbornness and ego."

"Tom has always said Barry is a fine architect. It just seemed to Tom that lately he's not putting his creative genius to work. He seems very protective of his projects as if he needs confirmation of his abilities. Tom is at a loss how to help without offending Barry," said Laura carefully. "I don't mean to sound negative towards Barry, but we both wanted to make sure you guys are ok. I'm glad we had a chance to catch up. We should try to make this happen every few weeks...you know we're the only ones that can keep these boys in line as they prepare to take charge of the firm."

"No doubt. And please don't think Barry is harming me physically...I really did drop a bowl on my face trying to get it down from the top shelf."

"I believe you, the story was actually hilarious and too bizarre to make up as an excuse. But remember, the mental part can be just as bad. If we can help or if you just need an ear to bend, call me."

"I definitely will. See you in a few weeks, Laura."

"Bye Christine. I look forward to it and have a great New Year's Eve."

Laura got in her car and called Tom to see how his day was going. "Hey honey, how's work going?"

"Good. I hope I can finish up early and head home. I should have everything caught up until the New Year rings in. How was lunch with Christine?"

"It was really good. I just love her! We agreed to do lunch every few weeks just to stay in touch."

"What about Barry and her bruise? Did she fess up?"

"She had a pretty viable excuse that I'm going to believe for now. They haven't been doing very well and she is worried about Barry. Something is eating at him and she can't get him to open up."

"I didn't know he had an 'open up' state to him?"

"She says he does and that over the last year he's become cynical about everything. She recognizes that it's affecting his work and the environment at the office."

"Well, she should know him better than anyone else. For all our sakes, I hope she can show him the error of his bitter ways before it's too late."

"We'll see! What time do you think you'll be home?"

"Probably around 3 o'clock or so. I need to make a few quick calls and pack up."

"Great. Maybe we can put the kids to bed early and have some 'us time'! Love you."

"Don't tease me unless you mean it! Love you too."

Tom wasn't convinced about Christine's excuse but he didn't hear the story, so he would trust Laura's acceptance of it for now. Barry had been on his mind a lot lately wondering if he would be an under candidate. It certainly would benefit plenty of folks in the office and maybe even Christine if she was suffering more than she indicated to Laura. But that choice would be very close to home. Probably too close. Tom wondered also if Barry would be worthy of an over miracle instead of an under? Maybe he could make the guy happy and productive? Could he even perform an over miracle without knowing what the problem really was? Did he have to have a hard diagnosis of a problem, a disease, a dilemma, or an issue before he could pass along an over miracle? This question had been rolling over in Tom's mind for a while. So far, there had been a clear problem for all the folks he had 'saved'.

Saved. Bad choice of words. It made him feel too powerful. And power usually corrupted people. Nope…how about improved their situation. That still seemed a bit egotistical. Gave them Hope…or rather confirmed the reality of Hope for each of them. Funny how it kept coming back to that…the validation of Hope.

Tom picked up the phone and dialed the critical care ward at the hospital in Louisville. "Hi. This is Tom Roddin. Is Miranda there...she was one of the nurses on duty last week when I visited?"

"Oh yes, Mr. Roddin. This is Catherine, we spoke about sharing some ideas about critical patient care."

"Yes, hi Catherine. Sorry, I only remembered Miranda's name, old age is my best excuse. I was calling to see how Tommy's surgery went?"

"The surgery went really well...actually a miracle some have said. He came through the procedure with remarkable ease and hasn't had any of the seizures or debilitating pain that normally accompany his condition. The doctors are holding out hope that the recovery is long term, and we are all ecstatic that Tommy has survived. You should see him...he is so happy, so full of energy. He keeps saying 'See, if you hope hard enough, then you can get your wish'. He certainly has given us reason to believe."

"That's fantastic to hear. Will he be able to go home soon? What type of after-care will he need to keep the symptoms at bay?"

"Well, that's the real miracle of it. The doctors have him here for a few more days for close observation, but they say that the tests are showing signs of a full recovery...potentially without any follow-on medication. It's almost as if the disease wasn't there in the first place. Other than putting some weight back on the boy, they feel he can go home without a medication regimen. For his condition and the type of treatment he was given, that is unheard of. They are baffled but very excited."

"That really is great. I'm so happy for him and his family. I'm sure this is a happy ending that comes none too often on your floor. Congratulations to all of you for helping Tommy survive what we hope is the end of a very long, hard road and the beginning of a normal life."

"Thank you Mr. Roddin. Isn't it funny…sometimes it takes the strength of a child to confirm hope for us. It's easy to succumb to the woes of the world as an adult, especially in our line of work. Then, the innocent come along with a positive outlook and validate that there is still some good left in the universe to grab hold of. It's an important reminder to all of us."

"Yes it is. Please tell Tommy and the family that I'm so happy for them and for him to jump out and seize the world! Thanks for the update Catherine."

Tom hung up the phone and could hardly contain his amazement. Certainly Tommy's story was a miracle and one Tom now accepted with joy. But it was what Catherine said about the validation of good in the world that really soaked into his mind. It was the first time he'd witnessed the validation of Hope from someone who was not physically part of the choice and how it permeated the souls of other people. It seemed the gift was working according to plan.

Chapter Twenty-Three

Peter Landstrom grabbed his little brother's hand and gave it a squeeze for courage. They both tried to hide their anxiety as the nice lady from the state rang the doorbell to their old house. Within seconds, the door swung open revealing their father dressed in casual khaki's and a University of Indiana sweatshirt. Despite the big smile and hugs from his father, Peter sensed these emotions were part of the overall deception his father purported during the bi-monthly visits. All three entered the house with the lady setting up shop in the kitchen and the boys retreating to the living room with their dad.

The familiarity of the house should have put the boys at ease. They had lived in this rental house since their birth, but their memories were both horrid and joyful. Looking around, Peter saw pictures of himself and his brother in varying stages of growth centered in dusty frames on the end tables next to the couch and in the bookshelves on either side of the TV. The pictures of their mother were free of dust as if they had just been put out for viewing. The normal dust bunnies of the house only mingled with her image every other Saturday. The boys and their father sat in the room and talked idly about school and sports while the TV provided relieving chatter in the background. Peter figured his little brother was too young to understand the purpose of the visits with the nice lady in tow. These trips for the younger brother were to visit a man he was supposed to call dad, but had no real affection for or fond memory of. Peter knew better. These visits were to judge the relationships the boys had with their father. Whether there was fear, anxiety, hatred, love, or longing. Even though the state lady stayed mostly in the kitchen, Peter knew she was taking notice. He was even more convinced of their purpose based on the questions asked during their drive back to his grandparent's home. *Home,* he thought to himself. *Grandma and Grandpa's house is more of a home than this will ever be again.*

Peter's memory of the night his mother went missing was foggy. At ten years old, he couldn't decipher reality from dreams. He wasn't certain that he saw his mother's limp body being carried to the car from his bedroom window, but the memory was vivid. He wasn't positive that he heard the argument that night, but it would have been no different from what he heard almost every night in his earlier years. A dozen people had asked him if the stories were real over the last two years and his answers had varied because of the doubts that dwelt in his mind about the truth. Most of the people—police officers, lawyers, counselors—shrugged off his inconsistencies due to his young age at the time the crime occurred. For Peter, his part in this nightmare had many layers he hadn't talked about. He had told no one of his 'dream' where his father made him drink an adult liquid that burned his throat and made him gag. Initially he had refused, but his father forced a full glass down his throat and made him walk around his room so he wouldn't throw up. The morning after, the same day his mother went missing, he couldn't piece together the reality of the night. All he really knew for sure was that his feelings towards his father that morning were neutral at best. More likely, his feelings were the same as the ache he had in his belly and head.

After an hour of talking, the father took the boys outside to throw the football around, while the state lady watched from the kitchen window. Peter had no memory of this having happened in the past. Their father never played anything with the boys. In their past life, when the father was home, which was rare, he was usually drunk. Theirs was a house filled with arguments and anger. Peter and his brother would steal away to their rooms and wait for the storm to settle. When the father was gone, there was usually a temporary peace. Occasionally, mostly Sunday afternoons, there was a period when the household called a truce and the four of them would exist without open pain. Those afternoons weren't the memories of joy that Peter reflected on when he entered the house on these bi-monthly visits. The memories of joy were from a time when he was much younger, before he knew what evil looked like.

Chapter Twenty-Four

The firm had been commissioned to do another strip mall re-
design in Memphis and the plans were well under way when
Tom made the trip for a zoning meeting. It was late February
and the team had been furiously working to meet a late spring
construction start date for the project. Tom always included at a
minimum the project's junior architect in the normal client
meeting, but for some of the zoning hearings he would travel
alone and present the material. A large team of architects
walking into a zoning meeting was like bringing a dozen
egotistical, high-priced lawyers to a bond hearing for a
speeding ticket. It sent the wrong message and just made the
committee members bow up in a confrontational stance. A
single, humble architect presenting material for approval was
much more palatable to a group of folks who always felt they
had more power than they really possessed.

He went to the afternoon hearing to present the initial design
and came away with several actions before the next
presentation milestone. Always the detailer, Tom spent the next
two hours making notes in the lobby of the government
building while they were fresh on his mind. Notes completed
and lists made, Tom packed his stuff and headed to St. Jude
Children's Research Hospital to visit the critical care ward.
Tom was in absolute awe of the facility and the level of care
they provided to some of the sickest children in the world. He
had known for years about St Jude's and their mission to save,
counsel, and comfort children with advanced medical
conditions. Many of the cases were so extreme that survival—
although never talked about—was a fleeting dream with
experimental treatments as a last-ditch effort to save an
innocent child. Despite the seriousness of the diseases, the
advanced stage of many of the children, and the experimental

nature of the treatments, St. Jude's had an incredible survival rate. The research and development of treatments for childhood illness was unmatched by any institution in the country, possibly even the world. On top of that, the staff was known for its compassion to patients and their families, who often times needed more comforting than the children undergoing debilitating treatments. Tom sat in the waiting room of the critical care unit observing the families of the sick children. *This is a good place for some miracles...more than they are already performing.*

Tom walked to the nurse's station when it was clear of people and asked the attendant if he could talk to her. Again, he posed as a Care Consultant to Vanderbilt and wanted to ask her a few questions about the model they used for care of critically ill children. Linda Smart was in her early 30's and had been working here for six years. She was more than willing to talk to him for a few minutes if he was willing to follow her around the wing as she checked the schedules at each station before shift change.

"I have my walking shoes on for just such an occasion," joked Tom looking down at his dress shoes hidden under his suit pants.

"We'll have to work on that with you," Linda joked back.

"How many children do you care for in this wing at any given time?"

"We have 24 rooms but we try to keep the patient load to about 18 to make sure we can give each one the attention they need without overwhelming the staff."

"How long do most of the kids stay in this ward before they are moved or...," Tom hesitated... "get to go home?"

Linda noticed the hesitation immediately and replied without missing a beat, "We get the most severe and advanced cases in this wing and despite our survival rate, we unfortunately don't get to send as many home as we would like. Time on this wing can last as short as a week during special treatments or as long as several months in more extreme cases. The average time is about three to four weeks."

"That's a long time to get attached to some of the patients. I can only imagine the tug that produces on your hearts on a daily basis."

"Well, yes it's difficult...by the way, we don't use the word *ward* here...it has a negative, impersonal connotation to it. We actually have a use/don't use list to make sure we speak in positive, encouraging, and soothing tones. It sounds kind of silly but when you think about it, those little details add up. Each detail feeds our mission statement, which is as much about the care as it is the treatment. Working in this wing is the most difficult and rewarding job a person could have. The dichotomy is exhausting. The losses are extremely hard to cope with, but the successes...wow, the successes...they are just pure! Pure is all I can think of ...no noun or adjective is needed to follow the word for me."

"I actually understand that. The word is strong enough on its own."

"Yes. I cry every week on this job...sometimes for death sometimes for life. Sometimes for both."

"Do you have any long timers on the wing now?"

"Yes we have two. They both have what is normally considered a terminal advancement of their disease, but they are undergoing some specialized treatment. They, along with us, are unwilling to give up."

"How long have they been here?"

"The boy, 13, has been here for seven weeks and he is currently not responding to the treatment which is more a stop-the-growth treatment rather than a cure. The girl, nine, has been here for eight weeks and was doing much better after a few sessions but has taken a turn for the worse these last few days." Linda was answering all these questions with thoughtful passion but with acute attention to the schedule boards she was inspecting.

"Are they still hopeful or can you tell when they've given up?" asked Tom.

"Honestly, the kids are more defeated and scared when they first come in than when they have been here for a while. These two, they have an amazing strength to their spirit. Despite the pain and discomfort, they seem to hold on to the belief that they will beat the disease. It's not an air of invincibility…it's a belief in hope that just won't go away. These two just like many of the kids that come through this wing are an inspiration to all of us. I have seen sick adults that don't have half the will to live the kids here possess."

"Isn't that odd," Tom mused. "We have seen this at many critical care units…kids and young adults have an innate ability to keep Hope alive while adults with lesser diseases seem to stop believing early in the treatment process. There are always exceptions, but in general, kids seem to have more faith in Hope being validated than adults do."

"Hope being validated…that is an interesting way to put it." Linda pondered the phrase for a minute as she stopped walking. Turning to Tom, she said, "I like that. It's so true. The successes certainly validate hope…not only for the sick but also for the families…and us!"

"Exactly," said Tom. "Linda, would it be ok if I met the boy and the girl? Only for a few minutes each. It wouldn't be an interview or anything like that. It's just to see their state of mind through the eyes of a complete stranger."

"We can't allow contact with the patients by anyone unless the family agrees. I am also supposed to get permission from the director of the critical care wing."

"Ok I understand. I don't want to make you go through a bunch of protocol hoops just for a quick hello. It's not worth all the fuss."

"Well, let me ask the family real quick. If you are just saying a quick hello then I think we can bypass the formalities."

Linda disappeared into a room a few doors away from where they were standing. Tom was getting a little nervous about his ruse as a Care Consultant and made a mental note to talk to someone at Vanderbilt to suggest a collaboration session with St. Jude and Kosair. Linda returned with a smile and said, "Both the mother and father are there and said that a quick visit would be fine. Her name is Monica Stapleton. As I said she is nine and her treatment is experimental. She did really great at first and her progress was encouraging. But lately the side effects have started taking a toll on her physically. She's been here for a while and I think she really misses being a normal 9-year-old girl. She should be experiencing middle school, going to the mall with her friends, having late night girl talk, watching boys grow an interest for her and her friends. She still has a lot of fight in her despite the recent setbacks. She asked me yesterday if 'feeling good all the time, felt good?' That night when I got home I cried myself to sleep…partly because it was such a sweet and innocent thought…but mostly because of frustration at my inability to help her."

"I know it's tough to see this every day, but you have to believe that the care you give these kids is your gift to life and Hope for them."

"We know and we keep reminding each other of that, but in the moments when they are down and wondering if they have a future, we want to give them the crystal ball and let them see that their future is brighter than most people who don't have the same trials and tribulations. Anyway…Monica seems to be in good spirits today… her next-to-last treatment is scheduled for the morning so I think she's ready to have 'hope validated' for her." Linda added the last bit with a smile and a wink to Tom.

She seemed to like the feel of the words coming out of her mouth.

"Thanks. I promise I'll only be a minute."

Tom walked into room eleven-eleven and couldn't ignore the significance of the number – it was the date when he got his note about the gift. "Hi there Monica! My name is Tom Roddin. I just wanted to stop by to say hello and see how you were doing?"

"Hello Mr. Roddin. Are you a new doctor here?"

"No. I'm just a helper at another hospital and am visiting to learn more about the wonderful things the staff does here. I hear you're one of their favorites."

"Well, that's only because I have been here so long," she insisted. "But I am ready to be home and writing them letters instead of asking them for more Jell-O and applesauce."

Tom laughed and approached the bed extending his right hand to take the girl's frail bony hand in his. As he gently shook her hand, he casually placed his left hand on the girls shoulder and said, "Are Jell-O and applesauce your two favorite foods?"

"Not really, but they are the only things that sound good when my tummy is sick."

"Well I hope your letter-writing will come soon. You are a special girl, Monica…and special things happen to special people. Is there anything we can get you?"

"No. Just a prayer for the other kids here with me. I don't want them to have to spend as much time here as me. I hope they get better quicker."

Tom glanced over to the parents who were both fighting back tears as they listened to their daughter's selflessness. "I can definitely do that. Thanks for letting me stop by and I hope you are home before they run out of Jell-O!" He nodded to the parents and left the room wishing again he could reassure them that miracles did actually happen. They only needed one more night of strength before things would turn around for Monica.

As he walked into the hallway, Linda was coming from another room three doors down and turned in his direction.

"The boy's name is Ronald St. Onge. He's not feeling very well and the father wants to talk to you briefly before he agrees to let you visit."

"If they have any concerns then I shouldn't bother them," said Tom.

"I think he just wants to make sure you're not going to ask questions that will remind him of his misery. It's been a long, hard stay here for him...I think their hope is starting to wane."

Tom followed Linda down the hall and waited outside the room while she brought Mr. St. Onge to the hallway. Tom extended his hand and introduced himself to Ronald's father. They exchanged a few quick introductory words and Ronald's father began explaining his concerns about Tom's visit.

"Ronald has had a rough stay here. They have been trying to slow the growth of the tumors over the last two months...not cure them, mind you...just slow them down. Then, last week we found out that they want to try some type of experimental treatment on him, but that it won't be ready for another three to four weeks." Mr. St. Onge paused, partly in thought and partly to choose his words carefully. "I don't want to sound cynical Mr. Roddin, but I am concerned about giving him too much false hope. He is being kept alive right now for the sake of a treatment that may or may not help. His current treatment makes him so uncomfortable, I'm just not always sure the potential for a cure and its uncertainty is worth the continued suffering."

"I completely understand your feelings. Hope is a thread that

128

we all like to believe in but we have to weigh the price of suffering versus the reward of Hope. I won't mention anything about the future to Ronald. I just want to observe his current state of mind as it relates to the care by the staff. I don't mean the food, the service, and all that...I am talking about the effect of the staff's compassion on him. He won't know what I'm looking for by the questions I ask him. I will just be another 'administrator' stopping by to say hello."

"I'm sorry if my concerns come across as unappreciative of the care and attention he is receiving here. It's just...my son is dying and I don't know how much longer I can watch it."

Tom was startled at the man's resignation. It was hard to accept that a parent would ever lose the fight necessary to make their child well. But at the same time, he could empathize with the difficulty of watching your own child suffer so much when promise after promise of treatment didn't produce a cure. He was curious to see whether Ronald's state of mind showed the same resignation as the father's.

"I know it's difficult to remain strong and confident for your son when you see him struggling. But let him believe in Hope...it may be the only thing that he has to look forward to right now. And save a little for yourself. Seeing the strength of Hope in your eyes will keep him encouraged no matter the outcome."

Tom walked into Ronald's room and introduced himself. Ronald was a good-looking kid, albeit skinny from his time in the hospital, who produced a large grin at the sight of the stranger walking into the room. His smile wasn't forced but it was obviously concealing his physical discomfort. To Tom, it appeared to be a genuine reaction to something new in Ronald's daily routine of monotony.

"The nurses tell me you are quite the pain in the rear around here," Tom said jokingly.

Ronald laughed and said, "They must like people who are

pains because they won't let me leave." He shot a loving glance toward nurse Linda who was in the room looking at the spider web of tubes running in and out of Ronald's body.

"We'll let you leave when you learn some manners!" she joked back.

Tom was in complete observant mode as he asked Ronald a few benign questions about his stay, his favorite foods, and what he was doing for entertainment. Ronald seemed to be taken away from his pain for a brief moment as he thought up clever answers to Tom's questions. Never did Tom notice the slightest hint of defeat or resignation about his condition or his future prospects.

"Sounds like I'll be here for a few more weeks before we begin a new treatment. I've always got my fingers crossed and I trust the doctors when they tell me I have as good a chance as any to come through ok. If its 50-50 then I might as well believe I'm on the side of the good 50," said Ronald with matter-of-fact believability.

"You're absolutely right," said Tom a bit hesitantly because of the talk with his father earlier. Tom reached up and touched the boy on his shoulder and gave a slight squeeze. "Take care Ronald. You're a special young man. I hope I can get back here soon to see your progress."

Tom walked out of the room followed by Ronald's father. Tom stopped and took the man's hand. Looking directly in the eyes, he said, "You have done a wonderful job keeping his spirits up. He hasn't lost Hope that he'll get better and that says a lot about yours and your wife's strength. As I said, keep some of the Hope for yourself so it doesn't always feel like pretending. He feeds from you and that may just keep him alive for a long time." Tom spoke these words with a compassion that carried no hint of instruction, scolding, or condescension towards Mr. St. Onge. It was delivered as a heart-felt pep talk like a minister would give to one of his congregation members.

Mr. St. Onge's eyes diverted downward with a sadness that reflected some guilt at showing the defeated side of himself to a stranger. "My wife is the strong one. She has a very positive outlook in all difficult situations. These last few weeks have been especially difficult for me. Sometimes it takes a stranger to come in and remind me of what's important…his happiness and comfort are all that matters now, whatever the final outcome. And to keep providing that comfort, I have to show him I believe. Thanks for the reminder."

Tom shook the man's hand and said his goodbyes. Linda walked him back to the front desk and he wrote down the number of the direct line to her station. On his way out the door, he couldn't help but wonder why he was only limited to 10 of these life saving miracles. He could sit in this wing and hand out hundreds for the rest of his life.

Chapter Twenty-Five

A few weeks later Tom was in the small conference room with his Memphis project staff when loud voices and arguing interrupted their meeting. He stepped into the hallway and glanced toward the large conference room to see Barry and Lisa Harrington standing face-to-face exchanging unpleasantries in front of the three other project personnel. Barry was red-faced and barely controlling his temper when Tom walked in to mediate the fight.

"What's going on?" Tom said with calm authority trying not to be confrontational.

Lisa, a bit embarrassed, immediately backed away from Barry and melted into one of the high-back conference room chairs.

"This doesn't concern you Tom," retorted Barry.

"Well, actually Barry, it does concern me. When the whole office can hear raised voices while we're trying to work, you bet your ass it concerns me. Now what's this all about?"

"We seem to have some members of the junior staff who believe they're in charge! I will not tolerate disrespectful behavior or the constant questioning of authority that seems to now be the norm around here."

"Disrespectful?" shouted Lisa as she jumped from her chair back into the fray. "I merely made a few recommendations on our approach when you started on your tirade about how incompetent we were. Why are you so insecure that you feel every idea that isn't yours is a challenge to your authority? These are recommendations that the client has brought up more than once."

"That's another thing! Why are you talking to the client without my knowledge? I should be the sole point of contact. I can't work in an environment where I'm constantly being undermined by 'secret' meetings where I'm certain you're painting me as an obstacle."

"Those meetings were requested by the client and you didn't even show up for the conference calls. It was put on your calendar six days ago, so don't accuse me of setting up 'secret' meetings."

"You are fired effective immediately! I will not be talked to in this manner."

Lisa inhaled a roomful of air in preparation of a loud protest, but Tom waved a hand to silence her.

"Will everyone excuse us for a moment. Lisa go back to your office and calm down. Barry and I need a few minutes to talk this through," said Tom with steely calm.

"There is nothing to talk about. I have made a decision and that is that!" shouted Barry.

Looking Barry straight in the eyes and with a very stern voice Tom said, "Sit down, Barry!"

Barry, a little startled at Tom's command, descended heavily into the nearest chair as the rest of the staff exited the room. Tom was furious at the situation and knew Barry had struck the wrong chord with Lisa and vice versa. Once they got to this defiant position, neither would back down despite the difference in age and level of authority. Tom tried to steady himself for the awkward conversation that was imminent. Despite Tom's previous talk with Rodney, Barry was still his senior and a partner in the firm. He doubted that Rodney had told Barry of his intentions to make Tom a partner and eventually let him take over management of the firm. Even so, Tom felt compelled to make Barry realize what his arrogance was doing to the firm. They couldn't afford another defection of a talented young architect. Not only would it affect their current workload but it would create an insurmountable challenge when trying to recruit new or replacement talent.

"What started all this Barry?" Tom tried to use a calmer, rational voice to draw Barry away from his defensive posture.

"That uppity bitch thinks she knows everything!"

"That's not what started it. Where did the conversation go south?"

"She has been meeting with the client without my knowledge and scheming changes to undermine my work and involvement. As a senior partner in this firm, I find that unacceptable."

"Apparently the meetings have been at the request of the client and you were invited."

"All coordination of changes should come through me. I am the direct line of communication for Roger Malty who last time I checked is the owner of our client's company."

"Roger Malty is a figurehead and lets his people run the day-to-day project operations. If you consider him your equal then you should let your team handle the details of the project on our end."

"You would love that wouldn't you Tom," Barry said with dripping sarcasm. "Get me out of the way so you can take over the firm and baby all your precious 'team' personnel. Well, I won't sit by and let you or any of the other snotty-nose little twerps put me out to pasture."

"No one is trying to get rid of you Barry. So knock off the self-pity drama." Tom surprised himself with this blunt retort but couldn't hold back his frustration any longer. "We have some great young talent in the firm and one by one you are chasing them all off. Who's gonna be left, Barry?

You...me...we need these folks to run a business and help carry the workload. Your arrogance is getting in the way of our being successful...even profitable. Recognize that they are the ones that make us look good...not the other way around. So back off!"

"I will not be spoken to in that tone!" Barry slammed his fist on the table and abruptly stood up. With a red face and every vein in his neck strained to the bursting point, Barry said, "I am a senior partner at this firm and the only reason we have stayed afloat the last few years. You, Tom, are NOT a partner and have no say in this matter!" Barry stormed out of the conference room slamming the door into the back wall with enough force for the doorstop to pierce through the solid wood door panel and send a loud signal to the whole office that he was not willing to back down.

Tom sat at the conference room table for a few minutes trying to calm down while debating how to bring this to Rodney's attention and save Lisa from her firing. If they lost Lisa, they would be in big trouble. *Dammit! Why couldn't she have been more civil with him...at least through the end of this project?* Once this project was finished, Tom would see to it that she never worked on another of Barry's jobs. Tom couldn't understand why Barry had become so hostile the last two years. He had always been passively arrogant but it was tolerable then. Now it was affecting the firm's future, the people that Tom cared about, and possibly even Barry's wife. Something had to give! He couldn't stand by idly anymore and watch Barry destroy people's lives.

Leaving the conference room, he turned towards Lisa's office to find out what prompted the argument knowing he would need the whole story in order to save her job. After 30 minutes of listening and counseling, he left Lisa reassured that the firm would not allow her to be fired on a whim from Barry. Lisa made it very clear to Tom that while she appreciated all that he did for her, she would not stay at the firm unless something was done to resolve the issues that the entire staff had with Barry. "I can grow professionally somewhere else if this firm decides that Barry Johnston is a critical element to its future," Lisa stated with true conviction.

He hated to go back to Rodney with another problem related to Barry. Rodney would quickly tire of the childish bickering between Barry and the staff. He also wouldn't play the babysitter every time Barry and Tom had a disagreement. Tom walked back to his office and noticed his Memphis team had retreated to the comforts of their own confines to let the situation settle. His anger had not yet subsided when his phone rang. *What now?* he snorted to his empty office.

"Hello. This is Tom."

"Mr. Roddin. This is Linda Smart from St Jude Children's Hospital. I was returning your call from yesterday."

Quickly changing gears, Tom found his calm voice. "Oh yes. Hi Linda. I just wanted to check in on Monica and Ronald. It's been a few weeks and I was curious how they were progressing?"

"Well, it seems that we could use a few more of your visits! The other nurses and I have come up with a theory that you are a miracle worker. Monica is doing very well and her last few treatments have shown real signs of improvement. More importantly, her body is not rejecting the treatment as it had been. In fact, she has been feeling remarkably well and eating regularly. She has put on almost ten pounds in the last three weeks and looks fantastic."

"That's great but I certainly can't take any credit for that. How's Ronald doing?"

"Well, he is the real story behind our theory."

"How so?"

"Ronald's tumors have definitely stopped growing over the last two and half weeks which has been very encouraging. The research team put together his treatment regimen earlier than expected so he had his first experimental treatment three days ago. Ronald has experienced what can only be described as true modern medical miracle. Not only have the tumors stopped growing due to his regular treatment over the last several months but also several have been drastically reduced in size just in three days and from only one treatment. He's getting his second treatment today."

"That's remarkable! Well it sounds like the doctors have hit a home run with this new method. The treatment designers should be commended for their work. Science is a wonder isn't it?"

"Yes, but...Mr. Roddin, I've seen a lot of experimental treatments in my time here. Some work and some don't. I have never seen a treatment work this quickly and without having to make adjustments on the fly for the dosing, the percent combination of drugs, and/or changes to the mechanism of administering it. All of these take time and an incalculable toll on the kids physically and mentally despite the hope their condition may improve. Ronald's treatment has so far shown miraculous results without any medical adjustments. What's even more unusual, his body...well, physically he is experiencing no side affects, no signs of physical degradation that almost always accompanies new treatment. Normally there is a downward physical trend, at least temporarily, before there is positive progress. Ronald seems to have by-passed the downward trend in favor of the positive progress."

"Ronald is a strong kid and I didn't see any signs of his letting go when I was there. Call it luck, call it perfected science, call it a miracle...this one worked out the way it should work every time. You and the staff provide the care and love to these kids so they can continue believing in a good outcome. You should be proud of that."

"We are but we also can't ignore the fact that you came to us out of the blue and then two of our worst cases, two of our

137

longest staying patients miraculously began a healing process that was only a hope and a prayer at first. I can't get out of my mind what you said about hope. It has certainly been validated for those two kids and we all carry around a little more belief in hope than we did previously."

"Thanks Linda but I have no healing hands. I've had some things happen in my life that lets me lean on Hope more than I did in the past. Hopefully it is contagious! Thank you for calling back. I'm so glad both Ronald and Monica are making progress. You've really brought some great news on a day when it is sorely needed."

"You're very welcome. Come back to visit anytime and bring your healing aura with you!" Linda made this last comment with a bit of irony that wasn't lost on Tom. She had called him a miracle worker. That hit a little too close to home for Tom and he started getting nervous about being too obvious with the gift. Unbelievably, this type of situation raised his anxiety levels much more than the office drama. The fear of being exposed frightened him. Where most people accepted this type of praise as a compliment, Tom's social anxiety made him shy away from the spotlight. The presence of the gift only compounded his discomfort. What if someone, like Linda, had an awareness about the gift and started telling other people that she thought he was a healer. Things could get crazy very fast if something like that became a public phenomenon. He would be sought after constantly to perform miracles and then denounced as a psychotic fraud once he couldn't produce them. A thought flashed into his mind...*I wonder if that is how Jesus felt?* He immediately regretted making the comparison and felt guilty for his arrogance. He had no illusions about the gift of Hope and what it meant for a mere mortal like himself. He was a normal person...a human...just like Aarzu, Marina, and all the other gifters before and after him. They were just spreading Hope one small miracle at a time. The Christian angle of the gift that seemed so definite to him at first was waning quickly with the progression of his journey leading him farther and farther away from the one-dominant-religion mirage. With

138

himself, the Jewish man, Aarzu, and Marina all in the picture together, it seemed selfish to associate the gift of Hope to Christianity. This was *something* larger, more universal. *Have I been living with tunnel vision all my life believing that God belonged only to one religion?* Tom began to think about the universal concept of religion with a new perspective…one that would never have entered his mind in his previous life. With each passing day, he took two steps closer to his wife's understanding of the world around them.

"Tom, can I talk to you for a minute?" Rodney Turnage was standing in the threshold of Tom's office with a disturbed look on his face. Tom was startled out of his thoughts and immediately wondered if he had been thinking out loud. It took him a moment to resurface from the depths of his confusion about his lifelong religious beliefs. Finally, he looked at Rodney and invited him to the two chairs opposite his desk.

"You look a little shaken," Rodney declared.

"Sorry. I was just sorting through some difficult thoughts."

"I'm not exactly sure what happened today but Barry stormed into my office ranting about the lack of respect provided to the partners in this office."

Tom took a deep breath to switch focus back to the office crisis. "He and I had a difficult discussion earlier in the conference room. Maybe I was out of line, but I can't continue to stand by and watch him run off every good architect we have left in the firm."

"He told me he fired Lisa Harrington and wanted her out of the building by the end of the day."

"Yes he did. I was going to come talk to you about that…see if he could be persuaded to reconsider. I don't believe…"

"He also told me that he wanted you fired effective immediately and that we should go out and recruit some established talent that would be more conducive to a respectful atmosphere in the office. What the hell happened?"

"Rodney, I'm going to be blunt despite the risk of jeopardizing my job. Barry Johnston is destroying this firm one talented person at a time. You know he's always been arrogant but it is turning vicious now. Over the past two years we have lost four very talented architects because of his inability to work with the project teams. He can't do it alone yet he refuses to treat his team with any amount of dignity."

"What happened this morning?"

"He and Lisa got into a heated discussion—something about meetings she had scheduled at the client's request but he seems to think he wasn't invited. He feels like she's trying to go behind his back on the final project designs. She claims he has been included in the meeting invites but that he hasn't been participating. Apparently, he came in at the end of the teleconference this morning and didn't like the changes to the design that had been agreed upon with the client over the past two weeks. He came in to the picture late and then just started putting Lisa and her work down in front of the client. When the call finally ended I think Lisa's frustration level went over the edge and the discussion got a bit out of hand."

"Lisa needs to learn to control her temper with more grace," declared Rodney. "I understand where she's coming from but unfortunately we all have to tiptoe around Barry's personality. I have no doubt that she was provoked, but she must learn to work with Barry and all his nuances if she wants to grow here."

"I agree and have talked to her about this. But, with all due respect Rodney, something also has to be done with Barry. I understand and agree that we all have to adjust to special personalities in the office...but it must include Barry also. He's an angry man with intentions of belittling people. I would be more than happy to try and talk with him, but he sees me as no more than an underling...he won't listen to any advice from me."

"I understand…that's my job unfortunately. I should have made some adjustments in the firm personnel before now. It might have softened some of the growing tension that is occurring. But my own reasons for procrastinating were and still are valid, so no bother whining about it now. I'll talk to him today and set some things straight."

"What about Lisa? Can I make good on my promise to her that she really isn't fired?"

"Yes you can, but be careful about those promises. As of right now you don't have the authority to make those kind of guarantees," Rodney said with a bit of sarcasm. "As for you, I am still considering whether to honor Barry's request to fire you!" Rodney couldn't keep a straight face while delivering this final tension-breaking joke.

"I'll pack slowly to give you plenty of time," declared Tom pitifully. "Rodney, I apologize this couldn't be resolved professionally with an adult conversation between myself and Barry. He just refuses to recognize me as an equal…well, not an equal…but an…"

"I understand. I'll talk to him and then hopefully we can make some announcements soon."

"Thanks Rodney. How much do we owe you for the babysitting?"

"Oh…have no fear! I'll make you pay."

<u>Chapter Twenty-Six</u>

Tom arrived home that evening with some disturbing thoughts running through his head. First was the business at the office with Barry. Second was the conversation with Linda Smart at St. Jude's. He and Laura made some idle small talk about her day as they ate dinner with Anna and Brady. Laura put the kids to bed while Tom sat blankly in front of the TV. When she came down, she snuggled up next to him on the couch.

"What's on your mind?" she asked with a voice that knew he was lost in thought and troubled about something.

Startled out of his daze Tom casually said, "Nothing." His attempt to hide his troubled thoughts was not confident enough to throw Laura off the scent. She knew her husband well and he was struggling with something.

With eyebrows raised and an investigating voice she said, "Really. Nothing at all? I'm not buying it. Spill the beans or there will be no peek inside this dress tonight."

Tom glanced at Laura, her exposed cleavage, and smiled. He knew he couldn't keep up the ruse with her. "There was another incident with Barry today. He and Lisa really got into it and he fired her on the spot."

"What?"

"Yep. Then he marched into Rodney's office and told him that he wanted me fired effective immediately. Seems he thinks the office is totally devoid of respect for the partners."

"Are you serious?"

"Yeah. It got ugly."

"Well I hope Rodney told him to find a nice hole in a tree and fu…"

"Whoa now sailor! Rodney came and talked to me about the whole thing and promised that my and Lisa's jobs were safe. He was going to talk to Barry this afternoon and mentioned making an announcement soon. I was a little distracted when I was talking to him, but I think he was referring to making me a partner and beginning the transition of me running operations at the firm." Tom made the statement as if that was the first time he realized that it might actually happen. It hadn't dawned on him at the office that this might have been Rodney's intention.

"Honey that's great! I mean I'm sorry you had the blow up but maybe that was the catalyst needed to set things in motion. Why are you so troubled about that? We should be celebrating."

"Yep…it's great…but something is wrong with Barry and it's not going away just because Rodney makes an announcement. As a matter of fact, it may just make things worse. Barry will feel like he was defeated…overruled which will make him dig his heels in even more as he tries to challenge me about every decision. I just don't know what's going on with him."

"I had lunch again with Christine this week. She still doesn't seem very happy but she didn't talk about Barry at all. As a matter of fact, she seemed content just to hear about the kids and us. She really didn't talk much about her life."

"God bless her for putting up with that ass on a daily basis. It doesn't surprise me that she wouldn't talk about herself given her miserable existence with him."

"I know you think that, but she loves or loved him for a reason. Maybe she is trying to ride through the storm right now. Every marriage has its bumps in the road."

Laura had such keen insight into people's lives and minds

that Tom knew she was right. Barry at one time had probably been a decent guy. He was always a bit arrogant, most likely always would be, but his arrogance was tolerable when he wasn't so defiant about accepting help from other people. But over the last year, Barry had taken a hard turn towards intolerable. It wasn't just his arrogance but his determined meanness to virtually everyone, including Christine that bothered Tom the most. He didn't like mean people and he certainly didn't want to deal with one as a partner for the rest of his professional career.

His day in the office had taken a toll but in the forefront of his mind was the gift. His conversation with Linda Smart had made him realize he needed to be more cautious. Also, he was struggling with the debate that questioned his belief in the singularity of a Christian God. There was no doubt his mind was being stretched to perceive a new spiritual order. Maybe that was the purpose of the gift being given to him...to challenge or even correct his longstanding beliefs.

"Do you believe in miracles?" he asked Laura.

Laura stared at him for an unnoticeable second, recognizing the abrupt change of direction in the conversation. Adjusting, Laura replied with hesitation. "I do."

"Who do you think creates them?"

"I think you know where I stand on that. I believe people create miracles. Miracles of morality where a person helps or encourages another person to become better or improve their own soul."

"So you don't think miracles are created by God?"

"I believe there is a presence, an order to the world that is guided by *something*. But you know I don't believe this *something* belongs to one religion. I believe there is an omnipotent one that serves all religions with many different disguises. That *something* may make miracles possible through

144

the hands of good people, but I also believe the miracles are produced by everyday, common people. Someone explained to me once that we are all like ants in an open field marching in the same direction when we stumbled upon a mountain range. Groups of us looked at the mountains and decided that certain paths were the only ones that successfully and safely led over the mountains. Each group believed they were on the only path…the chosen path and that the others would perish in their own foolish attempt to cross over a different peak. Once we reach the other side of the mountains, we will be surprised that we are all once again marching together in an open field. We started together and we end together, we just separate for a period with each group believing their path is the only one that will get them to salvation on the other side. There is only one deity or *something* on the other side greeting us. I can only imagine at that point we realize how silly we were to think that there was only one path over the mountain."

"It sounds so logical when you put it like that but it goes against everything I have been taught from my first memories. Salvation is through Christ and only through that faith can one achieve the rewards of heaven."

"You are right. You have been taught to believe in Christianity as THE path over the mountain. Same for a young Muslim girl who has been told salvation is achieved through Islam. Can you blame her for believing in the teachings of her culture? Do you think there is a God that would punish her because she was born to a Muslim family and found comfort in her beliefs? If Allah is the 'true' deity do you think you will be punished for being born and raised in a Presbyterian family?"

"I hope not…on both accounts. I just feel foolish sometimes when I realize my beliefs may be all wrong. I feel a little betrayed."

"You and millions of other people who begin to think of a more omnipotent presence that encompasses a huge mass of different cultures and beliefs. In the end does it really matter? I think certain teachings about morality found in many organized religions or even just from life experiences have a common bond…a message of kindness or helping others that is universal and without bias."

"So you believe this *something* is responsible for creating miracles or giving ordinary people the ability to create miracles?" Tom asked gently.

"Maybe. Maybe it's *something*, maybe it's just a person's innate belief in a moral code learned apart from religion. I don't know. It's the people with good, pure hearts that can use this power to create good—or miracles as you call it."

"What about real miracles, like the healing of the terminally ill?"

"I am not so sure about those cases. Maybe it is *something* reaching its hand down to intervene. Sometimes I think it is luck or science or something else." Laura presented her answer with smooth confidence but was reeling back to some very familiar memories while the words where exiting her mouth. She wasn't ready to let Tom know that she definitely believed in the type of miracles he was describing and that certain people could create them.

"What about miracles of death? Like someone dying to help others from suffering?"

"You mean like a martyr?" asked Laura.

"No, more like someone being killed to keep them from continuing to harm other people. Or someone dying to relieve the family of long-term care issues and watching them suffer through terrible diseases like dementia?"

"Well one sounds like a killing for mercy's sake. Like the girl in the accident who ended up dying three weeks after her whole family was killed. She suffered so much only to die in the end anyway. But the other is more like a justification of murder for the good of a larger sct of people."

146

"Could you justify murder for a good outcome?"

"Could I? I don't really know." Laura thought for a moment to better hide her lie. "I think I probably could but I wouldn't want that power of reason to be in the hands of just anybody. Hitler thought he was justified in killing six million Jews. Islamic extremists believe they are justified in killing infidels. Could someone with a pure heart justify killing Hitler to save six million people? In my little brain I could justify it. But for some people killing is killing. It's up to each individual to decide if *something* allows us to justify murder as a defense in the battle of good versus evil."

"Do you think there are people in the world, ordinary people with, as you say, pure hearts that should be given that power of reason? Given the power to create miracles in the form of both life and death for the good of mankind?"

Laura immediately froze inside at the delivery of the question...the wording. His comment conjured up memories that nearly left her speechless in front of him. For a moment she wondered if her only secret in life had been discovered and Tom was trying to find a gentle way to elicit a confession of her past sins. Laura studied Tom's face and could see the internal struggle he was having with his deep-seated religious beliefs. The logical part of her brain pushed aside her guilt and concluded that Tom was fishing for something else. She had often wondered if Tom would ever reach a point in his life when he questioned his strict, conservative Christian upbringing. As her memories reminded her, she had discovered her universal religious beliefs when she was a teenager. Later, when she and Tom began dating, they had debated religious ideals once or twice before Laura realized she couldn't convince him to open his mind on the subject. If he ever would, it would be of his own accord. When they married, she agreed to raise the kids in a formal church setting in exchange for permission to raise their awareness about other opinions when they became adults and could decide for themselves what spiritual path they would take.

"I do think there are special people like that in the world," Laura replied with gentle conviction. "People who could make decisions based on a spiritual moral code. Maybe those are the ones we should call angels."

"Angels of death?" retorted Tom with a smile.

"Well, I think we have plenty of those...they are called child molesters and serial killers. If someone had actually killed Hitler when he reached the 100,000 mark, I think that person would have been revered as a saint or human angel with courage that God would have been pleased with. But, would Hitler's evil had been so evil if it had stopped at 100 deaths? Someone could have argued that he never would have reached six million and would have seen the light and stopped the massacre. So, the person who kills him at 100 might just be called a murderer. We couldn't have known Hitler would take it to six million. At what point does someone decide how evil a person's potential really is? And if that person should be stopped before he is guilty of anything more horrific? It's a difficult decision to try and predict evil." Laura almost seemed to be convincing herself at this point. She looked up to Tom and asked, "What's bringing all this up? Why the sudden interest in exploring miracles?"

"I'm thinking about killing Barry for the good of everyone in the office!" he joked to Laura while hiding his real question to himself about whether Barry might be a deserving candidate for an under.

Laura smiled, "While that would serve a good purpose, I don't think Barry's evil runs as deep as Hitler's. I think a good flogging might be better served on Barry."

"I've just been thinking about how God justifies death as a means of good. There has never been a good Sunday School lesson that discussed that justification. It's always been about being a good neighbor, help the weak, don't fornicate with sheep, stone a woman who is in her menstrual cycle if she lies with sheep or something like that. I just wonder about modern-day miracles and if death can be justified as a means for good in our modern world."

"Times have certainly changed since those scriptures were written. But I believe there is an interpretation that can be made to justify how we are good neighbors...how we help the weak. And in some cases, if that means stamping out evil with a death sentence, then I think it can be justified. But, as I said before, I don't like that power of choice resting in the hands of politicians, courts, or even clergy. That leaves too much room for corruption. I believe those choices should be resting in the hands of anonymous individuals chosen by a *something* ...if that is even possible." Laura added the last phrase and quickly glanced at Tom to gauge his initial reaction.

Tom was stunned at how close Laura was hitting to the mark of the gift. She was advocating a scenario that was exactly his reality, which made him wonder if somehow she knew about the gift. He was certain she had no idea about the note and the choices he was making, yet she sincerely believed that such a gift would be ok in their society. Tom adored Laura and her willingness to selflessly help others. She had as pure a heart as he did, maybe even purer because she had clarity of human nature and how good should be able to overcome evil. He was comforted by the thought that if someone like Laura was ok with the gift being present in their world then the gift was probably a good thing. So far, his own miracles—both overs and unders—had played out in the manner that Marina had instructed him. They had validated Hope for someone. They had made people believe in Hope and the power that Hope has in everyone's lives. Still, he struggled with using unders on people who had potential for evil as opposed to those who had already openly committed atrocities. As she put it...how can you predict evil potential? The consideration of Barry as an under just placed the debate very close to home.

Chapter Twenty-Seven

Laura comforted Tom a while longer as she pushed aside her own dark thoughts and the curiosity their conversation had aroused. Once in bed, Tom fell asleep immediately letting his dream state wash away the day's troubles. Sleep was less accommodating to Laura. She went to the kitchen and brewed a mini-pot of tea while examining her memories in private. She was in complete shock at the revelation she was reaching. Could it be that Tom wasn't fishing for a confession from her but rather that he was a gifter? This was the only explanation she could think of based on the questions he asked and the specific words he used. Logic was against her but the gut was burning in support of her conclusion. She never dreamed in a million years that two people who knew each other, much less who were married to each other, would ever share the common bond of possessing the gift of Hope. Tom was certainly deserving of the gift. His heart was as large as anyone she had known…almost too large. He was forgiving and trusting to a fault and it was obvious he was struggling with making choices for the minus 10's as she had called the denominators. Tom's compassion would make the choices for the plus 10's easy, but the minuses would go against the grain of his Presbyterian upbringing.

It was 24 years ago when Laura Conklin's views of the world changed forever. Long before she became Mrs. Roddin. Exactly five days after her 15th birthday she received her note. The next day an elderly woman she had met, oddly enough, in the bleachers after track practice, quietly instructed her on the gift of Hope. For a typical 15-year-old girl, this information or gift would be far too overwhelming. But Laura was an exception to the rule. She managed to understand, avoid, and mediate normal high school drama unlike even the most grounded teenagers. She had a unique capability to manage the people around her in a way that eliminated the typical feelings of revenge, jealousy, and social status. Her friends spanned many of the competing social cliques and she was generally accepted by all of them. When drama arose that remotely included her, she would wave it off and move on so quickly that the girls who generated the drama wouldn't get any satisfaction out of the mess. After a few attempts, the girls quit trying to create 'Laura-drama'. They realized she wasn't going to commit to any one group and therefore was never going to be a social threat. Laura belonged to everyone and no one at the same time.

Laura's understanding and acceptance of the gift at the young age of 15 opened her eyes to the ugliness of evil in the world and confirmed her already growing curiosity about universal religious beliefs. Except for one horrendous incident with another adult a few months earlier, she never let revenge become a teenage emotion. After her instruction with the older woman, Laura spent weeks trying to understand where or from whom the gift came and what its real purpose was before she ever used it. She had already begun to question the religious doctrine assigned to Christianity as the one true religion and the sole means for salvation before the gift was given to her. Her journey with the gift confirmed her migration toward a belief in a spirituality that encompassed the goodness from many organized religions and was guided by a universal *something* that may or may not resemble the Christian God. She wasn't denying God's existence, she was just universalizing a Divine presence…giving it an open forum on which to exist that was not constrained by one religion. She believed more and more in the philosophy that salvation was garnered by kind, selfless, heartfelt acts toward others, rather than disciplined prayer and religious study. Practicing religion to Laura meant protecting innocence and helping people in order to make the world a more tolerable place to exist. This included, for her at least, a fight against bigotry, bullying, and other social actions that demeaned a human's status in the world. She couldn't stand the arrogance of children and adults alike when it infected their psyches with a sense of justified dominance over others. She understood that, in general, those who felt the need to punish 'weaker' people usually suffered from an underlying insecurity...especially in teenagers...but there was no excuse for someone to continue abuse after their actions were exposed as mean and degrading.

This conviction led her to choose her minus 10's with a clear conscience. It wasn't based on the 'eye-for-an-eye' parable...that was too vengeful. While she tried to choose her minuses under the premise of whether she thought the person had the ability to change or not, she wondered later in her life whether she had created death for someone who actually had potential to turn their life around. It was something she would never really know since the person wasn't given the opportunity to correct his or her path. She struggled mightily with this unknown and tried to comfort herself by saying that she also may have saved many people from years of continued abuse or even death by removing an evildoer from the life equation. Maybe, just maybe she eliminated a Jeffrey Dahmer from the world before he could act on his aggressions. This circular thought process of justifying the minuses was one backlash of the gift that she was certain plagued everyone who had been tapped as a gifter. Depending on their own religious beliefs and moral code, some would be haunted more than others.

Laura worried that Tom might not have the strength of conviction, given his own strict religious beliefs, to justify the deaths. In his religious order, murder would be difficult to justify as means for good. She knew she had to resist the temptation to openly discuss the gift with him...that could be detrimental to both their marriage and his own ability to maintain the purity of the gift. She could never tell him she knew or that she had also possessed the gift...at least not until he finished making his choices. But she desperately wanted to comfort him in his struggles. Laura loved her husband dearly but knew he was more naïve about right and wrong than her own black and white definition. Maybe naïve wasn't the correct term. He was just less aware of evil than she was. He always saw the good in people and tended to close his eyes to evil, writing it off as bad decisions by people who didn't understand consequences. While this was partially true and certainly a positive way to view the world, it sometimes allowed inaction that encouraged further evil or abuse. Their differing views gave a balance to each other, which, in turn, had strengthened their bond over the years. Laura vowed to remain aware of Tom's moods over the next several months to see how she could comfort him without revealing her secret, or that she was aware of his.

Chapter Twenty-Eight

Several months had passed since the confrontation in the office with Barry. Although Rodney had made the announcement that Tom was now an equal partner in the firm and would be, over the next seven months, gradually taking over more and more of the operational decisions in the office, the tensions between Barry and the rest of the office staff had not diminished. In fact, it had gotten worse. Barry seemed to be on a rampage to offset his frustration of the announcement and made it clear to everyone that he was not on board with the decision. He constantly degraded his team in meetings and worked around them with clients to create a false picture that their work was substandard. To this effect, the firm's design team and the client were completely frustrated by the back-door discussions conducted by upper-level management at both places. It was clear Barry was trying to get the executives in his Rolodex on his side of the argument to save face and lay the blame on both design teams. The junior architects working for Barry made Tom aware of this but rarely backed it up with any concrete proof. He didn't doubt what was happening but he couldn't accuse Barry of mismanagement based on the he-said she-said argument going on. Something had to be done.

Tom had asked Laura about Christine's physical and mental state after each of their monthly get-togethers. Up until last week everything had been normal. After a lunch with Christine on Friday, Laura told Tom she noticed a mark on Christine's neck that looked like a bruise. Christine didn't mention anything about it and Laura was hesitant to broach the subject. Laura was still convinced that Christine was too strong a woman to let someone physically abuse her and said there was probably a reasonable explanation. Laura wasn't completely aware of Barry's actions in the firm over the last month, so

Tom disregarded his wife's intuition and came to the conclusion that Barry was taking his frustration out at home as well as at work. His belief that Barry had turned abusive at home certainly helped justify his consideration of Barry as an under candidate. Could he really make a choice for someone who was so close to his own life? Would it be a selfish choice made only to ease his problems at work? He wasn't ready to make the decision yet but his suspicions of the abuse compelled him to think more seriously about a choice. Whichever way the argument in his head turned something had to be done to resolve the issues at work. Tom made a mental note to set up a meeting with Barry in the next few weeks.

As the end of the day approached, Tom was busy getting his documents together for a trip to Terra Haute, Indiana. He was traveling with his core team to present preliminary designs to a client for another strip mall renovation project. In anticipation of the trip, Tom researched the Terra Haute area to identify hospitals, nursing homes, prisons, and the top headlines from the area over the past eight or so months. This exercise became a standard activity for all cities he visited for work. Since the gift's arrival, his second job was to investigate the possibility of validating Hope in an area where he could perform miracles without getting noticed or put under suspicion. He didn't want to have a string of miracles in one city that could be threaded together and possibly place him in a position to explain his actions, whereabouts, or coincidental 'relationship' with people who had recently died or miraculously been cured.

For Terra Haute, one headline a few months old caught his eye. The article laid out the history of events beginning in 2010 when a man's wife was found dead at a nearby lake. Six weeks earlier she had been reported as missing by the husband, which led to an exhaustive search and an investigation into probable suspects. Although he had a solid alibi at the time, the husband was still under suspicion by authorities based on accounts from friends and family of severe strains in the couple's relationship. Three times in the two years prior to the murder, police had been called to the residence for reports of domestic violence and disturbing the peace. Each time, the couple admittedly had been fighting but no charges were ever pressed. In the year and half after the body had been found, police suspicions grew as the husband continued to run afoul of the law. After an altercation with neighbors and two DUI arrests, the husband lost custody of his two young children to the state. The two boys were living with their grandparents while their father was undergoing counseling and trying to hold down a job at a hardware store. He had supervised visits with the boys once every other week for four hours. Tom had read as much as he could about the man, the crime, the investigation, and the kids to sort out his own judgment of the risk the man posed to his children and society in general. The more he dug the more he felt the man was guilty of his wife's murder but he had nothing to go on except his own gut. He desperately wanted to carve out time during his trip to either meet the husband or talk to the children. A chance meeting with the boys was not very probable but a 'coincidental' meeting with the man could be pulled off. He found the man's home address and place of work with a little investigative work—which Tom was becoming quite adept at—and tucked the information into his briefcase.

That night, Tom and Laura talked again about Christine's mood and physical appearance. Tom didn't want to sound overly curious but he also had a legitimate reason to wonder if Christine's situation was related to Barry's abhorrent behavior in the office. Thankfully, he didn't have to bring up the subject out of the blue. Laura told Tom after dinner that Christine had cancelled a trip to a new antique store in town that the two were planning tomorrow.

"She didn't give an explanation but she sounded rather defeated and depressed on the phone. I didn't want to press her but she really seems to be hurting...mentally I mean, not physically."

"Has her mood changed during your last few lunches?" Tom asked relieved that Laura had volunteered the information without being prompted.

"A little. It's hard to tell with Christine lately. She is so good at putting on a happy face in public and making it seem genuine. But recently it's been harder for her to hide. I've never seen her not sell a happy face."

"Well I can tell you that if Barry is bringing his work mood home with him then she must be miserable. He has become intolerable at work and the office environment is awful. I know it is...or at least will be my responsibility to settle things in the office but with Rodney out all month on vacation, Barry will not accept my authority to engage him and his staff."

"I just can't believe she would allow him to physically abuse her," Laura said in reference to the mark on Christine's neck she'd noticed last week. "I know how the stories go with abused spouses, but I don't see her as one to keep herself in the way of harm."

"I'm at a loss for what to do. I have to make a choice soon or everyone in the office will leave."

Laura froze at the word 'choice'. He really was thinking about using the gift on Barry. You couldn't just Hope for someone to be happy and not grumpy and poof they were pure sunshine. The gift didn't work like that. Unless there was a known and obvious affliction that could be remedied to save someone—give them a life miracle—then the only other choice was the minus 10 miracle. Could Tom really give a minus to someone he knew so well and who was part of his daily professional life?

"I'm going to set up a meeting with Barry in two weeks when he gets back from his trip to Pennsylvania and lay it all out there. God, I dread that meeting," Tom said with little conviction of finding a resolution between the two professionals.

"I'm sure you will find the right things to say. Maybe he has some sort of demon he just needs to talk about and get it out of his system? Remember, at one time you two were actually friendly to each other," said Laura, trying to remind Tom of Barry's once human existence. *Stop it,* she thought to herself. *This is his decision…don't try to influence it.*

"We'll see. Maybe he'll come around and realize he is making himself miserable along with entire office. He has to be feeling the tension. Anyway, I'm meeting the team at the office around 7:30 in the morning to drive to Terra Haute. We should only be gone one night unless I decide to stay an extra night to scope out some other opportunities. We're taking two cars so everyone will be comfortable and in case they want to head back early."

"No problem. I think the kids and I are going to Mom's house tomorrow night for dinner. We may just go ahead and spend the night there."

"Sounds good. You want to have a date night Friday? Dinner and then pretend we are not too tired to still love on each other?"

"I'll have to check my calendar. I may have plans with my boyfriend that night," Laura added with a mischievous smile.

"Well, you two work that out and let me know."

Chapter Twenty-Nine

The planning session with the client went well and the team put forward several design options for consideration. Tom treated his comrades to a nice dinner at the Saratoga Restaurant and they were settled into the hotel by 10:30. Waiting for his mind to succumb to the desires of his body for sleep, Tom sorted through his plan to randomly meet the father of the two boys in state custody, the husband of the dead wife. His first option was to go by the man's work place and interact with him as a normal customer. If that didn't work, plan B was to meet the father at his residence. Given the publicity the father had garnered from the investigation, custody battle, and recent arrests, it was unlikely the guy would invite a stranger in for a friendly chat. Tom decided he could pose as an inspector representing the property owner—Tom knew the father was a renter—to evaluate the condition of the property. The premise was a bit far-fetched but Tom could think of nothing else as a second option. He desperately hoped he wouldn't have to employ plan B. Despite having defined his options, his mind would still not succumb to restful slumber. The thought of considering someone for an under who might be innocent of any real crime or abuse was hounding his conscience as if it were already guilty. He had no idea if this guy was on the straight and narrow and turning his life around. He may have been dealt a bad hand, made a few mistakes, and was trying to reconcile things so he could regain custody of his kids and manage a new life with the boys. Maybe that was how Hope came into play without Tom's intervention? He would have to wait until tomorrow's encounter to see what his heart and gut told him about this man's capabilities to be a murderer or a chameleon.

Tom woke without even realizing he had fallen asleep.

159

Unrested and groggy, he knew making it through a full day would be a challenge. After meeting the team for breakfast and sending them home with the excuse that he was going to scout some new commercial property on the north side of town, Tom set out to the father's workplace. The Lowe's Home Improvement Center was located off S 3rd Street, highway 41 just south of Terra Haute. Having no idea which department the father worked in or what his work schedule might be, Tom was prepared to wander the aisles in hopes of finding the man. He planned to dissect the building from left to right starting in the garden center and finishing in the lumber 'yard'. To the casual observer, Tom appeared to be just another homeowner looking at the possibilities of improving a patio or aggressively contemplating a new flowerbed for a weekend project. For Tom, he was intensely evaluating every employee's face, trying to find a match with a mug shot that might not be representative of the man's true appearance. After 45 minutes of browsing in the garden center, Tom couldn't find a single possible match. His next move took him to the kitchen and bath area to look at cabinet and countertop options. This area was far less populated and the staff included only a handful of people, none who matched the face or age range of the father. Strike 2. Moving over to plumbing, he browsed through two aisles of pipe-fittings, elbows, and water heaters. He was about to abandon plumbing and head for the tools section when he spotted a guy walking toward him who might fit the bill. As they passed, he glanced at the employee's nametag—Roger—but couldn't get a good look at his face without being overly obvious. The man took a left turn down the plumbing aisle where Tom had just been admiring toilet seals. Tom immediately hung a U-turn and followed. 'Roger' stopped about half-way down the aisle and was looking for a pipe fitting to match the used one he had in his hand.

"Excuse me. I was wondering if you could help me with something?" Tom asked politely.

"Let me find this coupling and finish with my other customer. Then I can help," Roger said impatiently.

"Sure thing. Sorry to interrupt."

Roger found the coupling and walked away without saying a word. He returned an agonizing four minutes later and asked Tom what he was looking for.

"I was wondering about the tankless water heaters everyone is bragging about. Are they really that great and are they hard to install?"

"How old is your home?" Roger said flatly.

"About 55 years—late 1950's I think," replied Tom.

"Have you replaced your old water pipes with copper or new PVC that's approved for water distribution?"

"Copper, about five years ago."

"Do you have gas at the house or do you currently use an electric water heater?"

"We have gas but the water heater is electric and old. I need to replace it and was thinking about going to the tankless if they are all they're cracked up to be."

"Like anything they have advantages and disadvantages." Roger continued in a steady stream of pros and cons associated with tankless heaters but without any passion or excitement. He wasn't rude. He was just flat, very monotone and didn't seem to care one way or the other whether the customer actually bought one.

"Do you have one at your house?" Tom asked trying to engage the guy or get some sort of reaction by which he could assess the man's character.

"I rent."

"Oh. Are they difficult to install?"

"Not if you know what you're doing. It takes about three

hours once the gas line has been run to the area where the unit will be installed."

"Do you guys have an install team?"

"Yes. Well, we contract it out but we have approved and designated crews for that kind of stuff."

Tom couldn't get much out of Roger. He was hoping to find a friendly enthusiastic employee who would relish the chance to show someone how much he knew about plumbing and tankless water heaters. It could have led to some house plumbing project story swapping and given Tom a little more insight into this guy's state of mind and stability. Just two bubbas swapping stories about their wife or kids clogging up toilets or not knowing how to turn a water valve off when it's spraying all over a bathroom. Nothing. Nada. Bland as a bowl of ramen noodles without the little packet of sauce.

"Well, thanks. I need to weigh out the cost between replacing our old unit or converting to this tankless thing. It's just me and my son in the house so we may not really need the endless hot water supply that the tankless system provides," Tom lied.

"Ok."

"Thanks for your help. You gave me a lot of good information."

"No problem."

Roger turned without haste or hesitation but also without being in a hurry. He just turned, like a robot, and walked down the aisle out of sight. Tom stood in the aisle, alone for a few minutes and analyzed the encounter. The father seemed to be numb, just going through the motions of everyday life and not feeling the need to cover the doldrums of his life with a smile. He wasn't rude...he was just absent of any feeling or emotion. His situation had obviously taken a toll on him and he didn't see the need to hide it. Tom thought that maybe a guy in that situation would try to be more positive if he was turning a corner and trying to improve his lot...especially if it meant getting his children back. He found himself at a crossroads with his decision to intervene in the name of Hope for the children and possibly the dead wife. This guy definitely didn't seem to have much to offer life in return for living, but he also was the only living parent to the two boys. Even if he was capable of abusing or murdering his wife, he might be capable of being a decent father. Could he recover enough of his human instinct and dignity to lead a normal life from here on out?

Tom walked down the aisle and took a left in the direction that Roger disappeared. He saw him two aisles over inventorying toilet fixtures and walked steadily toward him. When he got within three feet of the father he hesitated, placed his hand casually in the middle of the man's back and said, "Thanks again for the help. Have a great rest of the day."

A bit startled at the contact, the father said, "No problem. You too."

Roger kept performing his duties without any thought of his last customer. He walked through the building materials section of the store on his way to the break room and crouched down under the caution tape of an area where two co-workers were unloading a half-ton stack of plywood with a forklift. Nodding at the co-workers through the noise of the lift and the alarms, Roger walked under the edge of the stack as it levitated nine feet in the air during a turn maneuver by the forklift. Less than 20 seconds later he bent underneath the caution tape on the safe side of the danger zone and headed through the swinging doors to the employee area.

<u>Chapter Thirty</u>

Tom rolled the car windows down to let the early summer heat escape. Contemplating the encounter, he took a few deep breaths and tried to relax his mind. At the last minute, he had decided that he couldn't give the gift of Hope to this father...or rather to his boys. His gut was aflame with warning signs, but he didn't have enough evidence to justify death in an effort to spare another victim or improve the lives of the two boys. He couldn't get out of his mind the slight possibility that the father had the potential to turn his life around or even the fact that he might be innocent of his wife's murder. Tom wasn't comfortable making a decision based solely on his gut and decided to keep his unders for known criminals and elderly folks suffering from diseases degrading their mind and bodies to a point of no recovery. While this somewhat satisfied his guilt of justifying murder for Hope, he felt like he was copping out of a responsibility to address the risk posed by inherently mean people doing bad things to other people. The gift gave him the opportunity to stop aggression and violence before it actually happened. Unfortunately, it required him to take an even larger risk by guessing whether a candidate was going to cause irreparable harm to someone. If he was wrong, then he was killing potentially innocent people. If he was right, he could save numerous people from pain and anguish and even prevent the death of innocent victims. The thought of either scenario weighed heavily on his mind. But for today, he had made a decision and erred on the side of caution.

Tom spent the four-and-a-half-hour drive home trying to take his mind off the debate and focus on the weekend ahead. Hopefully, he was getting a long-overdue date with his wife and some pool time with the kids to escape the summer heat and humidity. But his mind kept coming back to the gift and what his number was. Eight months after the gift entered his life, Tom was 4/6. After the gang banger gift in the winter and Ryan Miller the real-estate slime ball, Tom had visited a full-care nursing home and found another candidate who was obviously in the solid stage of dementia or some other neurological disease that rendered her quality of life to almost zero. Family interaction had been reduced to pressured courtesy visits by loved ones whose own guilt and frustration kept them in turmoil as they struggled to show love and compassion for someone who didn't recognize them as kin. It was curious to Tom why his denominator number remained higher than his numerator. From the beginning he always thought he would rush through the overs with the greatest of ease and find himself left with so many unders that a haunting morbidity would take over his soul. Maybe that was why he had been so reserved about using his overs. The overs gave him so much pleasure. He believed he really was spreading Hope into the world through validation. But the unders...he just didn't find the same satisfaction despite his discussions with Marina and Laura. He didn't feel the same sense of validation for Hope. For all the unders he spent too much time justifying the action rather than accepting the Hope they provided. Shaking himself from the depths of thought, Tom relaxed his grip on the wheel and tried to enjoy the remainder of the scenic drive. He was looking forward to the distractions at home to give his tormented mind a rest.

A month later, he and Laura finally made time for date night. In the cozy and quiet atmosphere of the Fire Fly, they talked about their upcoming schedules and the start of a new school year for the kids and herself. His attempts at a casual, flirtatious conversation were constantly interrupted by the questions from his drive home a month earlier. He wanted more than anything to share his struggles with his best friend and partner in life. She was so clear on the matter of good versus evil that he wished he could pass the remainder of the gift's choices to her. It would release him from confronting the questions of making a choice that was not completely rooted in known facts. Making decisions based on reading tealeaves was not part of his natural

DNA.

"How do you think *something* justifies allowing atrocities, large scale atrocities to happen to so many innocent people...or even if it was just one person?" Tom asked thoughtfully realizing he was introducing a serious discussion into their date night conversation.

"I don't really know." Laura noted that Tom used the phrase *something* rather than his normal reference to God. "I've heard the arguments for martyrdom. I've heard that you have to have suffering in the world in order to recognize and cherish good or love, a balance if you will. I've even heard and considered the possibility that the Divine has abandoned humans and that the human race is just in motion without any intervention. I don't believe that, but I also don't have a clear understanding of why there is so much innocent suffering. *Something* must have the guilty weight of the world on Its shoulders to think there is a purpose for suffering."

"And yet we think our own burden is heavy when we make a decision to sin and kill one person who is creating so much obvious evil." Tom didn't mean to let the implication slip out that someone had that power.

"Well, the courts are the ones to decide that unless you want to be a vigilante," Laura said to let Tom off the hook. She could see in his expression that he had not meant to show so much ownership of his burden. "Have you ever heard the term 'situation ethics'?" asked Laura.

"No, but I can probably guess its meaning just from the two words."

"It's a concept that was formally introduced by Joseph Fletcher in the 1960s. He was a theologian who preached that love is ultimately the only real law of life and that all other scripture, spiritual guidance, and even judicial law is secondary and should only be followed if they served the purpose of supporting unbiased love. Basically, secondary moral principles could be cast aside in specific situations if a certain action strengthens true love. Theologians took the principle and expanded it beyond love and debated situation ethics as a means to justify what would otherwise be sinful behavior to create a larger good. There is no right or wrong decision based on prescribed rules, but rather each individual situation dictated the flexibility of theological rules. The concept stirred up feverish debate among theologians. Some deemed the concept heretical. Others argued that approaching a solution based on a general set of moral principles was better than creating a strict moral code to follow no matter what the situation. Basically, a one-size-fits-all set of rules was not realistic. This allowed people an avenue to justify certain behavior to create a common good."

"That could also allow certain groups to justify a massacre based on preserving a race's purity—hence the Hitler philosophy."

"You're right," she confirmed. "And several groups have hijacked the concept to justify actions they deem right when, in fact, it is abhorrent in the eyes of those who suffer or to those who have a better moral compass. It can certainly be played on both sides. But in its purest form, it maintains a moral standing even if it abandons a biblical or judicial code."

"That leaves too much room for error. Anyone—good or bad—can claim situation ethics as self-defense for their actions."

"No doubt. But those with pure hearts and a good moral foundation can use it to justify committing murder if their family is threatened. They can use it to justify a lie to avoid hurting or demeaning someone. Just because it can be used in an evil way doesn't mean it is not helpful when applied for good. Only those with pure hearts and a strong moral compass should use situation ethics without guilt or worry of divine judgment."

"I believe in miracles, Laura. I think we see them every day. Hidden under the guise of the strangest actions and sometimes from the most unlikely people. Finding someone alive who has been buried in the rubble for seven days in the aftermath of a disaster. That's a miracle. A dying patient who suddenly responds to treatment and gets better. That's a miracle. They exist. But is it a miracle when someone is freed from suffering because of the death of their abuser?"

"Yes." Laura said calmly but with profound confidence. "I believe those are some of the most spectacular and deserving miracles. But it's a fine line to distinguish between relief from abuse and the act of revenge. I'm not sure how to define that line other than to say that the person who is abused should not be the one to cause the death. That at least keeps the revenge factor out of the equation. Though, as I say that, if I were on a jury, I would probably never convict a person accused of murder for killing someone who has repeatedly abused them. I just don't think I could justify killing someone myself merely for revenge." Laura thought for a moment back to some of her own dark memories.

"Victims of abuse see their abusers in human form," she continued. "I can't think of anything more degrading. Sickness hides behind bacteria or viruses or biology. Natural disasters hide behind location and circumstance. Nothing can be more painful, physically and emotionally, than to suffer at the hands of another human. Yes, I believe the death of an abusive human is a miracle more inspiring than the healing of a terminally ill patient." Laura realized after a long silence that she had spoken her truths with a little too much conviction. She had tempered her opinion the last time she and Tom talked on the subject. This time she didn't hold back. She didn't want to influence Tom's perspective on the denominators but, then again, he brought the subject up. He obviously was reaching out to her for an opinion while he waded through his own indecision. Tom seemed relaxed with the conversation and his expressions didn't reflect any shock at her blunt defiance of guilt associated with the death of an abuser. As a matter of fact, he seemed content to give weight to her answer.

"How do you 'predict evil' as you so aptly put it the other night, so abuse can be stopped before it actually begins?"

"Everyone can't. Only certain people can, special people with a keen sense of understanding of another human's intentions. Mostly that comes from a snap judgment or first encounters. It's an ability to read or feel a person's soul at a first meeting, an answer to a question that reveals something good or bad. Not many people have that gift to read another person's book so clearly and without the person knowing. I think you have that ability, Tom. You can see through a person's bullshit without ever revealing it to them."

"You give me too much credit. I would just try to sit down with Hitler and talk him out of his evil. I would always want to believe that the last victim was actually going to be his last."

Laura smiled sweetly with a soft giggle. "No. You'd see right away he wasn't willing to listen. Then you would go tell his mother!"

They both laughed and the conversation shifted to a much lighter tone and soon they were back discussing schedules, school, and kids. Tom was grateful for the time with Laura even though the topic that consumed him daily was only a brief part of their night. Laura's words always had a way of confirming what he already knew and believed but just couldn't fully accept when his mind argued evenly both sides of an issue. She always helped tip the scale for him, not always in a direction that she wanted. She was good about not trying to form his opinions for him. She was kinder than that and he was stronger than that. She simply knew how to present her opinion as a realistic and legitimate option. Take-it-or-not was her presentation style and she respected both results as long as you weighed the options equally. In this case, he accepted her reasoning for death as miracle and had a renewed conviction to try and use the gift to protect innocent victims. But he still had trouble trusting his gut. Trusting that sixth sense that Laura was convinced he possessed. He certainly didn't trust it when he made the decision for the father in Terra Haute. With the father, he had choked down his gut feeling and convinced himself he hadn't spent enough time with the man to come to a conclusion. The risk of harming an innocent man was too great for Tom to let his intuition make the call regarding the father.

<u>Chapter Thirty-One</u>

With Barry out of town, Tom spent the next week immersed in his current projects without the distraction of office drama. Things ran smoothly when he could focus on his own work without the other responsibilities. Not that he was dreading taking on more responsibility for the daily management of the firm's activities and staff, he was just distracted by the 'Barry' dynamic in the office. Life would certainly be a lot easier if Barry wasn't in the picture. However, life wasn't that simple. He knew there would always be some personality conflicts in the office with or without Barry. But right now, Barry was the issue. He couldn't postpone the dreaded encounter any longer, so on Friday he confirmed the lunch appointment with Barry for the following Tuesday. He'd give Barry a day to get caught up in the office then sit down with him on Tuesday, in a public place, and just be honest with him. He knew honesty would be a hard reasoning tool to use with Barry but it was the only way to approach their predicament. He couldn't use force…Barry would take that as a challenge and go toe-to-toe with him. Barry would certainly win that fight. Honesty might actually catch Barry off-guard and let him realistically assess his recent attitude and the effect it had on the office. He would give Barry the chance to make things right. Otherwise…well, Tom was prepared to consider Barry for a choice.

Tom anguished over the pending meeting for the entire weekend and went over and over in his mind the possibility of using the gift on Barry. The debate rolled on until Monday afternoon when Tom finally decided what the 'otherwise' would be. Barry stormed into Tom's office Monday demanding to know why the lunch date had been put on his schedule. Tom calmly told Barry that some decisions needed to be made concerning the firm and that he simply wanted his opinion.

Barry, a bit suspicious that Tom would ask or consider his opinion on anything, asked why they couldn't just discuss the issues in the office. Tom said he felt it was better discussed outside the office and that it would give them an opportunity to catch up on the different projects currently on the books. With a huff, Barry agreed to keep the date leaving Tom more comfortable with his 'otherwise' conclusion. He was ready to face the dreaded consequences of the meeting.

Tuesday rolled around and the office staff was in a state of bewilderment when Tom and Barry left the office together around 11:45. Tom had told no one except Marge about the meeting but even she didn't know its purpose. Speculation immediately occupied the still airwaves in the office as the staff discussed the oddity of the event. By 12:10 the they had a pool in place, guessing who would come back the bloodiest. Despite their admiration and respect for Tom, most thought Barry would eat Tom's lunch—no pun intended—and Tom would come back defeated and depressed. Only a few believed Tom could hold his own and tame Barry to a point of tolerance. The jury was out and the entire staff ate their lunch in the office so they wouldn't miss the moment when the two returned from battle.

Tom and Barry sat down at MaCabe's Pub in a corner booth against the windows looking out to the golf course. Tom was quite nervous but hid it well under a cool demeanor of old friends catching up with the comfortable confines of the restaurant. Barry seemed agitated from the moment they sat down and barked his order at the waitress without any guilt for his rudeness. Tom had thought about how to open the conversation and concluded that calm directness was the best approach.

"Barry, we obviously have our differences and they've shown themselves lately. I just wanted to settle some things so we can move forward productively."

"I don't know what you are talking about," snorted Barry

while looking out the window already bored with the conversation.

"I think you do, so let's cut through the bullshit and lay it out on table. First, I had no idea that Rodney had intentions of making me a partner in the firm this year and I certainly didn't ask for the daily management responsibilities."

"I find that hard to believe. It seems that's been your goal lately, to get me out of the picture and diminish my role in the firm."

"Well if you want to be a pompous ass and believe that, then be my guest. But I have no reason to lie and, quite frankly, I don't give a shit whether you believe me or not." Tom's sternness raised an eyebrow with Barry and he was ready to lash out at Tom. Before Barry could start his defense, Tom continued with his opening arguments. "Barry you are a good architect and have a solid base of clients that are critical to the firm's success. But your treatment of the staff is causing tension that is not conducive to a productive work environment. We need these folks to be successful and there are some really good minds at work over there."

"They're all insubordinate in their actions," Barry interrupted.

"They're doing their jobs, Barry. They have to interact with the client to make progress on a design and it's up to us to determine the balance of communications between us and the client, and them and the client. You're going to have to learn to trust their capabilities and help them along when they need guidance."

"How can I do that when they're constantly going behind my back and belittling me to the client! I won't tolerate it!"

"Barry they're not going behind your back, so lose the whole conspiracy theory attitude. They're inviting you to the meetings and you don't show up. They move forward with the blessing of the client's team, then you turn around and call the top dog and together you convince them to change the plan, seemingly just for spite. Do you not see what kind of tension that causes for our team AND the client's team?"

"My schedule is very busy and I don't have time to babysit them every time they want to make themselves look good without my input. I realize they don't want to work with me because my design criteria are more disciplined than theirs."

"Barry, they don't want to work with you because you're a prick!"

"Watch yourself young man!" Barry warned with a condescending tone.

"Based on the way you've treated me and the staff lately, I'm going to ignore that warning and be honest with you. You've been in this business long enough to know that one person can't do a large job alone. It takes the entire team to jump through all the hoops necessary to make a client happy. We're a full-service architectural firm and that includes services that you and I don't have the time or knowledge to provide. We need these folks and there are some really talented people here willing to invest their time to do things the right way."

Barry's posture was still defensive but his fight seemed to be relaxing a bit as he stared out the window in silence for moment. "They need to understand who is in charge at the office. They run all over you and I won't allow that insubordination on my projects."

"They know good and well who is in charge in the office. Despite what you may think, they don't run all over me, Barry. They work WITH me." It was time for Tom to start softening his approach and take advantage of Barry's weakening defenses. "I lay the groundwork for a campaign and then let them use their skills to move a design forward. I give them guidance along the way and always have final say on decisions. They respect me, Barry, because I work with them and allow them to learn, grow, and stretch their own wings within the bounds of the ground rules. You have so much to offer these kids if you would just be involved and listen to some of their ideas. Teach them. Make suggestions instead of tearing their ideas down. You will garner a level of respect that is far more satisfying than bullying people around."

Apparently the softer approach didn't work. Barry found a new fighting spirit and started on the attack again. "I don't bully anyone. I set high expectations and hold all of them to it."

"And how can you judge their adherence to those high expectations if you're not involved in the daily activities of a project?"

"I don't need you or any of the tattletales on our staff to see when things are all fucked up!"

"And what has been fucked up by the staff? Name one thing they have screwed up on your last four projects that you have had to go in and fix?"

"Well I don't like them changing the design without my approval."

"When has that happened Barry? When have they instituted a major design change without your approval being solicited? You are invited to all the team meetings and you don't even show up. If you were more involved you would realize that most of the changes are at the request of the client or the construction firm to conform to the design criteria."

"How would you know? Have you been sticking your nose into my projects and listening to their complaints without knowledge of the truth?"

"Yes I have been looking into your projects and have sat in on a few team meetings when the client's design team was involved. I was only a silent observer but at least I was there to understand what was going on. That's more than I can say for you." Tom regretted revealing this fact but he was getting tired of Barry's baseless arguments. "Barry, what's really going on here? Is there some reason for your attitude lately that I should know about? Something that might explain why you have turned from a very good architect into someone who is impossible to get along with?"

Tom's directness surprisingly seemed to strike a chord with Barry. The taut muscles in his neck and face seemed to relax into a defeated look of exhaustion. Barry contemplated the last remarks, trying to decide whether to open up to Tom. After a prolonged silence, Tom decided to open the door a little wider.

"Barry, we all know you are a great architect with a wealth of experience. No one is trying to replace you or put you out to pasture. We are genuinely concerned for you and want to help where we can."

"I think I am losing Christine," Barry confessed in a very solemn tone. "About 14 months ago they found a tumor on her breast. She was scared to death. They did some testing and we waited longer than expected to get the results. During that time I was not very supportive. I basically shut down and couldn't comfort her because I didn't want to face the real possibility of losing her. Instead of putting on a happy face and giving her hope, my initial reaction to the news was frustration and denial, which manifested itself in me being distracted, angry, and unsupportive toward her. In the end it turned out to be benign, but the damage to our relationship had already been done. She couldn't understand how I could be so callous about the threat. It wasn't that I didn't care…quite the opposite, I love Christine with all my heart and realize that I probably don't deserve her. But for some reason I couldn't accept the fact that I might lose her. I dealt with it by giving her the cold shoulder at a time when she needed me the most. I lost all hope for her survival while we waited for the test results."

Tom listened in stunned silence. He didn't want to interrupt the flow of emotions that Barry was sharing.

"My lack of sympathy hurt her deeply and she became resentful of my mere presence. I haven't been able to find the courage to apologize. I've made a few pitiful attempts but I couldn't dig down beyond my own ego to really show her how sorry I am...to let her know how frightened I was about possibly losing her. And the irony is that I'm probably going to lose her to life instead of death."

"Barry, I know Christine loves you deep down. You have made a life together and raised two wonderful kids. I doubt she's willing to throw that away because you are an insensitive, stubborn SOB."

"I've made her miserable and we hardly talk now except to throw jabs at each other. I can recognize my own shortcomings but I am paralyzed to do anything about them. It all comes at a time when I am already questioning my worth in life. What have I done? What have I accomplished...I mean really accomplished? Call it a late mid-life crisis but I don't know what I have to show for years of disciplined work and living."

"Well, I can tell you several things you have accomplished. You've raised two remarkable kids. That in itself should be satisfying enough. You've also done some great work professionally and are well respected as an architect... notwithstanding the current staff," Tom added with a slight grin to lighten the moment. "Barry, I've always known how much you value Christine and your relationship. You have it in you to be compassionate and loving. All men have a macho side that often gets in the way of showing sensitivity to a woman. It usually rears its ugly head when the women in our lives need it the most. It's an unfortunate stroke of bad timing that challenges us all. But that doesn't mean we don't have the capacity if we're willing to step out of our hard shell for the good of a meaningful relationship."

"I think it's too late. I can see the way she looks at me with utter contempt."

"It's never too late. Sit down with her and admit your

mistake. You have to make yourself vulnerable in order for her to believe you're sincere. Be honest with her, Barry...completely honest and let her know that your fear of losing her drove you to be an ass."

"Easier said than done, said the ass," Barry admitted with self-deprecating humor. "Tom you are a good architect and deserve to be the one managing the firm. It's just a hard pill for me to swallow. Watching your meteoric rise in the firm and becoming the darling child with Rodney and the staff...I always felt that was my destiny within the firm. I recognize I don't have the personal skills to run the office and that you are far better suited to excel in this role. I guess the cumulative effect of Christine's diagnosis and my own insecurities with the staff has made me a bitter person to deal with. I apologize but I am still bitter about the way everything was handled."

"I appreciate the apology but the staff is more deserving of an apology than me."

"Probably, but as you well know my pride will make that difficult."

"Barry, don't take offense at this or think I'm trying to get rid of you, but why don't you take a couple of weeks to reconcile things with Christine. Go somewhere, visit the kids, or stay at home, but just take some time to spend with Christine and let her know how you really feel and that you're sorry for the way you coped with her illness. By the way, how is she...I mean physically? Is the threat gone?"

"Yes. She's fine. The mass was benign. Instead of removing it by surgery they decided to give her medicine to dissolve the mass. It has made her a bit moody and she tends to bruise easily, but she's fine. The medicine has obviously worked because the mass has gotten significantly smaller. It's just taken a long time. She goes back next Thursday for what should be her final appointment."

Barry's 'bruising' comment caused by the medicine was not

lost on Tom. It certainly explained a lot and for now he chose to believe the explanation. Christine's bruising and the departure from her normally light and playful demeanor had been the main reasons for Tom's decision to use the gift on Barry if today's conversation went awry. Thankfully the conversation eventually took a positive turn and Barry opened up to reveal a softer side Tom didn't even know existed under the egotistical armor Barry always wore. Tom couldn't help but feel that he talked Barry down from a ledge that he didn't even know he stood on.

"That's great news, Barry. All the more reason to take some time off. Let her know how you feel and go with her to the final appointment and show you support her."

"There are some critical milestones coming up on two of the projects that I don't think I can miss."

"Real life situations trump work crap every time. I can help guide the team through the next few weeks and we can postpone some of the milestones if you feel you really need to be involved."

"That will put me in a weak position with the team and disintegrate what little respect remains."

"You can't disintegrate from zero." Tom regretted the statement at first, then realized Barry's ego still needed to be shot down one more rung before he could recover. He was being brutally honest at this point and from Barry's reaction, it was the best way to move forward. "If you approve, I'll talk to the staff tomorrow and explain to them what's going on without revealing the personal aspect of your situation. I can make the apology for you in your absence. But when you return, you have to show them the apology actually came from you and that I didn't just make it up to cover for you."

"That seems so cowardly."

"Barry, no one expects a person to make a complete

179

turnaround overnight, much less over one lunch. When you come back, it will be a fresh start and you can show them through actions that you are neither a coward nor an ass."

"Easier said than done, said the ass again," Barry repeated the phrase with a slight hint of humor. "Is it really as bad as I imagine…the office tension and what they think about me?"

"Yes it is, but it can be overcome. I promise they will have more respect for your change than they will if you are too proud to admit a mistake. I do have one exception on the apology."

"You are taking this captain of the ship thing seriously. What are your demands of my surrender?"

"I would ask that you apologize to Lisa today. Privately. Sincerely. She will be taking the lead on your projects while you are gone and she deserves an apology and a vote of confidence from you that she can make smart decisions. She's really very good Barry and I am afraid we are about to lose her if she doesn't feel some worth from someone other than me."

"Now you're the ass! You're asking a lot of a beaten down mule. I know she's smart Tom and she didn't deserve my wrath, but that is a pill that I don't think my ego can swallow right now."

"You don't have to kneel down and kiss her ring or anything. Just let her know that you're taking a short leave and that she will be leading the team in your absence. She'll get the message even if an apology doesn't form on your lips."

After a long sigh Barry agreed to talk to her privately this afternoon before he left. "So what now? We go back into the office holding hands and singing hymns?"

"No. Let's go back to the office like we just had lunch. Finish up our day like normal, but without the tension. Talk to Lisa and let her know what milestones you're willing to trust her with and which ones you want to postpone, if any. Talk to Allen just to let him know and leave a note for Rodney. You don't have to go into detail…you've earned the right to disappear for a few weeks without them questioning you. I'll wait until tomorrow to let the staff know."

"Tom," Barry hesitated for a moment while he looked out the window, "I'm sorry it has come to this. I'm not good at showing any weakness but I am relieved to have it off my chest. Now I just need to focus on giving my wife what she needs and deserves."

"Don't be embarrassed…everyone needs a little push to get through difficult times."

"For the first time in many years, I think I have the courage to show my wife how much I care about her. Let's just hope she's still willing to listen."

"I'm sure she is. All women are willing to accept an apology if for no other reason to prove they were right!"

"You realize that I'm still an ass by nature, don't you?"

"Oh yes. I don't expect that to change. I just expect it to be back to normal…the old ass is tolerable." The two men laughed quietly as they settled the bill.

When Barry and Tom returned to the office, all eyes were on the door to judge the victor. They entered without frowns, anger, or smiles. They just entered and went to their respective offices. The staff, disappointed at the stoic faces of the two partners, resumed their normal work activities, afraid to ask any questions of Tom. Anticipation was high but the staff resigned themselves to wait for an answer when the men were ready to reveal any outcomes from the meeting. Barry settled into his office and reviewed the schedules for his current projects in preparation for his meeting with Lisa. He knew this would be a difficult meeting for him but he agreed with Tom that Lisa needed to hear about his absence directly from him. He actually did respect Lisa and he knew she was very smart. He trusted her to keep the projects on track, he just didn't trust her to keep from throwing him under the bus if she got the chance. That was something he would have to work on when he returned. Hopefully she could learn to respect him and his experience even if she didn't truly like him. He could live with that as long as their professional relationship was…well, professional.

At 4:00 in the afternoon, he asked Lisa to come to his office. Lisa was taken aback a bit as he usually came into her office or the conference room and yelled at her in the open. He rarely invited her to his office to talk about anything. As she walked in he asked her to close the door.

"I'm going to be away for a few weeks and I would like you to take the leadership role on four projects in my absence. You know the clients and the team respects your authority on decisions. I have printed out a list of upcoming milestones for each project. You can make the final decisions for each milestone except the initial presentation for the Horner Quarter's project. I'd like you to request a schedule change for that item and push it until mid-September. I would like to be involved in the final internal review of the alternatives before we present to the customer. This will give you and the team time to develop options that may be more outside the box than what we originally discussed."

"Yes sir." Lisa was stunned by the conversation and tone that Barry was using to present the scenario. She could hardly form a complete sentence and didn't trust what might come out, so she sat there in silence listening to his instructions.

"I recognize that there has been a lot of tension in the office lately…mostly between me and you. I take partial responsibility for causing the tension and I apologize for that. When I return, I hope we can start on a fresh note and find a common understanding of how to work together more effectively. Keep Tom posted on all progress and lean on his experience if you run into a difficult spot. Better to get a second opinion than take an unwarranted risk."

"I appreciate your trust in me to take care of things while

182

you're gone. I will do my very best to represent you and the firm with our clients." She hesitated for a quick second before saying, "I don't want to pry but I hope everything is ok?"

"Everything is fine. I just need some time to take care of a few personal matters. I'm confident things will run smoothly under your command."

"Thank you, Mr. Johnston. I appreciate the vote of confidence."

Lisa left the office in a state of utter shock and excitement. Something very serious had obviously taken place during the mysterious lunch and she certainly approved of the outcome. As she walked by Tom's doorway on her way back to her own office, she leaned in with raised eyebrows and a look of—what the hell just happened? She didn't even have to say the words as Tom knew from her expression that Barry had fulfilled his promise. Tom looked straight at Lisa and with a nod of his head and wave of his hand said, "Not now. Keep it quiet and we'll talk tomorrow." After a quick pause and a look of confusion, she marched to her office to wrap up the day. She would be celebrating tonight!

<u>Chapter Thirty-Two</u>

Laura spent the entire afternoon on pins and needles wondering how the meeting with Barry went. She knew Tom was probably considering Barry for a choice and was scared of receiving a call that Barry had been sent to the hospital after a sudden heart attack or other unexpected fatal incident. She didn't believe Barry was worthy of such a drastic decision, but it wasn't her call. Deep down she felt Tom would make the right decision but the thought of comforting Christine with such an unexpected loss would be difficult to do, given the knowledge she had. Desperate to hear the results, she had left a message with Tom earlier, but so far had received no reply. It was past six o'clock now, so she relaxed a bit knowing that if something bad had happened should would have heard.

While cooking dinner, Laura's memory kept falling back to one of her own choices that she questioned to this day. She had worked as an intern at a small insurance agency doing filing, shredding, and front-desk reception work during her junior year of high school. She was at the end of her gift cycle and had deliberated for almost a year about using the gift on the owner of the agency. He was generally a cynical person and treated his staff with less than kindness. His cold looks, condescending comments, and unappreciative remarks made the agency a revolving door for turnover in the staff. He never paid much attention to Laura as a young temporary intern, but she occasionally saw and mostly heard about the deprecating environment in the office that had sent more than one staffer home in tears, only to call the next day proclaiming they would not be returning. The rumors extended themselves to his behavior with his own family, which Laura could never confirm. Despite her lack of conclusive evidence, her gut told her that the owner was not a nice human. She had seen enough to convince herself that most of the rumors were probably true and that his presence in this world would not be missed. Eventually, Laura decided to use her next to last 'under' gift on the man. Shortly after his passing, she saw his wife and children at a restaurant. They seemed happy...almost to the point of relief. Maybe this was a perspective that she created in order to justify her decision, but he was still one of the few choices where she didn't have direct knowledge of someone's life improving. She often wondered if the decision for the insurance agent was too rash and based on too little understanding of the situation and whether he had the capacity to change. She could only imagine it was a similar struggle for Tom if he decided to use the gift on Barry.

Finally around 6:30, she heard Tom pull in the driveway.

"Well? How did it go?" Laura was trying to seem as calm as possible to hide her anxiety.

"Looks like we both will live to see another day," Tom said not realizing that Laura would completely understand the reality of the pun.

"I don't see any stitches or broken bones so it appears you came out ok! How does the other guy look?"

"His ego is a bit bruised but I think he may have turned over a new leaf. Did Christine ever mention anything about being sick?"

"No. Is she?"

"Apparently she had a tumor show up on her breast that gave them both quite a scare. It turned out to be benign, but I think it's what sent Barry into his rage over the last year."

"So her bruises were from him?" Laura said with disbelief and concern.

"No, from the medicine she was taking to dissolve the cyst. He was mentally abusive no doubt, but I don't believe he physically abused her. He went into a state of shock after they found the lump and apparently shut down. He was beating himself up for not supporting her better and was afraid he was losing her. In typical Barry fashion, instead of realizing his mistake he went deeper underground."

"I can't believe she didn't tell me. I could've helped her through this while that ass of a husband went on his cruelness bender."

"Easy, Florence Nightingale. You know Christine is very private about personal matters. She doesn't accept help any better than Barry gives it."

"True." Laura stated, a bit dejected that her helping hand wouldn't have been received well. "It's just...I wish she had told me so we could at least recognize what was going on and helped. Barry revealed all this to you at lunch today?"

"Not at first. We had a very difficult conversation before he finally softened up and confessed his sins."

"Well, Father...do tell how you got the devil into the confession booth."

Tom told Laura about the conversation and how surprised he was at his own ability to be frank with a guy like Barry. As good as Tom was with people and getting them to open up, Laura was shocked that his 'brutal honesty' approach had actually solicited an apology from Barry. Laura listened as Tom explained the course of their talk and how Barry resisted arrest early on. As he came to the turning point, Laura was reminded again of Tom's gift for dealing with people. She didn't always have the patience to be slandered by people without reacting with aggression. Tom had stood his ground but waited for the perfect moment to let force and compassion merge, creating a comfortable space for Barry to let down his guard. It was a space Tom had been creating from the very beginning of the conversation without Barry being aware of it. By the time Barry realized he was sitting in the comfortable space, he was worn down from pitching his own line of defense that wasn't really gaining any traction. Laura knew that space all too well. Tom had created it for her on several occasions where her own anxiety had caused tension in their relationship. The space was a point in a conversation that allowed someone to break down without fear of judgment or abuse. Most people would create a space like that to show dominance and control. Tom did it to give an individual a safe haven where two people could admit mistakes and find common ground.

The family ate dinner together and spent the evening watching dull TV which was a welcomed, mindless activity after a day filled with high anxiety. Both Tom and Laura, without the other's knowledge, had spent the time before his meeting worrying about a choice that might have to be made. Each had their own set of anxieties associated with the choice but there was no denying that both sets were legitimate and of equal degrees of concern. Laura made a note to call Christine in the morning to see about a lunch date this week hoping she would say she couldn't make it due to an unexpected get-away with Barry.

Chapter Thirty-Three

Tom was as upbeat as he could remember during the next two weeks. After explaining to the staff about Barry's short sabbatical, Tom could feel the tension in the office begin to lift. The staff was working with a renewed sense of purpose and ease. Rodney seemed very impressed with Tom's handling of the situation and Tom felt more confident than ever in his ability to manage the firm. As the days passed several of the staff members began to look at Barry's return with positive anticipation, curious to see if the new and improved Barry was going to be as advertised. Tom made no promises to anyone about Barry's attitude once he returned, but he did tell them that a door had been opened for Barry and him to resolve issues without the staff having to suffer the consequences. Barry was a proud man, but he realized his mistakes when it came to the treatment of the staff. Tom assured them that at a minimum, Barry would be more engaged in the details of the project, which meant he would be more willing to consider suggestions. At the surface this would sound like an awful predicament...a nasty boss being more involved could be miserable for the staff. In reality, it meant fewer surprises and back door challenges, which was really the crux of the issue.

When Tom had time, he kept up his research to discover opportunities for his remaining choices. He would randomly select cities based on certain news articles and read the local papers to dig deeper into good news stories and articles revealing potential bad apples. One article that caught his attention was a football coach in Camp Hill, Pennsylvania who had been with Cedar Cliff High School for just over 20 years. He had a remarkable collection of victories and two state titles, but was best known for his dedication to athletes at the school. The article praised his work with the teenage athletes at a time when bad headlines were swirling around coaches and the trust parents put into them. This was an honorable man with no dark shadows who deserved some praise in a state suffering from the sexual abuse scandal at a major university program. Unfortunately, the praise came in light of his recent diagnosis with advanced prostate cancer at the beginning of a very promising season. The article told how Coach McMillan had made men out of teenagers in preparation for their journey as they went to college or entered into the workforce. The loss of a man with such dedication to a program that developed youth instead of just counting wins and losses would affect

"...so many people in this community and across the state where students he has inspired are living successful, productive lives. His influence is spread far and wide and has taught young men what it means to be honorable in victory and defeat."

The article went on to talk about his team's solidarity in preparing for a season where the 51-year-old coach may not make the sidelines during a single game. The entire team shaved their heads in preparation of "...Coach going bald..." from the treatment and the student body was raising money to help pay for the medical expenses with some innovative fundraising techniques to be presented at each home game. It was the kind of story that made you want to be a better person. A story that made you think...why does this happen to good people? It was a story that Tom recognized as an opportunity to validate Hope. He would work on an excuse to travel to Camp Hill in the fall.

In the short term, Tom was preparing for a trip to Birmingham to visit a friend from college who had been diagnosed with ALS, or Lou Gehrig's disease. The diagnosis had been a complete surprise to everyone and Tom had found out only recently when he called Adam for advice on a sketchy real estate deal in Montgomery, Alabama, that a potential client was trying to get the firm to represent. They wanted the firm to do the architectural design for a major retail section of a mixed-use development. Normally this would be a great project, but when the firm did its due diligence on the financial status of the developer, they ran into some potential red flags. Adam was a real estate genius and knew everything about every project by every developer in the whole state of Alabama. Tom trusted Adam and knew he could shed some light on the developer's reputation. He and Adam were good friends in college and roommates for one semester their sophomore year. They kept in touch talking two or three times a year when one or the other came to town for business or pleasure. When Tom called Adam last month, he told Tom of his diagnosis. He was having a difficult time coming to grips with the disease and the finality of its outcome and he had not told anyone outside his immediate family.

Through some quick research, Tom discovered ALS was a horribly debilitating disease where the body rapidly lost function while the mind continued to operate with clarity. The dichotomy between physical paralysis and mental awareness was the worst element of the disease. Physical and mental deterioration when running hand in hand was a palatable concept. Even mental deterioration with no physical change was somewhat acceptable. But having a normally functioning mind when the body crumbled to a mass of useless limbs and an inability to speak was a nightmare no one should have to experience. Tom had no idea what stage of the disease Adam had progressed to, but he wanted to spend time with his friend while he could and scheduled a road trip to Birmingham that Saturday.

On Friday afternoon, Tom walked to the reception area to give Marge a package of drawings for their Memphis project to be delivered by courier to the client on Monday. In the background, he heard a CNN reporter on the lobby TV mention a tragedy in Terra Haute. Tom turned to the TV and watched in horror at the story being told.

"…the details are still a bit sketchy but Terra Haute police have told us that Roger Landstrom, a suspect in his own wife's murder, who had lost custody of his two young sons but was granted supervisory visitation, locked the state case worker out of the house when the boys arrived for visitation. Almost immediately, the house went up in flames killing the father and both sons. It is believed that no other occupants were in the house at the time of this tragedy. We're told the caseworker called her supervisors immediately when the father pushed her aside and pulled the boys into the house locking it behind him. While on the phone with her supervisor, she noticed the flames inside the house and immediately disconnected and called 911. According to the caseworker, the house was consumed with smoke and flames within minutes and she had no opportunity to attempt to save the boys or the father. As we mentioned...police and emergency officials confirm that there were no survivors..."

Tom immediately felt the bile rise in his throat as he stared at the picture of Roger Landstrom on the screen. His range of emotions went from disbelief to anger and finally guilt. He could have saved those two young boys. He could have stopped this evil from happening. He could have trusted his gut, his instincts and the boys would be grieving the death of their last surviving parent...maybe grieving....maybe not. He could have validated Hope for the two boys without their even knowing they needed to believe in Hope. Marge broke Tom's nightmare when she asked if he was all right. All the blood had suddenly rushed from his head to his toes and Tom felt weak and lightheaded.

"Tom do you feel ok? You're white as a ghost."

Struggling to form the words Tom replied, "I think I'm going pass out."

Marge immediately put her arm around him as his knees began to buckle. She guided his almost dead weight onto the couch only a foot away and landed him in an upright position.

He didn't completely black out, but for almost 30 seconds he could see nothing but white dots. As they started to clear, he heard Marge asking someone to call an ambulance. Another 30 seconds and the white dots had disappeared and he seemed to be breathing again.

"Don't call an ambulance….I'm alright," he stuttered.

"Bullshit, you passed out. We need to get you to the hospital," Marge stated with motherly determination.

"No really. I'm ok. I haven't eaten much today and I guess the coffee on an empty stomach just caught up with me." Tom managed to say this with more confidence as the blood re-circulated through his entire body instead of just his toes. He forced a smile toward Marge and said, "I just need some food and to sit down for a few minutes. I'll be fine."

Marge seemed to relax a bit and backed off her insistence to cart Tom off to the hospital. "Well, I've got some leftovers in the fridge. Let me get you a bite and then you are not to move from your office until you get your blood sugar levels up. Then I'll consider whether I drag your ass to the hospital willing or unwilling."

Tom half-heartedly laughed and gave Marge a wink as he succumbed to her instructions. After a bite to eat and time on his couch, Marge came into the office like a nurse on a mission to examine a patient who was not readily cooperative.

"How do you feel now?" she asked as she felt his forehead and looked into his eyes.

"Much better Nurse Ratched," Tom retorted making reference to the Big Nurse from *One Flew Over the Cuckoo's Nest.* "I really did just need a little food."

"That may be, but I could have sworn that little episode came on from watching the news report. Did you know those people?"

"What people?" Tom asked trying to feign ignorance.

"The family that was killed in Terra Haute? The story was on the screen when you passed out."

"I don't even remember the story. I started feeling weak and seeing dots when I walked up to your desk. I guess I just stood there trying to focus on not passing out."

"For someone trying not to pass out you sure seemed interested in the news. Did you know those people Tom?" Marge inquired.

He looked at Marge and with his most innocent face said, "No. I didn't. I only remember hearing something about a fire and three people killed. My focus on the white dots froze me. I felt like if I moved I would have fallen right down."

Marge wasn't 100% convinced but she let it go and continued to 'examine' him to make sure the spell had passed. After a thorough interrogation, Marge declared Tom fit to go home. She promised to get the package out with the day's courier and instructed Tom to call her the minute he arrived home safely. Tom agreed and said he needed to tidy a few things up but he promised to leave in the next 30 minutes.

After Marge left his office, he allowed his mind to absorb the news. He immediately Googled the story and read three articles related to the breaking news. All three had the same minimal information since the story was so fresh. Only one included detailed background information on the story of how the father had been arrested recently for his second DUI, had an altercation with neighbors, had been considered a suspect in his wife's murder, and the state taking custody of the kids with supervised visits. All the things Tom already knew about the father. When Roger's actions were presented all on one page and tied to the latest tragic events, the warning signs seemed obvious. Tom felt foolish that he hadn't realized this man's potential for evil was so real. But Tom's face-to-face interaction with the man led him to second-guess his instincts and err on the side of a possible recovery for the father. Needless to say that ended tragically for the boys, the father, and for Tom. As promised, Tom left the office to go home. Physically, he was feeling better but mentally he was still in shock as he absorbed the news from Terra Haute.

When he entered the house, Laura could tell something was bothering him. His mood wasn't driven by anger, he just seemed overly concerned about something...distant, even exhausted. She asked if everything was all right, expecting him to brush it off with an issue at work. Instead, Tom was silent and sat down on the couch and took a deep breath. Laura knew something larger than work was going on so she pried gently to find out what it was.

"You ok, Hon?"

"Yeah. I just had a little episode at work. I didn't eat all day and got lightheaded in the afternoon. I almost passed out, but Marge saved me. She sent me home with a scolding," Tom confessed.

Laura sat down next to him and pressed a hand to his forehead to see if he had a fever. "You've never had an episode like that before. Have you felt sick lately?"

"No. Things have actually been great at the office. Everyone has been clicking along nicely and we're actually looking forward to Barry's return to see if he's changed. Really...everything's been good. I think I just needed to eat. "

"Why don't you go lie down for a few minutes before dinner and relax. Brady is spending the night with Alex and Anna is getting her nails painted with Danielle and her mom. She'll be home in a little bit. Go rest and I'll start dinner."

Tom went to the bedroom and lay down to clear his mind and put the tragedy away for a while. He awoke 45 minutes later without realizing he had fallen asleep. He changed his clothes and strayed to the kitchen with the determination to present a new mood.

"What's for dinner tonight, Chef?"

"Chicken over pasta with a light cream sauce. How's the nap?"

"Didn't even think I was tired but apparently I fell asleep anyway."

"Good. You feeling better or should I stay close enough to catch you just in case?"

"Much better," Tom declared.

Tom helped Laura with dinner preparations while they talked idly about their days. "Can you get the butter out of the fridge, honey?" Laura asked. When Tom didn't make a move or respond she looked his direction and noticed his face, frozen in an expression of pain and guilt. Tom stood motionless staring at the TV in the kitchen where the nightly newscast was reporting a horrible story in Terra Haute, Indiana. Laura noticed Tom's expression resembled the confused looked he brought home earlier today. As she listened carefully to the story, she began to understand that Tom had some connection. Maybe not directly with the father and the boys, but with a more general sense of evil that couldn't be predicted.

"Tom, can you get the butter out of the fridge?" she asked again when the story finished. She didn't want to question him about the relationship, but it was clear it had affected him tonight and was probably the cause of his episode today.

Tom shook himself away from the TV and retrieved the butter. "I heard about that story earlier today when it first broke. It's just awful," Laura said casually but with a compassionate tone.

"It is. I heard about it briefly today but didn't really understand the whole scenario," Tom lied. "How can someone do that? Or, better yet, how did people not see it coming?" The last statement seemed more of a question to himself than a message of blame towards the police or the caseworkers.

"It sounds as though the authorities did all the right things. They took the children and only allowed supervised visits. He was just determined to leave this world and unfortunately take his children with him."

"If only someone could have stopped him before this last desperate act. It makes it all more surreal having just been there." Tom took a deep breath and tried to return to his after nap mood. Laura played along and didn't mention anything else about the tragedy. Anna came bounding in the door a few minutes later and helped erase his recent memory. Lying in bed that night Tom decided that he would trust his instincts for his next considerations and not let the fear of judging incorrectly keep him from sparing other victims. He was given the gift for a reason. Him. He was. Trust that he was worthy of such a gift. *Use it to help others.* He fell asleep thinking about his trust that Barry had made a breakthrough. Only time would tell, but Tom's instincts felt correct about his decision for Barry. Not so much for the Terra Haute father.

Chapter Thirty-Four

After a night of restless sleep, Tom left for Birmingham to visit Adam. During the drive, he sorted through the shallow knowledge he had accumulated about ALS. He had learned about the symptoms and the disease's progression but had no idea what state Adam was in. The most disturbing fact was that there was no cure for ALS. There were treatments that could extend life but eventually the respiratory muscles would succumb to paralysis causing death. The fact that there was no cure made Tom question the gift's ability to intercede in the life versus death struggle when no scientific evidence would be available for explanation. People beat cancer and other types of diseases with drug treatment and surgery. People overcame addiction and other ailments. But ALS basically had a near-zero survival rate. Once the degeneration started it couldn't be reversed. It could be slowed in some cases, but very rarely. There were no cases where the disease had done a reversal with no lasting effects on the patient. Could the gift actually be used in this scenario? How would it ever be explained? Tom realized that miracles in the truest sense were...well miraculous...without logical or physical explanation...divine. But the gift he temporarily possessed and the choices he had made so far seemed to be disguised with a hint of possible explanation. He realized that was the way it should be. Otherwise skepticism would turn to fear and doubters would hunt down explanations that might eventually reveal the gifters. That would cause a firestorm of disbelief, discontent, doubt, polarization of people and groups, basically utter chaos and the need for influential groups to commoditize the gift. Tom started thinking about the witch-hunts that would take place. This realization further confirmed the need for secrecy. The exposure of the gift to the entire public on a global scale would be ironically disastrous. Here was a group of 'special' people with the ability to cure the sick, treat the afflicted, and kill the wicked. They would be studied, prodded and probed, rounded up for exclusion, hunted by differing religious groups…the public reaction would be detrimental on so many levels. Based on this thought progression, Tom wondered if an 'over' miracle would be effective on Adam. So far he had encountered no restrictions on the use of the gift. But he had never considered a choice like this. With his anxiety level rising, he spent the rest of the drive fishing for an explanation that would pass scientific scrutiny.

Tom arrived at Adam's house around 11:00 a.m. on a beautifully clear, cool fall day. He spent an hour or so talking with Adam and his wife, the kids running around the house showing off cartwheels, favorite stuffed animals, golf swings with miniature plastic clubs, and everything else that 7-, 8- and 10-year-old kids did on a typical Saturday when a guest stops by. They were oblivious to Adam's condition as the symptoms hadn't really become noticeable to them. The parents had not yet told the kids the whole truth about his condition. They were postponing the inevitable so they could first absorb the tragic scenario that would play out and find a way to explain to young kids the mortality of a parent. It was heart-wrenching to contemplate and Tom couldn't imagine how difficult that conversation would be. After Adam filled Tom in on his potential client's reputation and missteps, the two went to the backyard to talk privately.

Adam was still walking normally although with a slower gait. His only real outward physical symptom was limited control of his arms – particularly in the hands and wrists. He had trouble holding small objects as his fingers lost mobility and strength. Adam confessed to Tom that the diagnosis had been given four months ago after Adam began having spasms in his arms and a growing discomfort in his neck and throat. According to the doctors, there was no timeline they could give Adam since the disease progressed at varying rates for different patients.

"I'm scared Tom. For myself sometimes, but mostly for Ginny and the kids. I'm going to leave them without a father, without a husband, with a lot of their life left in front of them."

"Are there treatment options available, even experimental ones?" Tom asked.

"Not really. This has been a disease that's puzzled the researchers for years and years. They're studying the cause but not so much the cure because it's still such a mystery and deals with the part of anatomy that we don't understand very well. Not that they aren't working on a cure, but they need to understand its origin and progression better in order to figure out how to stop it."

"Are there cases where the disease has reversed itself?"

"Only very few cases where the progression has stopped, very few. But even then the symptoms and damage to the nervous system have not reversed themselves. The patient lives with the damage to that point for the rest of their lives. The only hope is that the progression halts itself in the early stages. There is only one case that my doctor knew of where the disease stopped when the patient had only experienced what he considers minor permanent damage. Most of the cases where the disease has halted itself, and again these are very rare, the patient's symptoms had reached a point where their quality of life had already been drastically altered."

"Well, maybe you will be one of those rare cases."

"I guess there is a slight chance of hope. But I'm not sure I could live with the conditions if they get worse. The muscle pain is already unbearable at times and I'm having difficulty breathing. It's not too bad yet but I've talked to other patients and the breathing issue is really scary. They say there are times when they think they're going to asphyxiate and die right there on the spot. It's like being underwater and never knowing if you're going to get to the surface in time to breathe air or just inhale a mouthful of water."

"How fast have the symptoms come on you? Do you wake up every day with a new issue or clearly noticing something has gotten worse?"

"No, not daily. It's a bit slower than that. I'll notice that my arm strength is less than it was last week and that my finger coordination requires more focus and effort. But it's not daily yet."

"Do they perform scans or tests regularly to gauge how the degradation is progressing or is it basically just by observing your own muscle control?"

"There is an experimental blood test they're using now to help determine the pace of damage. It has to do with a protein detected in the blood that's used to monitor the rate of nerve fiber loss. They do the blood test every two weeks. The more precise way to monitor this protein is by cerebrospinal fluid, but that requires a serial lumbar puncture, which is dangerous and pretty invasive. The blood test method is still a bit untested, so most of the progression rating is done by gauging muscle strength from month to month."

"When is your next blood test?"

"I just had one yesterday, so it will be in two weeks. Depending on the numbers they may consider another lumbar puncture depending on how quickly other symptoms progress."

"Adam, I'm so sorry for all of this. I wish there was something I could do. I can only imagine what Ginny must be worrying about, much less what you are going through both physically and mentally."

"It sucks. It really sucks. I don't know if I can live with the decline of my body while my mind is still active. I don't know if I want my kids to see me past a certain stage. I'm supposed to be superman to them. They're too young to watch their indestructible father become a vegetable. Ginny and I have talked about...options when this reaches a certain state. She's not ready to go there yet, but I have to think ahead knowing this probably doesn't have a good ending."

"Don't give up yet my friend. I've learned lately that Hope is a powerful thing. Hope is real in this crazy world and it comes in the most unassuming forms."

"I appreciate the pep talk. I still hold out a little hope, but I also can't bury my head in the sand. My fight now is with upholding dignity through all of this. If the disease halts itself, I'll be grateful. But this is different than cancer or other diseases where drugs, therapy, and perseverance give you a chance for survival. The disease either takes its course or doesn't. All I can do is manage the physical disabilities as they come."

"Could you manage the conditions now, if they stopped?" Tom asked with a curious motive.

"Yes. I think I could if I knew they wouldn't worsen."

"Then that's what we'll do!" Tom said this with such finality that Adam snickered at the thought of Tom willing the disease away.

"If you say so," Adam said with a laugh.

Adam talked a bit more about the plans he had made for Ginny and the kids when things get worse. He talked about when he would no longer be able to work and how he would find innovative ways to interactive with the kids when his condition completely confined him to a wheelchair. Tom was only half listening through the end of the conversation. His mind was occupied with the joy of knowing that the scientific explanation he needed to give Adam the gift was that the disease could be halted. Complete reversal of the symptoms was probably more than could be asked for but stopping the progression was an option without making the miracle too miraculous.

Tom stayed the night and they kept the conversation light

during dinner, talking about their college days and catching up on who was doing what. He left early the next morning and headed for home. During their goodbye's, Tom hugged Adam and gave him a firm squeeze on the shoulder.

"Don't let resignation get in the way of Hope just yet. You're still at a stage where the symptoms are tolerable. If you can live with that, then plan on trying," Tom told him. Adam appreciated the words and partially accepted the challenge although most of his thoughts wandered around the path of decline that was certainly ahead of him. Adam promised to keep him updated and they agreed to have another visit soon.

Chapter Thirty-Five

As Tom drove home, he wondered how the doctors would react to the halting of the disease. They would do a thousand tests on Adam with probably no explanation. He wondered if the gift had an element to its healing power that might provide the doctors with new insight to an actual cure of the disease? Could the gift stop a disease like ALS by introducing a protein or enzyme that could be shown to stop and possibly show promise for a cure? Somehow, that thought didn't seem feasible to Tom. The gift wasn't meant to find miracles of medicine. It was more human than that. It seemed more individual than that. The gift wasn't meant to solve world hunger, it was meant to motivate people with a desire to solve world hunger. To validate Hope one miracle at a time.

Traffic was Sunday-morning-light with only a minivan in sight about a half a mile in front of him. They had been cruising along at about the same speed and were just crossing the Alabama—Tennessee border still an hour south of Nashville. As he crested a hill, Tom noticed a car in the median sitting on a graveled authorized-vehicles-only path that connected the southbound lanes of Interstate 65 with the northbound lanes. Tom's first reaction was to slow down thinking it was a state trooper that had set up a speed trap. He was too far away to see lights on top of the vehicle but the color didn't match the standard marked car of the state police. He assumed it was an unmarked vehicle and continued on at a safe speed. The minivan in front of him had flashed its brake lights in an effort to slow down as well and they both seemed to be moving at a safe pace that would disappoint any radar gun looking for violators. As the minivan approached the cross-over, the car unexpectedly pulled out in the northbound lane in the direct path of the minivan. It seemed to take a slow turn onto the interstate without any urgency for speed. Instead of staying in the left lane closest to the median where it came from, it casually swayed to the center of the road unsure which lane to occupy, thus taking up parts of both. If it had stayed in the unoccupied left lane, then disaster could have been narrowly averted. But given the indecision of the driver, the minivan approaching in the right-hand lane was left with nowhere to go. Even at 70 miles an hour, the collision seemed to happen in slow motion and Tom watched the disaster unfold. The minivan slammed on its brakes and tried to swerve first left, thinking the car would move to the right lane, then again right when the car stayed indecisively in the center. The minivan careened off the car's passenger side door and was propelled by momentum toward the emergency lane on the right side of the interstate. After impact, the driver of the minivan had no control of the vehicle and it launched itself off the road, over the drainage ditch, and went nose first into the grassy embankment. After the initial impact, the minivan flipped several times crushing the metal frame like used tin foil. When it finally came to a stop, the van was on its side in the ditch almost 300 feet from where it originally impacted the car. Tom was far enough behind the collision to slow down and avoid slamming into either one of the vehicles, but close enough to imagine what might be left of the inhabitants of the minivan.

Tom's instincts overwhelmed any anxiety or fear his body tried to exhibit and he immediately kicked into controlled first responder mode. He pulled into the emergency lane and jumped out of his car while dialing 911 on his cell. Glancing over to the car still in the middle of the road, he noticed an older gentleman sitting in the driver's seat, stunned but seemingly alert. Tom yelled for him to quickly pull the car off the road and out of the path of traffic coming towards them. A southbound car was stopping across the median and a young man jumped out to help. Tom gave instructions to the new arrival to help the old man while he ran towards the minivan. His heart was racing faster than he could ever remember as he approached the van, terrified of what he might find. When he reached the mangled mess of metal, he peered inside the broken windshield and saw the driver and one passenger in the front seat. There were no noises except the hissing of steam as the vehicle's fluids floundered over the hot parts of the engine. Tom looked first at the driver. It was obvious he was dead as his head was contorted back and to the side in a way that was wholly unnatural. The passenger, a woman based on the length of her hair, was bloodied and occupying a very small space in what was left of her side of the vehicle. There was hope for her. Tom jumped on top of the side of the van and clambered over to the blown-out rear driver-side window. Sitting in the back-seat, snug inside a car seat was a girl about 4 or 5 years old. Her eyes were wide open but she wasn't making a sound. She looked at Tom with an expression of fear and shock that would burn in Tom's memory forever. He reached out, touched her carefully on the arm, and with a staged smile said, "You're gonna be ok. I'm going to get you out of here. Do you have any boo-boos that hurt?"

The girl shook her head side to side but didn't utter a word. "Good. Let me help your Mom real quick then I'll come get you. You are safe in your seat right now. Ok?" Again the girl shook her head acknowledging Tom's instructions. He raced back to the front of what was left of the van and reassessed the woman's condition. She was barely conscious and Tom began to pull the remainder of the windshield away from the car so he could get access to the mother. She began to groan and Tom spoke to her in a calm voice.

"Stay still. I'm coming in to help you. Your daughter is fine…she's still snug as a bug in her car seat and doesn't seem to have any injuries. Are you hurt?"

Slowly the mother raised her hand to her midsection and said something barely audible. Tom thought he heard the word baby.

"Your daughter is fine. She's not hurt and I'm going to get her out safely."

Struggling to speak, the woman again tried to form a word,

"Preg…"

Tom froze when he understood. "Are you pregnant?" he uttered in a monotone voice.

The woman nodded her head and Tom looked down to see if her body was trapped by the configuration the wreck had created. He noticed blood in her seat but wasn't sure if it was a discharge from her vagina or blood from another wound. The woman rolled her head sideways and saw the lifeless remains of her husband for the first time. She immediately began sobbing quietly, too injured to make much noise. Tom reached in his pocket for his knife and cut the shoulder strap of the seatbelt to relieve the pressure on her extended belly. He was afraid to move her before the paramedics arrived, uncertain of the injuries she might have. So he decided to comfort her and keep her conscious.

"It's going to be ok. Do you have any pain that you can isolate?"

"My legs," the woman said slowly appearing to become more aware of what was happening. "My legs hurt, but I can't feel my feet. And my belly…I'm having sharp pains in my belly."

"Do they feel like labor pains?"

"No. Sharper and constant," she whispered slowly.

"Ok. I'm going to raise your arm. Can you do that with me?"

The woman nodded as Tom raised the arm that was not pinned between her side and the door of the car. He examined her exposed side to see if there were any objects that had penetrated her belly. He gently let her arm back to a comfortable resting spot.

"Ok, that side looks good. Nothing has pierced your belly on that side." Tom looked at the woman's bloodied face and began wiping it with his bandana. Her eyes were partially shut and he could tell she was struggling to remain conscious.

"Stay with me," he said. "What's your name?"

"Rose," the woman whispered.

"Ok, Rose. You're doing great. My name is Tom. How far along are you in your pregnancy?"

"Seven."

"Seven months. That's great." Tom kept talking to keep her attention while he was examining her for injuries on the other side of her body. She was pinned against the car door on her right side and he couldn't quite get his hand in between her body and the door to feel if anything was stabbing her. He reached up to her right shoulder and worked his way down under her armpit when he felt a cold metal object. When he traced the object from the car to her body the woman groaned. The door release lever had pierced her side on the lower part of her rib cage and was still embedded. He couldn't tell how deep the intrusion was and didn't want to move her or the handle and make things worse. He surveyed the blood on her seat and became even more concerned for the baby and the 'home' it was currently inhabiting. Her eyes began to close again. She was losing consciousness.

"Rose. Stay with me. What's your beautiful daughter's name?"

"Em…Emma."

"Emma is a perfect name for a brave little girl. She is fine, so I need you to stay with me and we'll all be fine." Tom could finally hear the sirens in the background.

"Rose, the paramedics are here and they're gonna get you, your baby, and Emma safely out of here. OK? Rose, I need you to listen to me. I promise that you and the baby will be fine. Have Hope Rose. Keep Hope alive in your mind and heart. Can you do that?"

Rose nodded slowly. Tom reached over and gently squeezed Rose's shoulder…twice. He then slid his hand down to hers and held it firmly until the paramedics came to take over the triage.

Chapter Thirty-Six

Tom stayed long enough at the accident for the paramedics and other emergency crews to get Rose and Emma out of the car and safely into the ambulance. Before they left, he asked the paramedics about the wound and the risk to the baby. As for Rose, the paramedics said her pierced side could be critical depending on the organs involved and the depth of the penetration. They were worried about the lower lung area, kidneys, and liver. Any one of those could be life threatening if the penetration was not clean or too deep. The possibility of damage to a combination of any or all three could be too much to overcome. As for the baby, they believed they still heard a faint heartbeat but only an ultrasound would determine if the womb was still a viable haven to support life. The closest hospital was only 10 miles away but Vanderbilt's Life Flight Services were already on their way to pick up Rose and take her to a trauma center in Nashville. Emma, virtually unharmed physically, was put in the ambulance with her mom and would fly with her until they arrived at the trauma center where she would hopefully be united with a friend or relative since the father was dead. Tom was comforted when he saw the license plate on the minivan had Davidson County tags meaning the family lived in Nashville and therefore probably had friends or family in the area that could comfort Emma. He made a note of the family's last name while the police and emergency personnel were investigating the scene. He could contact the hospital tomorrow and see about Rose's progress.

Exhausted from the adrenaline rush, Tom got back on the road and called Laura to explain why he would be later than expected. Laura gauged his state of mind during the brief conversation to make sure he was safe to drive himself. Reassured by his calmness despite the shock of what he had seen and done, Laura was convinced that Tom had been present at that moment for a reason. She had no doubt that he had used the gift to ensure the mother and baby would survive. From his explanation, it didn't sound like the similar situation they had encountered a few years ago when an accident had left an entire family dead except for a critically injured child that eventually died days later. This time, Laura was confident that the miracle of life had been given instead of the miracle of mercy.

What Tom had done that day with three human lives was a bit overwhelming. During the drive he had emotions peaking with a feeling that the gift should be allowed to go on forever so more good could be done. On the lower end of the emotional scale, he didn't know if he would survive mentally with having to continue making choices for an eternity. It was a bittersweet gift for sure. Choices of great satisfaction followed by choices of extreme guilt or questions. The dichotomy of emotions brought on by the gift was brutal to the gifter's psyche. But in the end, Tom concluded that the gift was truly a gift, allowing an individual to recognize human existence in a way that could never be taught. No theologian could ever provide the explanation of humanity one got from their experience with the gift. He wondered if other gifters had this same revelation or if they just went about their giving with no real change. Surely not. All the gifters were people with "pure hearts," as Marina had put it. They certainly would have long-lasting and positive effects from their experiences. Something dawned on Tom that had not entered into his evaluation of the gift before. There were tens, hundreds, maybe thousands of people in the world over the course of time that had been given the gift. People who went on with the rest of their lives with a totally different perspective on life and death. An army of humans that had an upper hand on the human experience without a sense of superiority. He could only imagine that these were the people you heard about in everyday life that exemplified the good deeds done on behalf of true goodness with no ulterior motive. These were people with a secret so powerful they were compelled to live in a manner that was based on a moral code over which no religion could claim sole dominion. It propelled them through a life of managing their actions to give other people a chance at believing in Hope. The thought that he would be, in fact is, one of these people, gave Tom a sense of long-term purpose he had not felt before. The omnipotent purpose and effect of the gift on his life had finally come together in perfect clarity.

By the time Tom arrived home, still in his bloody clothes, he felt relatively calm. The day had been too traumatic to be excited about giving life, but a sense of serenity balanced his emotions in a steady plane of satisfaction. After a long shower, he came into the living room and hugged his family, seemingly for no good reason other than to reassert his protection over them. The rest of the afternoon and evening was spent with idle family activities that allowed Tom to let his newfound existence sink into his soul.

The next day, Tom called Vanderbilt Hospital to check up on Rose and Emma. Unable to get any information over the phone from the nurse station, he decided to go to the hospital during lunch. When he arrived at the ICU ward, he asked about Rose Wertleft and was told that she was in fact a patient but they couldn't give any details about her condition unless he was a family member. As he was explaining the situation from yesterday to the head nurse, Emma came down the hall holding the hand of a woman who was not her mother. She stopped in her tracks when she saw Tom and gave him a wayward grin of recognition.

"That's him," she proclaimed to her surrogate mother. "He's the one who helped."

"Hi Emma," Tom said with a soft, kind voice. "How are you doing?"

"I have a baby brother," she squeaked with excitement. "But he's too little for me to hold right now."

"Hi, I'm Tom Roddin." He introduced himself to the woman still holding tightly to Emma's hand. "I was at the scene of the accident yesterday and I wanted to see how everyone is doing."

"I'm Carla Mansfield, Rose's sister. Thank you so much for your help yesterday."

"How is Rose doing?"

"She's stable now but it was a long night. Emma, why don't you go over to the couch while we wait to see mommy."

Emma looked at Tom and said, "You were right. You told me everything would be ok and you were right. I'm glad about that." As she skipped over to the couch in the waiting room, Tom noticed Carla's eyes welling up.

"Is Rose going to be ok? And how is the baby?" Tom asked with a compassionate calmness to try and steady Carla.

"Rose is going to be ok. She was in surgery for hours yesterday to treat her wounds. She had damage to her right kidney, which couldn't be saved and her spleen was ruptured. The door handle also punctured her womb so the baby had to be taken out. Despite being six weeks early, he is doing pretty good in the infant ICU. Rose died twice on the table during all the procedures but miraculously revived herself both times. As you probably know, her husband, Jim, didn't survive."

"Yes. That was unfortunately determined at the scene yesterday. I am so relieved Rose and the baby came through ok. Are her legs alright?"

"Yes. She still doesn't have full feeling yet in her feet but the doctors believe that will come back soon. They didn't detect any permanent damage."

"That's great. Does Emma understand about her father?"

"No, not really. She asked about him once but I didn't tell her the whole truth. It's odd that she hasn't put it together yet that he's not here in the hospital. But I thought it best for her and Rose to have that conversation, as long as she doesn't ask about it again before Rose is well."

"Yes, I imagine that is going to be difficult conversation for them."

"Rose has only been conscious for a brief time today, so we haven't had much time to talk through the tragedy. But she did say that you were an angel."

"Well that's sweet of her but I really didn't do anything."

"No, she didn't mean a nice person, she meant a true angel...in the life-saving sense," Carla said with a seriousness that frightened Tom. "She told me a man came to the van after the accident and told her about hope...about keeping hope alive. She told me they weren't just words; they were feelings. She actually felt hope come to her and it kept her calm. I shrugged it off as a drug-induced euphoria until Emma told me something that I'll never understand. She told me that while you were talking to her mother, she heard another voice, felt another voice that told her to believe everything would be all right for her mother and her brother. She said she wasn't afraid after that and she knew her mother and brother would be ok."

"Well, sometimes it's easier to convince kids than adults that things will be ok in the face of tragedy. She was probably still in shock from the accident. But I'm glad I was able to tell the truth in this instance."

"Yes, she probably was, but she said she heard the other voice with a conviction that I have never heard any child use. Also, no one knew whether they were having a boy or a girl. It was going to be a surprise. She said the voice clearly told her she was going to have a brother."

Tom had no explanation for the woman and was completely at a loss for words.

"Whether you believe it or not, you did and said all the right things to save their lives. We are all very thankful that it was you there instead of someone else."

"Thank you," Tom managed to say with a hint of disbelief. "I just tried to comfort both of them until the real help could arrive. I'm glad they are ok…all three of them."

"Can I get your contact information? When Rose gets better I am sure she would like to thank you herself."

Tom left the hospital wondering if the voice the little girl heard was just an echo in her mind of what he had told her when he first reached the van. She had probably already set her mind on having a brother and used the moment to confirm her own desires. Nonetheless, he was pleased that the gift had been given and that the family, minus the father, was ok. He'd given his work number to Carla but in the back of his mind he hoped Rose wouldn't call. Her gratitude was already extended by Emma in a way that was more comforting than any adult could convey. Also, he was afraid Rose might be looking for an explanation of the events that he couldn't provide. Hope had been validated for Rose and Emma. That was enough for him.

Chapter Thirty-Seven

The first time Shanta Stricker was approached by the seemingly harmless guy from apartment 315, she thought nothing of the encounter. His face was familiar as a resident of her complex, but they had had no interaction. Returning from work one evening, he had popped out of nowhere in front of her building and asked if she had seen or heard anything unusual in the previous nights. Startled, she replied no and casually asked if something was going on that he knew about. He simply stated that some of his neighbors seemed to be keeping strange hours and he was concerned about illegal activity taking place in the complex. Their conversation was brief and she continued on to her apartment to end her day.

On two other occasions, he had approached her and asked if she could see his building from her apartment windows. Only one of her windows faced his building and she rarely opened the blinds in this second, unoccupied bedroom that was mostly filled with boxes and old clothes. She assured him that the last thing she wanted to do was spy on their neighbors and interfere with their lives. With a nervous look on his face, he walked away both times in silence. The night of the second peeping tom inquiry, curiosity got the best of her and she entered the second bedroom and lifted the blinds. Sure enough, her view was straight towards his building and she could see into an apartment where the blinds were up and an interior light was on. Curious, she watched as shadows passed in the background of the room but revealed little information about what was happening in the room. Suddenly, her buddy from 315 appeared in the window and looked straight at her. Caught off-guard and feeling like a peeping tom, she moved away from the window and turned off the bedroom light. Carefully, she walked toward her window and slowly shut the blinds without looking through them.

Thankfully, a month passed without encountering the neighbor, so she didn't have to explain the awkward window moment. Then, late one night she arrived at the complex's parking lot after a double shift from her convenience store job. Mr. 315 jumped out from the shadows and startled Shanta as she approached the walkway to her building. Fronting her face-to-face and impeding her path to the safety of her apartment, he grabbed both her arms just below the biceps. In a soft tone but with wild eyes, he whispered, "I know about your past." Still gripping her arms he maneuvered his thumbs to rub against her breasts, gently massaging her nipples in a circular movement. "If you want to keep your past a secret, then I suggest you do me some favors…just like the favors you used to do, only this time without getting paid for it." The expression on his face revealed a wicked smile.

"I don't know what you're talking about," Shanta feigned.

"Don't play coy with me. I'd hate for your mother, neighbors, and co-workers to find out how you made a living before your pristine existence now. I'm not asking for anything that you don't already enjoy. Plus, I've seen you looking at me through your window."

"You're a sick fuck. Get the hell out of my way before I scream."

"You don't want to do that. Your parole officer wouldn't like to hear my story."

Shanta froze for a moment thinking about the implications of his lies and half-truths on her already shaky reputation. She was walking on thin ice with her parole officer simply because she had refused him the same favors Mr. 315 was asking for now. She couldn't risk the exposure and knew her parole officer would find a way to twist the situation against her. It would jeopardize her job, her schooling, and make the blemish on her record a permanent mark. She was too close to freedom.

"I'm going to let you think about it because tonight not's the night. But next time I come calling, I expect you to be a good girl...well a naughty good girl, and keep me happy. Understand?"

Shanta just nodded her head and gave Mr. 315 an icy stare. He kissed her cheek making sure his tongue found its way across her hidden dimple. Letting go, he turned and walked towards his building and disappeared into the darkness. Shanta collected herself and hurried to the apartment. She got lucky tonight but knew this wouldn't be their last encounter. Mr. 315 seemed like a persistent bastard and it was only a matter of time before he came collecting on what he thought was a debt.

Chapter Thirty-Eight

For the next several weeks Tom was consumed with work and family events with little time to administer the gift. He had not forgotten about it, but rather wanted to let the gift sit for a while. It was now mid October of 2012 and the change of season had energized his soul as the fall months did every year. There was something about the cooler weather, the color of the change, and the impending winter dormancy that excited Tom like no other season. Many people began a depressing cycle with the onset of the long, dark winter months. But Tom relished the season's harshness and countered other peoples' somber tone of solitude with cheery excitement. He could hide his own depressed cycle in the summer when everyone else was occupied with happy sunshine and unaware of his downward mood swing. With his upbeat winter attitude, he unintentionally fooled everyone into thinking he was a year-round psychologically steady being.

He had been back to Birmingham twice since his first visit with Adam and was grateful for the news he was hearing. Adam's symptoms were not progressing and he was living with only the minor damage that had been done to that point. Adam and his family were thrilled with each new checkup as the doctors reported a miraculous halting of the disease. He was that rare case where the disease's progression halted on its own. Adam was encouraged with a sliver of hope and it had paid off. Pleased with the prognosis for his friend, Tom was relieved that the miracle was not so miraculous that it drew attention to itself. Adam's minor physical handicaps had not been reversed, but at least the progression had been halted. Adam's current disabilities from the disease were certainly manageable considering the alternative.

Despite his short 'sabbatical' from the gift, Tom thought regularly about his last few choices. The encounter with Roger from Terra Haute and the disastrous outcome gave Tom the courage to trust his instincts and waive the guilt associated with the moral justification of his under choices. Recognizing evil before it manifested itself into tragedy was now a goal for at least a few of his unused choices. To that end, Barry had made little effort to change his ways in the office since his return from leave. He participated more in team meetings but his scorn towards the office staff was not much softer. Tom wondered what had happened during his time off but hesitated to bring the subject up for no other reason than he dreaded the pending conversation. If Barry had returned with a new attitude, the conversation would have been welcomed. But given the bitterness Barry was still showing, Tom decided to postpone his conversation until Laura had a chance to gather some intel from Christine at their next luncheon. The two wives had a lunch date scheduled for tomorrow, their first since Barry and Tom's lunch at MaCabe's Pub, and both Roddins were anxious to hear about the 'vacation'.

The following day, Tom was examining front elevation plans when Lisa popped her head in his office.

"Tom, do you have a minute?"

"Sure Lisa, come on in."

Lisa walked cautiously to the chair opposite his desk and sat down with a concerned looked on her face. "I don't mean to bring more problems to your plate, but things aren't going very well on the Trident project with Homebrook Builders. Barry lit into one of the client's engineers yesterday for presenting an idea that had some merit. It would have caused some delays and a bit of rework on our part, but overall, the idea was a good one for the whole development. The client was a bit surprised at 'our' reaction and didn't seem to appreciate the way it was handled. I received a personal call from the project manager after the teleconference asking what was going on. He strongly suggested we change our approach when providing responses to their suggestions. He was trying to be diplomatic but I could sense his discontent with what happened."

"Does Barry know you received a call?"

"No. I haven't told him yet."

"Did he say anything after the meeting to explain his actions?"

"No. Nothing, other to say that the engineer was an idiot and that we should never bow to stupid suggestions, even if they were made by the client."

"So no remorse. No sense that he went too far?"

"No." Lisa hesitated but it was obvious she had more to say. Tom let the silence linger allowing her to speak her mind. "I truly hoped things would be different after your lunch with Barry and his return from vacation. But honestly, nothing has changed. He is participating more in the meetings, but his anger and unpredictable behavior are just as frustrating as before."

"I know. I've been putting off another meeting with him for selfish reasons, but it sounds like you're going to force my hand." Tom said this with a slight grin so Lisa wouldn't feel responsible for making him do the dreaded deed.

"As funny as it sounds, I'm also a bit worried about Barry's health. I thought he was going to burst a blood vessel right there in the conference room when he was scolding the client's engineer. He's wound up like a top and ready to explode. I don't know what you guys talked about at your lunch a few months ago...if he has some other issues going on, but something is causing this rage and it's gone beyond the office now."

"He does have some other issues and I thought he was ready to turn over a new leaf. But since his return, it's obvious the issues are unresolved. I'll talk to Barry this week. In the meantime, do what you can to appease and apologize to Homebrook. Keep the contact with them one-on-one for a week or so until Rodney and I can figure out how to formally apologize and reduce Barry's contact with them until the project is completed."

"Thanks. I must say, I was shocked and pleased at the initial result of your meeting with Barry. I truly believed things might change after his return. I'm sorry to say I was a bit disappointed." Lisa realized as soon as the words left her mouth that it was a slight towards Tom. "I didn't mean to imply…uh…I mean you…"

"No need to say anymore Lisa. I understand your meaning. I'm disappointed too. I may have trusted too much in my ability to talk Hitler into surrendering."

"What?"

"Never mind…it's an inside joke." Tom mused back to his conversation with Laura. Maybe his next step would be telling Barry's mother he wasn't playing fair.

Tom's ringing phone interrupted the conversation and Lisa left his office.

"Hello."

"Hey honey. You busy?"

"Nope. What's on your mind?"

"I just finished lunch with Christine."

Tom glanced at his watch. It was 2:15. "Long lunch. What about your class?"

"The student teacher has the class in the afternoon so it wasn't a problem. Tom, I think Barry was lying to you."

Tom's first emotion was a rush of pure anger. Trying to steady the emotion from anger to shock, he took a breath to

221

rationalize Laura's explanation. "About what?"

"Christine was sick, but it was more than a year ago and it was very minor. It was a simple out-patient procedure to remove and biopsy the lump. She said she was frightened at first but the whole thing was resolved within a month or so. It didn't linger on like Barry had told you."

"Wait, how did the subject get brought up? Did you tell her you knew about it…that Barry had told me?"

"No, not at all. I noticed another bruise on her neck. She tried to hide it with makeup, which by the way she has gotten really good at doing, but this one was large and covered most of her neck. Her turtleneck and makeup couldn't cover the whole thing. So, I asked her about it. At first she tried to make some excuse but she could tell I wasn't buying it. She finally confessed that Barry had caused the bruises in a fit of anger the other night. She defended him, saying he was drunk and that the stress of work had been building up on him. She lost her stoic demeanor for a moment and actually showed some emotion about their failing relationship. But, she quickly recovered and brushed it off as something that was a one-time thing. She actually said, 'all couples go through this right?' I didn't know how to respond without crossing over a boundary."

"I can't believe she admitted it. Did she actually say she was afraid or anything that hinted that she might want to talk more about it?"

"Not with those words, but I pressed her anyway. You know me, I can't let that sort of information pass without giving an opinion." Tom smiled to himself with that self-confession by Laura. She was the best at delicately giving an opinion without it seeming like an unwelcomed intrusion. "I asked her if this had happened before…the physical abuse. She denied it at first but then came around and admitted that it had happened once or twice before over the last few years. But there was no evidence of her accepting the fact that she was a victim. She played it off as a normal response to Barry's stress. She tried to be stern and tell me that she had warned Barry about continuing the abuse. But I think that was for me. Something tells me she wouldn't have the courage to stand up to him, which is shocking. I always took her to be a strong woman that would never put up with someone's shit. How wrong I was."

"Well, she fooled us both. I can't believe she would allow that, even from a guy like Barry. What was the rest of the conversation like?"

"Awkward. I tried to offer my support and help but she wasn't very accepting. In the end, I think she was a little embarrassed that she had told me. Tom, I just don't know if I believe her…the part about this being an occasional thing. She spent most of the time defending him and trying to lighten the conversation, but I could tell she was holding back."

"I can't believe that bastard lied to me. Even more, I can't believe I bought it. Damn him. Christine is a good woman, she doesn't deserve this."

"I know he has been on a tear in the office since his return and the homecoming wasn't what you thought it would be."

"It's getting worse. He blew up at a client yesterday. Lisa came to see me today and told me what happened. They want him off the job. I've been postponing a discussion with him but I can't hold off any longer. Something has to be done…I mean said."

Laura's thoughts stopped on the ending of his sentence. She had been afraid of how Tom might react to the news in light of the gift. She didn't want to give Tom any ammunition for a choice concerning Barry, but he had to know the truth about the lies. *Give him strength,* she said to herself. This is the kind of choice Tom may not be equipped to handle. She remembered the guilt and confusion she had suffered with a similar choice she had made a thousand years ago.

"Barry can't know Christine told me this."

"I know. I'll figure out a way to get him to confess his lies. Shit. This sucks."

"Would Rodney support you if you gave him an ultimatum?"

"Like what? Stop being mean or you're fired?"

"Well, with an ultimatum of some sort you may be able to coax from him what happened on his vacation? Whether he wants to continue the lie and say that everything went fine."

Tom thought for a moment. "Maybe asking about the vacation might be an introduction to the conversation. But I doubt he will confess to beating his wife."

"I'm sorry Tom."

"For what?"

"I don't know. Sorry that this situation has presented itself. Sorry that you have to deal with it. You can keep his personal life out of the conversation and just focus on the problems in the office. See if you and he can resolve that aspect of his miserable life."

"That is the professional approach. But there is a moral approach that comes into play as well. I am not sure I can sit by when I know he is abusing Christine. Let me see how the conversation goes. Maybe I address only the professional aspect now and we can work together on helping Christine. I need to see him this afternoon. Wish me luck."

"Good luck Sweetie. Don't let your anger of the lie cloud your professional judgment. Let's hope he comes around."

Hope…funny choice of words, he thought. Tom had *hoped* the situation with Barry would be resolved. But he wondered again if the gift of Hope needed to resolve the issue. Certainly from a professional standpoint, Tom was strong enough to bring Rodney into the discussion and resolve the issues in the office. Whether it was an ultimatum, or some other means of keeping Barry from raging against his clients and the staff…that was do-able. He hated to drag Rodney into this mess but professionally it was warranted since it affected the business end of the firm. But morally…a whole other scenario had presented itself. Barry was not likely to turn off his anger at home just because he had been admonished at work. It would probably only tip the balance harder toward home brutality. Tom couldn't look the other way. *Goddammit Barry. You've done this to yourself.*

Tom decided to first approach Barry alone. This afternoon. He would feel Barry out to see if he was willing to talk about the office problems. If it didn't go well, he would set up a meeting with Rodney, Barry, and himself to find a solution. Morality would have to wait.

Tom knocked on Barry's door and didn't wait for an answer before entering his office.

"We need to talk."

"What the hell about? If it's about Homebrook, save your breath. That engineer is an idiot."

"No Barry, that engineer is a client. And his ideas will be weighed equally and with courtesy no matter what you think of the concept."

"I knew that bitch would come crawling to you."

"What the hell is wrong with you? She had to let someone know so we can repair the damage you've done to a client relationship. Barry, this is unacceptable." So much for starting softly with 'How did the vacation go?'

"What is unacceptable is the way we coddle all of our clients. They hire us because we are professionals. They should shut up and listen to our opinions."

"Who the hell made you King of the universe? We're supposed to listen, then make suggestions as if the client thought them up themselves. That's how you get clients to come back for the next job."

Barry's veins were bulging so hard in his throat Tom thought he was going to burst his insides all over the office. "I will not sit here and tolerate the likes of you telling me how to be an architect! You little shit! You walk around here like you're a god and pat everyone on the head saying 'Good job' even when the staff is making stupid decisions. You don't know shit about running a firm!"

Tom had half expected this outrage but it still made his blood boil over. He took a deep breath and counted to 5 in his head. "What happened during your vacation Barry? Did you ever find the courage to apologize to Christine for being such an ass."

"Fuck you Tom! That bitch should have died with her silly tumor. All she does is cry and moan about a life she could have had with someone else. You two would be perfect for each other. You could sit around and coddle everyone in the world so they feel good about themselves despite their shortcomings. My kids, the staff here, everyone! Get the hell out of my office."

"You ungrateful bastard. You have no idea what a gift Christine is for a prick like you. You're the angriest person I've ever met Barry. You have fucked up everything that has been given to you. Your wife, your talent as an architect, your kids. Everything. People keep giving you chances and you just keep fucking them up! You are a total failure as a human being."

Barry came barreling across his desk at Tom with an outstretched hand aimed at his throat. For Tom, it all seemed to happened in slow motion. His mind raced around the conversation in a flash as he came to a very calm and definite decision. As Barry's right hand came close to his face, Tom countered by interlocking his left arm with Barry's. Leveraging his standing position, Tom drove Barry back onto his seat with his full weight leaning into him. Tom took an instant to the let the surprise of the counter attack sink in to Barry's conscious.

Out of the corner of his eye, he saw Barry's left hand reach into an open drawer revealing the butt of a pistol. Tom swung his free hand down with all the strength his now awkward position would allow crushing Barry's wrist between flesh and wood. The left hand went limp hanging uselessly by the side of the chair. Opposite arms still entangled, Tom returned his stare to Barry's eyes before leaning close to his ear.

"You lied to me," he whispered. "You lied about the medicine, the length and severity of the illness, about your true intentions to reconcile with Christine. You lied about it all. She doesn't deserve your beatings or your shit. So now she will be free of it. Say hello to Hope you son of a bitch."

Barry's eyes were open wide showing the bursting blood vessels running between the cornea and the back of his eyeball. He was stunned at the strength of Tom's counter and the knowledge that Tom was whispering in his ear. Tom quickly moved his right hand to Barry's shoulder and gave it a firm squeeze. Barry gasped for air with a painful look on his face as his body relaxed and slumped into the softness of the leather chair. Tom reached into the drawer and removed the gun, examining it with disbelief. With an unwarranted act of compassion, he slid the pistol into his coat pocket and called Marge from the phone on the desk. No living soul would ever know about the pistol or the violence that might have played out had Barry followed through on his intentions. Evil averted...a statement not a question.

The paramedics worked for 30 minutes to revive Barry from the heart attack before taking his body out on the gurney. Although no one had witnessed the actions, several people did hear the shouting from the office as the two confronted each other. Based on the ferocity of the argument, nobody questioned the idea that Barry's heart had just burst from the hypertension he internalized on a daily basis, much less from the encounter with Tom. Nobody blamed Tom directly, but it was impossible to ignore the fact that Barry and Tom's argument had probably been the straw that broke the camel's back...or heart in this case. Tom came away with more hero status than villain based on the staff's dislike of Barry. Tragic yes...sympathies would be the proper etiquette on everyone's tongue. But, in the staff's mind, satisfaction was the real winner.

At Barry's funeral, Laura and Tom sat behind Christine and the kids and comforted her as best they could. Christine said none of what she was thinking and played the role of grieving widow very well. To Laura, Christine periodically showed emotions of relief, but not in an obvious manner that anyone would notice. Tom was silent through most of the day, lost in a debate about his actions the previous week. Laura could tell he was struggling with his choice, if in fact, that was a choice he had made with the gift. She didn't question him about the incident. Instead, she let him tell his version of the conversation, about how Barry had collapsed in his chair as they were standing face to face across the desk. He told her Barry hadn't confessed his brutality toward Christine, but that he had had some choice words for her existence in his life. Laura knew if the gift had been used, it was a choice that Tom would revisit many times throughout his life. She wished she had some comforting words, but there was nothing she could say without revealing her own secret. She wasn't ready for that. Maybe she never would be.

Chapter Thirty-Nine

Early November weather was in the air in the weeks after the incident with Barry. As Tom began searching for new recipients he had been drawn to a series of articles about the safety of football for teens and adults, the serious long-term effects of head injuries to athletes from all sports. Earlier in the week, the local news had highlighted a high school senior who had been removed from his school's football team for his senior year because of the number of concussions he had suffered previously in his playing career. The boy had been showing signs of depression that were uncharacteristic of his personality. He had frequent headaches and the doctors, coaches, and parents all agreed that these symptoms were the result of numerous head traumas. He was a popular kid in school with a normally vibrant personality. He was a born leader who garnered great respect from his teammates and his peers outside of sports. All of this seemed to be slipping away as the boy now had trouble staying focused in school. He had dropped out of the social scene due to increased depression and anxiety, and seemed to be having trouble remembering the simplest information taught in the classroom. Information a normal teenager would absorb, memorize, repeat on a test, and probably forget later deeming it worthless information in the larger scheme of life. The boy noticed the change himself and didn't fight the decision by his coaches and parents to keep him out of sports for his senior year. Tom couldn't help but make the comparison to other, older athletes who began to see signs of early dementia and depression from repeated head injuries even years after retirement from their sport. Tom thought the boy's story deserved looking into and decided to try to visit the young man sometime in the next few weeks. He would like to assess the boy's mental state of strength and fight to determine if he needed help from the gift to return to normal adolescence or if he was on his way to recovery on his own.

Tom was finishing up work for the day when Laura called.

"Hey handsome. What cha wearing?"

"Well, Marge and I are sitting here in our underwear about to have afternoon tea. What are you wearing?"

"Just flowers in my hair! And maybe a smock with paint and glue all over it topped off with a series of pipe cleaners and Styrofoam balls. Janice and I are making a constellation model as part of a teaching lesson for her 6th grade class tomorrow. She was behind on her grading so I offered to help her with the model."

"Way to kill the mood, Miss Sunshine…although I like the flowers in the hair part."

"Maybe we'll give that a try sometime. Can you pick up some milk and Oreos from the store on your way home? Anna reminded me of a promise I made 100 years ago to reward her for the science fair project she completed. You know her, she never forgets a promise."

"Sure thing. I should be home around 5:30. What do we want to do for dinner tonight?"

"How about Oreos and milk?" she said with sarcastic enthusiasm.

"Perfect! I knew I married you for a reason."

Tom left the office later than expected to finish reviewing a design his team had put together for a client outside of Chicago. The team had done a good job with the initial rendering of the River Forest Public Library expansion just outside Oak Park, Illinois, but Tom wanted to add some features consistent with the retro but hip theme of a suburb that boasted several Frank Lloyd Wright designs scattered throughout the area. The team

230

had captured the traditional look and feel of the original library incorporating two additional bay-type windows on the expansion side. Tom added some curves and features to the new entrance and made some changes to the roofline of the expansion to merge Frank Lloyd Wright with the traditional, historical style. He was excited about this project despite its small size just for the opportunity to do something a bit funky with an already beautiful building. Also, he loved the Chicago area and especially Oak Park where he had spent a week some twenty years ago admiring the diverse architecture of the houses and churches. Since then, the Oak Park area had gone through several ebbs and flows of revival and depression but always managed to stay true to its architectural diversity as evidenced by the retail area along Lake Street. Within a mile's walk you could observe structures that took you back to 18th century England seamlessly transitioning into 1950's sock hop diners. The city's ability to meld together so many different traditional and modern structures was really a testament to its long-term planning capabilities while never losing the integrity of its charm. Thanks to this new project, Tom would get a chance to revisit the city soon and be a part of its ongoing transformation. Pleased with the changes he made to the design, he packed up around seven o'clock to head to the Oreo store before trekking his way home.

He pulled into a Mapco convenience store, surprised that the parking lot was nearly empty at 7:20 on a Monday night. As he walked in, he noticed there was no one behind the register and that the store was empty despite the single car parked in the space at the front door. Usually the employees parked on the side leaving the front spots for customers. Not overly alarmed, he walked to the cooler to grab a gallon of milk and searched the most obvious aisles for a package of Oreos. They didn't have the traditional Oreo variety so he had to settle for the double stuff package despite his guilt at contributing to the obesity of minors. He grabbed the package and headed to the still vacant front counter. Laying the contents of his shopping spree on the counter, he shifted down the counter past the heated glass container that housed old hotdogs and fried burritos to get a peek at the employee only area that was shielded by the huge cigarette wall. Just when he was about to ask if anyone was there, he noticed a pair of feet barely sticking out into the open visible area. The person was obviously lying on the ground with their legs about two feet apart. Thinking someone was hurt, Tom turned the corner around the glass container and started back to the restricted area. As soon as he made it around the counter he noticed another person in a sitting position on top of the person splayed on the floor. The body on top had been hidden by the cigarette wall and was obviously holding the other body down. Unsure whether the top person was helping or if the downed person was a victim, Tom yelled "Hey" and moved in on the two bodies. As Tom moved closer, the image of a man viciously holding a woman down came into focus. She was gagged with a red bandana and her shirt was torn open exposing her bare breasts.

Surprisingly the man didn't turn around or show any sign of being startled. Tom grabbed his shoulder to turn him, trying to knock him off balance, thinking he still had the element of surprise on his side. Suddenly and without sound, the man spun on his knees and extended his right hand into Tom's left side. Tom felt a sudden pain and realized too late that the man had plunged a knife into Tom's abdomen. The searing pain was icy-hot and grew worse as the man pulled the knife out and tried to stand up. Tom was unprepared for the attack but still had his hand on the assailant's left arm. Trying to steady himself and remain standing, Tom swung his hand down on the man's head but only managed a glancing blow to the left side of his neck. After the intended strike missed the mark, Tom quickly slid his left hand from the man's arm to his shoulder and gave it significant squeeze. A second later the man pushed Tom away, knocking him down and into the wall that originally had hidden the victim and the attacker. Unwilling to inflict any more abuse in fear of getting caught by another customer, the man spat on the woman, jumped over the counter and ran out the front door.

The woman was crying as she raised herself and removed the bandana from her mouth. She looked at Tom, now lying flat on the cold, concrete floor and placed the bandana on his side moving his hand in a position to hold it in place with pressure. She immediately ran to the counter and called the police then returned to Tom helping him keep pressure on the wound.

"Did you know him?" Tom winced in pain trying to keep his mind off the wound that he thought might be fatal.

"Yes. He's been harassing me for months. He usually gets me in my apartment complex...this is the first time he's ever come to my work to assault me. I'm so sorry. You're going to be ok."

"This hurts like hell! Can you see how deep it is?"

The woman removed the bandana and saw that it was more of a puncture wound than a slice. Although it meant less blood, it also meant the stab went deep and could have damaged internal organs. "It looks good," she lied. "An ambulance should be here any minute."

"Go see if he is out of the parking lot yet. Maybe you can get a license plate or something."

The woman stood up and rushed to the front door. Peering out she saw the taillights of a car screeching down the street but too far gone to make out the plates. She didn't need them...she knew exactly who the filthy prick was and this time she wouldn't be afraid to give up his name. When she turned to walk back inside, she heard a loud boom that sounded like a gun going off inside a metal dumpster. She spun away from the door and looked in the direction of the get away. Two vehicles at the nearest intersection were stopped in an unnatural way only explained by a collision. She couldn't make out the type of vehicles but it was obvious that one was a large truck and the other was normal sized sedan. Unsure of what the police would do once they arrived at the store and being in such close proximity to a serious accident, she moved to the center of the parking lot to direct the emergency crews to the injured man inside her store instead of to the intersection with the two mangled vehicles. As she waited for their arrival, she noticed a figure running down the dark sidewalk across the street from the store. The man appeared to be running away from the accident and was approaching a side street where he could find refuge in a wooded area nearby. Despite the darkness of the night, she instantly recognized the man as Mr. 315. The side street he was approaching was at an angle with the main street that allowed a car turning right to do so with speed. It was almost a Y instead of a right angle intersection. The runner was hobbling along at a trot, obviously injured from the car crash he was running from and approached the side street without slowing down, his head constantly turned back toward the wreck to see if he was being chased. Just as he began to cross the side street in a desperate attempt to make his escape to the nearby woods, a car came barreling down the main street and veered right to turn onto the side street at full speed. Hidden by the darkness, the runner was hit by the turning car directly in the center of the car's grill. The body was thrown into the air what must have been 15 to 20 feet in an unnatural acrobatic move with a landing that would have been a perfect 10 except for the 180-degree inversion of the body. The runner came down perfectly vertical with his head hitting the pavement first and compressing his spine like an accordion. The man lay motionless on the ground as the vehicle skidded to a halt after the impact.

The Mapco employee watched in wonder at the scene in front of her with equal feelings of disgust and satisfaction. Her life of torment from the attacker had just been simplified. She wouldn't have to deal with any more of his attacks and she didn't have to fear retribution for giving his name up to the police. An eerie silence engulfed the street for a brief moment before she heard the approaching sirens.

Chapter Forty

Tom awoke in a hospital bed with Laura holding his hand.

"Well, hey there Mr. Hero. How you feeling?" she whispered softly to no one but him.

"I'd be better if I knew who you were," he stated with a slight smile and a wince. "How long have I been here?"

Laura glanced up at the clock, "About four hours now. They knocked you out so they could run a series of tests to see if there was any internal damage. Looks like you'll live another day." Despite the comical tone of the discussion, Laura's eyes welled up with relief and concern for her husband. "I'm so glad to see you awake and...alive."

"What happened after the attack? I must have passed out when the girl left."

"Apparently the attacker was in an accident just down the street from the store and tried to run away. While he was running he was hit by another car and died after doing a face plant on the pavement. Seems it was a real mess trying to piece everything together with you sprawled on the floor, the attacker dead on the street and two innocent bystanders with wrecked cars wondering what the hell was going on. The clerk at the store witnessed most of the action and helped the police sort out the details. She told the EMTs to thank you for your bravery and that she was sorry that you got involved and injured."

"What do my insides look like?"

"They did an MRI before they closed the wound to see if the knife penetrated any of your internal organs. You were lucky, the knife missed your kidney and only lacerated the top part of your liver which the doctors said would regenerate by itself. So they closed the wound, put you on antibiotics, and said you need to do all the housework for the next month as punishment for helping out someone you don't know."

"What happened to doctor-patient confidentiality? I was sure I would get a prescription for sexual favors for the next month...a hero's reward for saving the earth."

"Well, as embellished as your side of the story might be, you did a brave, yet foolish thing. Next time you want to save someone just yell, run outside, and call the police. Promise me you won't walk right into that kind of trouble again."

"You're right. I shouldn't have approached the attacker, but I really didn't have much time to think after I realized the woman was being attacked. Plus, I wouldn't have been able to touch..." Tom stopped his sentence. "...who knows if he'd have killed her before running away. Then I would've felt totally worthless."

He stayed silent for a moment. Laura didn't react to his misstep but clearly understood now that Tom probably delivered a 'gift' to the attacker before he ran away.

"So the guy was hit by a car and died right there in the street, huh?"

"He did. Seems like fair justice to me. Apparently, he had been tormenting the clerk for several months. I don't know why she never went to the police but she won't have to worry about retribution now."

"Ahh...I remember her saying she knew him." Tom was silent as he thought back through the encounter searching for a tinge of guilt by the attacker's death. Nothing. This choice came with none of the questions that had haunted him with his previous unders. He was either supremely confident with the results of this choice or he was buying in to the overall objective of justifying death for the larger good. He had validated Hope for the clerk and probably several other past, present, and future victims. He was relieved his conscience wasn't questioning itself. "Where are the kids?"

"Molly came over and is spending the night with them. She'll get them off to school in the morning before her own classes start."

"Do they know I was hurt?"

"Just that you had cut yourself and needed to stay the night in the hospital."

"Do they know how I cut myself?"

"No. We can tell them in the morning. I rushed out the door pretty quickly as soon as Molly got there."

"Why am I spending the night here?"

"Just as a precaution. They want to make sure there is no internal bleeding. You should be free to go in the morning."

"You don't have to stay here you know. You can go home and let Molly get a normal night's sleep. Babysitting overnight is a new feature to our agreement with her."

"I know. But I am not leaving you…not tonight. Tom, I was really scared when they called. I couldn't imagine losing you."

In the morning, with the pain from his wound manageable, Tom insisted that Laura go home and see the kids off to school and he would take care of the discharge. Restless, he walked to the nurse's station to ask how long it might be before he was allowed to leave. Much to his disappointment, he was told it would be at least a few more hours. Tom decided to walk around to test his strength and ended up in the children's cancer ward. Unexpectedly needing a rest, he walked into a waiting room that was empty except for a small, frail girl sitting alone with a coloring book. Her head was wrapped with a scarf hiding the baldness that obviously was a byproduct of her treatment.

"Hey there," he said with enough futility to convey a patient-to-patient exacerbated sigh. "What are you doing out here in the waiting area?"

"Waiting!" The young girl cracked a huge smile as she looked up at the man with bedhead and hospital pajamas. "Just getting out of my room for a while. What brings you wandering down the hall looking like that?"

Tom glanced down at his attire and smiled. "It took me all night to look this good. I'm exhausted from all the primping."

"It shows," the girl said with a giggle.

"Are you getting treatment or are you here just for the food?"

"Definitely the food. I had to fake my cancer so they would admit me just for the yummy green peas. My name's Sophie. What are you here for?"

"Hey Sophie. I'm Tom. I tried to help someone last night and got stabbed instead. Nothing too serious though. Looks like I'll be able to leave in a few hours. How long are you here for?"

"Well, Tom. Today's a big day. They're doing more scans to see if I'm in remission. If everything looks good then I'll be able to go home and hopefully live a normal life. So, like I said, it's a big day...either way."

"How long have you been battling the cancer?"

"About a year and half now. Lots of chemo, a little radiation, and two surgeries. Hopefully, all that has done the trick." Sophie was stating all this like it was a spelling test and she was getting the results today. So resolute.

"What time do you get the results?"

"Around 11:00 this morning. I am either going to get a huge ice cream sundae or I'm going to beat someone up. Either way I should feel better by noon!"

"Let's hope its ice cream. If they haven't let me go home yet then maybe I'll come back over to help celebrate. I could use a sundae myself!"

"Sounds like a plan. I'll save you a ringside seat or a chair at the ice cream table."

Just then a nurse came out to the waiting room and told Sophie it was time to start the scans.

"Take care Tom. I hope your stab wound heals ok."

"Good luck Sophie. I am sure everything will be ok."

Tom sat there by himself for a few more minutes thinking about Sophie's plight versus his situation. He was lucky to have the healthy life he lived with his family. Yet there were so many people suffering in the world that didn't deserve it. Sophie was just one more example. He was amazed at how well they dealt with their individual lot in life. Here was a young girl who seemingly had lost a year and a half of her childhood fighting an invisible foe but still maintained enough dignity and humor to be a child. It surprised him how mature and grounded these kids were, fighting deadly diseases, abuse, and constant sorrow. He had noticed the same maturity and fight in the kids at St. Jude's earlier in the year. It was as if the pain and doubt administered by their situation made them find a strength most adults would crumble under. He liked Sophie. He would be back at 11:00 to share the prognosis with her.

Chapter Forty-One

Tom was signing the discharge papers when Laura called to see if he was ready to be picked up. He told her he was signing on the dotted line now but was going to wait around until 11 or so before he left the hospital. He briefly told her about Sophie and said he would call her after the ice cream. As he walked to the children's ward, he thought about how he would react if she received bad news. He was now 7/8 with his choices. He felt Sophie was certainly a good candidate for a numerator choice but he was struck with a sudden selfish feeling as his choices were dwindling. Should he save them for family members? Was he using them up too quickly? It had been just over a year since he'd received his note and had the surreal meeting with Marina. Yet here he was with only three numerators and two denominators left. The reality of his life without the gift brought on a feeling of emptiness that struck him as odd. He had done good things with the gift so far, after first considering whether to ignore or refuse the gift. Now he was immersed in its goodness and afraid to live without it.

The colored halls of the hospital passed by without notice as he thought about his recipients of the gift. Before he reached the children's ward he convinced himself that the gift couldn't be saved for the right occasion. It had to be given based on his encounters, both planned and unplanned. Just like the quick decision with the attacker, Sophie probably deserved the gift of life despite having just met her. Nonetheless, he hoped for her sake, and for the preservation of the gift, that her news was good and that this miracle would happen without his intervention. He approached the nurse's station and asked where Sophie's room was.

"What's the last name?" the nurse asked.

Tom realized he didn't know Sophie's last name. About the time he was going to stammer with an excuse, the nurse who had called for Sophie when they were together in the waiting room walked by and smiled at Tom.

"You looking for Sophie?"

"Yes, is she still here?"

"Yes. The doctor is meeting with her now. They should be done in a minute. They're in room 324."

"Thanks. I'll wait outside until they're finished. I just want to find out what the prognosis is."

Tom waited about ten minutes outside the room until the doctor came out. With a quick nod to the doctor, Tom knocked on the door and waited for a response before entering.

"Come in."

As he walked in, Tom noticed Sophie sitting on the edge of the bed with two adults who apparently were her parents. Sophie was smiling widely and the parents were teary-eyed with what Tom hoped was relief.

"Hey Sophie. Are you going to beat me up or are we going to get ice cream?"

"Ice cream it is!" she said with so much enthusiasm that Tom thought he might choke up. "The scans look clean and they believe we have beaten the beast. I come back in another month, but things look good now."

"That's great news! Hi I'm Tom Roddin." He extended his hand to the father. "Sorry to intrude but Sophie and I met in the waiting room early today. I just wanted to check back in to see about the prognosis."

"These are my parents, Larry and Martha...Mr. and Mrs. Chalmer," she finished with a giggle. "Tom was stabbed last night trying to help someone. By the way, is the person you helped ok? "

"Yes she is." Looking at the parents' concern about a strange man involved in a stabbing befriending their daughter, Tom explained the events of last night to set their minds at ease.

"I have a son about Sophie's age and was struck by her courage. Like I said, I just wanted to make sure she would be eating ice cream today."

"Tom will you join us? We can celebrate both of our victories," Sophie said before her parents could object.

"Well, I don't want to interrupt a great moment. You should celebrate with your family."

"Nonsense. We're going down to the food court here in the hospital. They actually have great sundaes there. Surely you can take a few minutes to eat with us."

Tom was struck by the forcefulness of the little girl's statement and the mother said, "You might as well give in and join us Mr. Roddin. Once she puts her mind to something, it's impossible to refuse."

"Ok. But just one scoop for me. I don't want to burst my bandage."

Tom spent the next hour talking with Sophie and the parents over ice cream sundaes. He had some time alone with the parents to discuss Sophie's struggles while she walked around and talked with other kids she knew from the ward. He also had some time alone with Sophie when she took him to an atrium next to the food court to show him where she came to think and pray during her stays there. There was an instant bond between the two of them and he was awestruck by her perseverance and hope for life given her past struggles. The parents were just like him and Laura…a bit younger but with a very similar story. Life revolved around their kids with the occasional interruption of work. The one difference was that life had punched them

242

squarely in the face with Sophie's disease. Something Tom and Laura had thankfully not had to deal with. Before he left to meet Laura outside the hospital, he exchanged numbers with Larry and Martha and asked if he could check in with them after Sophie's next appointment. They agreed and Sophie made him promise to have another sundae after her next checkup in a month.

Chapter Forty-Two

Halle Winford was relieved to have the ordeal over. If the situation had escalated to involve the police or worse yet her brothers, she would unwillingly let other peoples' doubts linger too long in her own heart. She knew she wasn't at fault, but the stigma of the situation could lead to suspicious thoughts by others. Thoughts she could never dissuade no matter how many truths she told. Her mother had finally agreed and sent her absent father's brother away with a sharp word to never come back to this house. Ever.

Halle internalized the situation but not before she analyzed it, accepted it, and finally evicted it from her mind. This process kept the events from the previous night, and all other wrongs done to her, from hiding somewhere in her soul only to rear their ugly heads later in the form of fury or life-changing mistakes. She knew the odds were against her—poor black girl, raised in the projects without a father, one brother dead from addiction, and two other brothers potentially on a path to gangs and crime. But somehow, deep inside, she expected a better outcome for herself. She wouldn't allow herself or her actions to conform to her environment. Rather, she believed she could conform her environment to her desires. Desires from her heart, which she allowed to control her thoughts, and thus guide her actions. Most girls coming from her background allowed just the opposite.

Her uncle came to their old apartment in the city often to visit with the boys and in hopes of snagging a free meal. He was basically homeless, sleeping from place to place with friends or fellow dealers, always staying one step ahead of nights in a cardboard box on the Chicago streets. Last night was the first time he had visited since their move to the Ryan

Farrelly Apartments in Oak Park, IL. Their new place was a move up in the world. It was described to her mother as a 'halfway house', somewhere between a typical housing project and full independence from government assistance. Based on her mother's new job and increased income, they had applied for only partial HUD assistance and been assigned an apartment at Ryan Farrelly. It was a step toward freedom that gave the family a sense of worth. For Halle, it validated her concept of conformity. The heart leads thoughts that result in actions, which gives life possibilities. This was how she lived.

When her uncle showed up at their door, the brothers were the ones who let him in. Halle's mother was still at work, otherwise the man may not have gotten past the dead bolt. He was drunk and probably high as well, but her brothers always gave in to his charisma. When her mother arrived home, she was furious but unable to get the man to leave. Late in the night, he found his way to Halle's room and laid himself on top of her in the bed. With a hand over her mouth and the stench of cheap wine on his breath, he began to whisper awful things into her ear. She knew her screams would garner a response from her mother and brothers, but the ensuing fight in the middle of the night would paint them as ghetto occupants in the eyes of their new neighbors. She didn't want to jeopardize their first month in Ryan Farrelly with a Scarlet Letter type incident. This place was a new start for them and it wasn't going to be ruined by the likes of her uncle telling lies about her willingness to bed him. Who would believe a teenage girl from the projects? "They were all whores," she could hear the neighbors saying. So, she decided to use his alcohol-induced state to her advantage. Without touching her uncle, she began to move her leg roughly against the pants he still wore in the bed. With her eyes closed as if she was asleep and no sound emerging from her lips, she managed to get the man to ejaculate without either one of them disrobing. Within a minute or two of his 30 seconds of pleasure, he was passed out. Dead drunk with wet underwear. He would never remember what had happened. Halle slid herself out from under him and went to the living room to curl up on the couch.

She refused to cry, but she did analyze the situation and conclude that her actions, while grotesque, would probably be best for the family. It wasn't the first time a man had tried to abuse her sexually. It probably wouldn't be the last either. But in this instance, she knew her heart could justify her actions and somehow, she believed that it would be the last time her uncle would try. She wasn't sure why, but something told her to believe his part was done.

The next morning, her mother found her on the couch and the uncle alone in her bed.

"Why are you in here and why is Ronald in your bed?"

Halle didn't tell her mother the whole story. "He came into my room and laid on the bed. He fumbled at me for a minute but he was too drunk. He passed out right away, so I got up and came in here."

"That bastard! I'll kill him!"

"No momma! Let it go. Nothing happened."

"I can't let this go. We have to call the police or something"

"No. If we call the police they'll have to report it to HUD and we'll be put on probation or something. I don't want our neighbors to think we're trash from the projects who don't belong here."

"But Halle, he tried to rape you! I can't let that pass."

"I can momma. We both have to. Get him out of here and tell him to never come back or the police will be on him."

"You shouldn't be so forgiving child. People must pay for their evils."

"I'm not forgiving him momma. I'm forgetting him. He'll get his payment from someone else."

Chapter Forty-Three

Tom spent several days in the confines of his home recovering from his injury. The kids were telling everyone at school that their father beat up a robber. The story grew way beyond the actual events leading some to believe Tom's skin was made of dragon scales that bent the knife when the assailant jabbed him. They were more proud of their super-hero father's actions than they were aware of the danger he had put himself in. Typical for kids that age. Now that he had time to piece together the incident, he realized how lucky he was not to have been wounded more seriously or even killed. He was certainly not prepared to be a hero in the spotlight. He was more than happy to make his choices in a less dramatic fashion.

By the time he returned to work, news of his heroics had swept through the office much to his chagrin. He laughed off the jokes and accolades and avoided as many questions as he could regarding the details of the moments before and after stabbing. Although he was healing well, every discussion regarding the actual incident seemed to open the wound with a new blade. So, he said as little as possible and brushed off the questions with an "I just reacted…stupidly" kind of phrase. Realizing Tom was uncomfortable talking about the incident, Marge finally, privately, told the staff to let it go. She knew Tom well enough to recognize that it wasn't so much a reminder of the pain or danger that bothered him, but more about his uncomfortable presence in that kind of spotlight. Tom was a leader and certainly had the charisma and skill to run the office. He was proud of his work and accepted professional kudos with humility and ease. But when it came to praise resulting from good deeds, kindness, or human compassion, Marge knew he got uncomfortable. She understood this stemmed from Tom's belief that general acts of humanity should be the norm and not something so out of the ordinary that it shocked people or was worthy of a parade. Every person should have reacted the way he did in the store that day. He would think it was a shame that it was made into such a courageous deal. All he needed to hear was that he made the right decision and move on. That was the kind of man he was. It was why Marge had so much respect for Tom and his genuine humility. She had been inspired by him within the first week of joining the firm and his inspirational track never wavered in her eyes. She was just one of a number of people in Tom's life who understood the pureness of his actions. She was glad to secretly unscrew the light bulb from the spotlight and let Tom get back to his humble sainthood ways.

Since returning, Tom focused most of his attention getting ready for a trip to River Forest and Oak Park, IL for the library job. He made plans to travel with his team the following week to review the designs with the client and make their first presentation to the city architectural committee for initial approval. He planned to spend an extra day or two there to re-trace his steps from twenty years ago and take in the architectural treasures of the city as well as Frank Lloyd Wright's home studio which had recently been converted into a museum celebrating the famous architect's life in middle America.

Before leaving the office that day, he checked the local on-line paper where the boy featured in the article about youth concussions lived. Tom was looking at the Grundy County Herald to see when the next home football game was for the Yellow Jackets. They had two games left in their season, one at home which was this coming Friday night and one away. Tom would talk to Laura and the kids about heading over to nearby Monteagle, Tennessee for the weekend as a fun outdoors getaway. They could hike, visit the historical city of Beersheba Springs, and sneak in a high school football game in hopes of meeting the boy with the headaches.

After talking it over with the family, the Roddins decided to spend the weekend at the Edgeworth Inn at the Monteagle Assembly, tucked in the mountains of the Cumberland Plateau in southeastern Tennessee. They had vacationed in the area for years and were familiar with the recreational choices making it an easy sell to Laura and the kids. They left after school Friday and were on the mountain in just under two hours. Even though Tom snuck the football game onto the agenda, he didn't expect to see or have an opportunity to meet Justin Skinner. He did hope to hear first-hand from some of the local folks their thoughts on Justin and the cumulative decision to leave a football life behind. He was interested to gauge the community's concern and its affect on a subject that ran deep in rural communities...the importance and pride of Friday night high school football.

As they entered Coalmont, the home of the Grundy County Yellow Jackets, they noticed signs, banners, and ribbons scattered across the town all supporting the Jackets in their quest for a playoff spot. This was a big night as they were playing their annual rival, Bledsoe County in a game that had serious post-season implications. The town was fired up and the excitement in the air was worth the trip alone. Tom, Laura and the kids positioned themselves in the packed stands next to some parents who had a daughter on the sidelines cheering and a son on the team as a freshman O-lineman. He wasn't a starter but from the looks of his size when the proud parents pointed him out, he would certainly make an impact in the starting rotation his sophomore year. As the game progressed, the parents freely shared information and stats about certain players, coaches, play calling, and all the other nuances of the team. It was a stereotypical night of high school football. People were cheering, fans were questioning calls or miscalls by the referees and coaches, parents were praising their children's performance, and all were talking about the high expectations of a playoff run to the Division State Championship.

During halftime, Tom asked the parent next to him if he knew Justin Skinner.

"Yeah, we know him and his family. Good solid folks. It's a shame what has happened to him," the father of the freshman said.

"I read an article in the Nashville paper about him and what he's suffering through. Seems like a good kid," Tom said without trying to sound like he was prying into a community secret.

"He's the best. A good-natured kid. Friendly with everyone and shows respect to his elders too," the man stated. "I can't imagine being pulled from something he loved so much. This football team meant the world to him. He's down there on the sidelines with them every game cheering them on."

"It certainly hurts him not to be playing, but I think it shows his courage to be down there still fighting with the team even though the noise and lights give him so much pain," the mother added with a concerned note. "I've known his momma and daddy for thirty years. They own the restaurant in Tracy City, the Sun Dial, just up the road a bit. They say it's all he can do to get out of bed in the mornings to go to school much less put on a happy face and be with the team. They have him helping out at the restaurant when he can just to keep him socially active."

"Wow, so he's with the team on the sidelines?" Tom asked.

"Yes sir. That's him walking out with the defensive unit right now," said the father pointing to a tall kid in street clothes walking with the coaching staff as the teams re-emerged from the dressing rooms. "He was a beast of a linebacker. Covered the field like the sidelines were only two steps away. People joked that he could cover the field from defensive line to the secondary all by himself—sideline to sideline. We only needed one linebacker instead of three."

"He must be really good. Is he thinking about playing in college if he gets better?"

"I hope not. He could do some permanent damage if he hasn't already. He's too sweet a kid to ruin his life for a game." The offensive lineman's mother said this without any hesitation and with little reaction from the father who Tom suspected might disagree. In a rural town, Tom expected the community to have less understanding of long-term disabilities caused by football injuries and more the attitude of 'get back out there and help your team'.

"Does everyone pretty much support the decision for him not to play?" Tom asked with a nervous voice not wanting to be labeled as the big city outsider sticking his nose where he shouldn't.

"Most of the folks agree with the decision although you have some parents grumbling about it hurting us in the playoffs. But we don't pay much attention to that. He's pretty messed up. He needs to get right and then decide what's best for him," the father pitched in. "He's a smart kid and can do other things if he puts his mind to it."

"Do you or the other parents worry about something happening to the other players?"

"We do now for sure. We've all had talks with the coaches and the kids about how serious head injuries are. Coach put in place a policy this year that when you get a serious head bang, you're out for the rest of the game. Then you have to spend some time with the doctors before you can be cleared to play again. Our doctors are now more aware of the signs of head trauma than they were before. Everyone seems to be giving it more attention these days."

"And thank the Lord for that," the mother proclaimed. "Football is a big way of life here, but not more important than our children being safe."

Tom let the conversation go and returned to talking about the game being played tonight. Laura, engaged with the couple as well during the game, took a pause and only listened to the conversation Tom had initiated about Justin Skinner. It wasn't until after the discussion that Laura realized what Tom might be doing. He was thinking of helping this kid with the gift. She brushed back a quick tear at the thought of his compassion and understood the real purpose of their trip. When they left the game amongst the celebration of a win for the Yellow Jackets, Laura wondered why Tom didn't seek out the young man to talk to him. Had he decided not to help the boy because of something the couple had said? Or was she mistaken about the purpose of the trip and reading too much into her knowledge of his secret? She didn't question Tom about the matter and they returned to the inn with a tired Brady and Anna in tow.

The next day the family had breakfast at the Edgeworth Inn then went for a short hike to the base of Foster Falls to take advantage of the beautiful autumn day atop the plateau. After the hike, they stopped at the Sun Dial café in Tracy City for a late lunch before making the obligatory stop at the locally famous Dutch Made Bakery for some goodies to take home with them. The Sun Dial was relatively quiet as the lunch crowd had come and gone. There were only three tables occupied but the dishes still lingering on many of the tables were evidence of a large Saturday lunch crowd. The family settled into a table near the front window and began browsing the menu when a large teenage boy emerged from the back with an empty tub. The boy went to the nearest table and began piling dishes into the tub and wiping down the surface, readying for the early evening crowd the family hoped would be coming in a few hours. Tom recognized the boy immediately and observed his movements while trying to avoid being caught staring. Justin Skinner seemed sad. He moved about the table with an awkward rhythm as if he wasn't sure whether to pick up the plates first, then the silverware or the other way around. It was a slow pace that seemed indecisive for such a simple, benign task. His face contorted several times showing confusion, frustration, and simple exhaustion in the course of the three minutes it took to pile dirty dishes into a plastic tub. It was a face whose expressions showed a troubled kid whose mind simply wasn't providing his body the confidence to move

252

with any synchronicity.

Laura noticed Tom's observance of the boy and saw Tom's own face crease with lines of care. In an effort to break his stare, Laura asked the kids what they saw on the menu that looked good.

"The macaroni and cheese sounds yummy," proclaimed Anna! "Do you think it's the kind with regular yellow cheese?"

"I'll bet it's homemade," replied Laura. "Yellow or white, I think it definitely will be yummy."

"I'm going cheeseburger and fries," declared Brady as if it were news. A cheeseburger and fries was his staple order anywhere they went only occasionally replaced by chicken fingers if the mood hit him.

"Tom, what are you thinking about?" she asked wrangling his thoughts back to the table.

Tom stumbled his attention back to the menu then looked to the white board near the checkout counter with the day's specials. "I think I am having the special. I can only imagine the meat and three here is to die for. What are you thinking about?" he asked Laura.

"I think I'm following your lead and going for the homegrown vegetables. Let's see…turnip greens, broccoli casserole, black-eyed peas, and cole slaw. That should leave me room for the treats we'll get at the bakery!"

The kids eyes lit up at the mention of the bakery as it was one their favorite things about coming to the mountain. "Oooohh…I'm getting the pastry thingy with the chocolate cream filling," claimed Brady. "And a chocolate chip cookie."

"I am getting some banana bread and a cookie too," chimed in Anna with excitement.

"You have to eat all your normal food here or your mean ole

daddy will not go by the bakery," threatened Tom with a voice like a Drill Sergeant.

"Deal!" exclaimed both kids in unison. Nothing would keep them from a trip to the bakery.

After placing their order with the waitress, the kids asked Tom and Laura about their family plans for Thanksgiving. They would trek over to Asheville, NC to visit Tom's sister, then head home to spend an afternoon with Laura's parents who lived just outside Nashville in Shelbyville. As Laura and the kids were arguing about when they actually got out of school—full day the Wednesday before Thanksgiving or just a half-a-day—Tom got up and approached the boy at the next table gathering up the dirty dishes. Laura watched Tom and the boy talking while trying to keep her attention on the debate at the table. She watched as Tom introduced himself to the high school senior with a handshake. The boy looked a little startled at Tom's introduction but as they talked, she could see Justin slowly relax his posture and respond to Tom's inquiries and his comforting tone. Tom was doing what he did best. Put a total stranger at ease with his genuine concern and easy speak. Laura couldn't hear the full conversation but knew that Tom was reassuring the boy that his condition would get better. Tom had a way of giving Hope to people who couldn't find a way out their individual dilemma. It was one of many reasons Laura believed Tom was the perfect match for the gift. He could provide the words of Hope and follow it with actions that validated that Hope. That was why she knew after the physical numbers of the gift ended, Tom would be able to continue the giving of Hope to people who needed it. The miracles would come as normal, natural occurrences.

Justin and Tom shared a quick laugh and Laura watched in amazement as Tom reached out and gently grabbed the boy's shoulder. With a big smile and slight squeeze, Tom told the boy to keep believing that this would pass with time.

"You'll get better with time," she heard Tom say. "Be

patient and start thinking about what you want to do with your life. You have the potential to be involved in sports, medicine, therapy…whatever you want to do. Just believe that you will be better soon."

"Thank you sir. I just don't want to let anyone down," Justin replied.

"You have already given folks what they want and need around here. No one is seeing your condition as a let down. They want you to get better, not just for football, but for you. Your teammates and this community are all behind you 100%."

"Thanks. I appreciate your concern and I'll take your advice to heart."

Tom returned to the table as the food was coming out of the kitchen. Both kids immediately asked if Tom knew that boy, having been unaware of the conversation in the stands the night before.

"He's one of the football players from last night," Tom whispered since the boy was still in the main dining room. "He's sick and can't play anymore so I was just telling him that I think he will get better soon."

"So that was Justin? The kid you were talking about to the couple last night?" asked Laura already knowing the answer.

"Yes. They told me his parents owned the restaurant so I figured it had to be him helping out."

"How do you know he will get better?" asked Brady.

"What is he sick with?" added Anna.

"He hurt his head playing football and the doctors said he shouldn't play anymore or he could have long lasting effects from the injury."

"What's wrong with his head? He doesn't have any cuts or

stitches." Anna mused as she looked at the boy walking back to the kitchen with a full tub of dishes.

"The hurt is inside his head. You can't see it. It's called a concussion. When you hit your head really hard on something like the ground or another player's helmet, it can make you sick…with like headaches, dizziness, and sometimes it makes you forget things. He's hurt his head more than once which makes it last longer. He stopped playing so he doesn't keep hurting it."

"Will he really get better or did you just tell him that to make him feel better?" asked Brady again.

"I think he'll get better. He just needed to hear from someone besides his doctors and parents that he'll get better. Sometimes it's easier to believe in Hope when hearing it from someone you don't know," Tom stated matter-of-factly.

"He probably just thought you were some weird old man telling him a lie," said Brady with a grin.

"Maybe," Tom retorted with a laugh at Brady's joke. "But I told him anyway. You should always try to give someone Hope when they are down on their luck."

"Well, I hope he gets better. He seems nice and anyway, he seems big enough to scare the hurt right out of himself," Anna said with a raised eyebrow referring to Justin's physical presence.

"Daddy's right. You should always help someone believe in Hope. How boring would the world be without Hope?" Laura said. Although directed at the kids, she reached over and gave Tom's hand a squeeze while she made the proclamation. "That boy deserves to believe in Hope just as much as we do. That's why I love your father so much. He has a special way of making people feel good about themselves."

"Uggghhh…gross," Brady scowled as he shot a glance towards Anna. "Here they go again talking about love!"

256

Anna laughed and made the finger-in-the-mouth sign like she was going to throw up. They finished their meal and headed to the bakery for treats. The rest of the afternoon was spent at the Inn and wandering around the Assembly grounds. That night when the kids were asleep and Tom had turned off the light, Laura whispered into his ear, "You're a good man for helping that boy."

Tom asked what she meant by helping him.

"Helping him believe that he will get better. Helping him believe in Hope."

Tom thought about her words for a moment and wondered if he could trust Laura with the truth. He so much wanted to tell her everything but then again, he liked the secret. He mused to himself that when he first received the gift, he didn't think he could make the choices on his own. Now, he liked having the decisions solely up to him. It gave him a sense of accomplishment and confidence and made him understand why the gift should remain a secret. The constant threat of approval or conflict with someone else would only cloud the decision process. Even with someone you loved and trusted. No, the gift should remain a secret. That was certainly one 'rule' he would emphasize when and if he became an instructor.

Chapter Forty-Four

After their escape to the mountain, Tom spent Monday in the office preparing for his trip to Oak Park and mapping out his solo trek around the city's Frank Lloyd Wright district. Tuesday morning he lingered at the house to see the kids and Laura off to school. After they left, he took a leisurely shower and again transitioned from CNN in the bathroom to Fox news in his bedroom while he dressed. Grabbing his worn-out suitcase from the closet, Tom began collecting the necessary items for his trip. He didn't travel very often but the process of packing had become methodical for him—four pairs of boxers, two suits or dress shirt and jacket combinations, appropriately colored socks, at least two bandanas, shoes, belt, toiletries and a jacket or overcoat to ward off the week's weather. Being a creature of habit, the items were always placed in the same location in the suitcase and were efficiently organized to preempt wrinkle-causing shifts inside the case as it rolled through the terminal, into a tight storage bin, into a rental car trunk, then finally into the hotel room. As he worked his way to the bathroom to pick up his toiletries, he glanced over to the bed. Something caught his eye that sent his mind reeling with fear, anticipation, and inexplicable suspicion. There in the center of the bed, was a piece of stationery, his stationery. His body froze in mid-stride while his mental presence evaluated the situation for a logical explanation. The house was quiet. He immediately glanced around the room for signs of another person, an intruder perhaps, thinking he might catch someone in the act of anonymity. He calmed his panic by suggesting that maybe Laura had left him a note wishing him well on his trip. As he relaxed his muscles, he moved toward the bed and hesitantly picked up the note. It was face down, so no writing appeared on the topside. Carefully, as if holding a 1000-year-old piece of rice paper ready to disintegrate in the flutter of sudden movement, he turned the note over to examine the other side. The instant recognition of the script made a flurry of tiny white dots appear in his vision. He steadied himself against the bed and quickly sat down to keep the anxiety from overwhelming him. It took almost two minutes for his mind to recover and for his eyes to focus on the message.

Tom – your journey has been maintained with integrity.
It's time to share your experience with another.

Halle Winford

Ryan Farrelly Apartments

Oak Park IL

Merry-go-round

Sincerely,

Hope

Tom stared at the message with disbelief, unable to process the real intent of the note. He had lived with the knowledge of the gift for over a year now and it had become somewhat normal to him. This strange journey began with a mysterious note that he had still not fully explained to himself. Here, for the second time, he was reminded of how bizarre the mystical appearance of a hand-written note was within the confines of our own reality. It was simply inexplicable. His encounter with Marina and the reality of his first choice had somehow distracted his curiosity about the origin of the gift and the note. How could he have forgotten that a physical piece of paper suddenly appearing in his bedroom was something that should have made him explore the depths of logic to provide an explanation? Normally, he would have driven himself crazy searching for that explanation. But something made him accept the mystery and move forward with action in the name of Hope. Now, after living in the bizarre reality of the mystery for over a year, the gravity of another note seemed almost normal. But still, how in the world could *something* transcend its purpose and manifest itself into a physical piece of paper? Notes just didn't come floating down from the heavens and land perfectly on someone's bed. After several minutes of blankly staring at the paper and trying to substantiate the argument in his head, Tom read it again. He actually read the note, putting aside the curiosity of the impossible. There was no denying that it was real and that it was in fact from "Hope". It was time. It was his time…his time to instruct someone else.

Throughout the day he struggled to stay focused on the library project. It didn't take much to dig into his memory of his initial conversation with Marina Kostitsen. He recalled almost every word. Until now, he had never given any thought to what must have been Marina's anxiety in having to approach a total stranger and share a secret so personal that it bordered on insanity. Facing his own encounter as an instructor, he was certain her outward confidence belied what she was experiencing internally. He hoped his own confidence and experience with the gift would keep him from fumbling his way through the upcoming encounter with Halle.

Both presentations to the library committee and the planning board went well as Tom made the early introductions and let his team leads do most of the presenting. As always, they did a great job staying focused on the elements of the design during both presentations and Tom chimed in occasionally only to emphasize the emotional connection of the renovation's design to the tradition of Oak Park's architectural integrity. Both committees were impressed by the out-of-towners' obvious understanding of the city's history and architectural nuances. "Your team has done a wonderful job striking the balance between new and old while maintaining the integrity of our community," one of the committee members said. "It's as if you've lived here all your lives. It's refreshing to see a group blend with us rather than force a change that would be out of sync with our natural growth."

The team celebrated that night at the Kinderhook Tap sports bar with Tom heaping plenty of praise on them for their presentation skills. He was fortunate to have a team he could trust especially since his own distraction probably would have diminished his ability to fully connect with the committee members. Thursday morning, the team flew home leaving Tom to have his 'walk-about', an endearing term his coworkers used to refer to his extra day there. He ate a late breakfast and made his first stop at the First United Methodist Church studying the building's interior and exterior wonders. The church, built from 1925 to 1932, was a piece of art in and of itself with strong, prominent arches and columns reminiscent of its modern English Gothic Revival style that the designers, Tallmage and Watson, had incorporated. The church included stained-glass windows created by Giannini and Hilgart, a local Chicago firm founded in 1899 and still producing sculptures and stained glass. The local firm had worked closely with Frank Lloyd Wright over the years, so the presence of the glass work in the church was comfortably at home in this small Chicago suburb. After taking in the beauty and mystique of the church, Tom wandered across the street to visit the home of Ernest Hemingway where his family had lived from 1931 to sometime in the mid 1940's. The home was built by a marine architect and salvage wrecker adding to the deep, diverse but very coordinated architectural history of the area. Throughout his walk-about, Tom was amazed how well the fusion of eras came together in Oak Park and River Forest. He was honored to have a small part in the renovation of an area that contained more Frank Lloyd Wright designs than any other concentrated area in the world. But his attention was constantly distracted by his upcoming encounter with Halle Winford. Lunch was on the agenda before driving to the housing project to find the girl who would undoubtedly be shocked by his presence.

The Ryan Farrelly Apartment complex was a fairly new development where residents could get HUD assistance to help pay the rent. It wasn't a true state or city housing development but rather a place that partnered with HUD to provide partial or gap assistance to residents who applied for help. At least one family member had to be employed full-time and they were responsible for at least 50% of the standard rent. It was equivalent to a half-way house for families trying to move from full-assistance housing projects to full independence. As their income grew and their financial situation stabilized, residents receiving HUD assistance would increase their percentage of responsibility with the eventual outcome of paying the full rate and being financially free from government assistance. It was a good partnership as the property's appeal was far greater than that of typical housing projects. The apartments were new, spacious, had nice amenities and certainly incentivized the tenants to make sure their financial progress kept them moving in an upward direction. One unique aspect of this development was the number of tenants that were not and had never been in public assistance programs. There were young professionals, transient families, local college students, and just married couples readying for an evolutionary move to family living. It was a mix of independents and half-independents that created an atmosphere where the have's and have not's were fairly anonymous.

As Tom approached the development, he noticed immediately that the design of the complex allowed it to blend seamlessly into the surrounding neighborhood. Another example of where the new was creatively mixed with the old so neither stood out as odd. He parked in the front lot and walked around the complex looking for an opening to get to the back courtyard where he was sure there was a playground. Finding the courtyard, he noticed a few benches, a picnic table, and two large permanent grilles. He was standing in a common area for the residents' use, but with no playground in sight. Earlier Tom's anxiety level had hit an all-time high as he prepared for today's encounter. Hardly touching his food at lunch, Tom had a quiet conversation with himself to calm his nerves. He must have been a sight sitting in front of a full plate, mumbling to himself, with a distraught expression unwillingly controlling his face. An on-looker would have pegged him as schizophrenic and moved to the farthest table they could find. Fortunately, the restaurant was mostly deserted and Tom was left alone with his struggles. He had managed to talk himself down to a level of calmness that was reasonably sustainable. Now, standing in the courtyard of the apartment complex unable to find the playground, his anxiety level rose again.

This is something you can do. You advise and counsel people everyday Mr. Roddin, he reminded himself. *Settle down or you will scare this poor girl to death.* He put one foot in front of the other and moved out of the courtyard past another set of buildings. Following a pathway around the left side of Building C, he came to an open space that was obviously still part of the complex. Shading his eyes from the sunlit day, he saw several picnic tables in a circular pattern scattered around a central area that housed a new, wonderfully fun-looking playground. Tom took a deep breath, hardly able to swallow the air. On the left side of the playground, he saw a merry-go-round centered between two swing sets, a blue plastic slide, and a set of monkey bars. Sitting alone on the edge of the still merry-go-round was a young teenage girl. From somewhere other than his own consciousness, a serene feeling overcame him washing away the anxiety of the second note. It was a moment of clarity very similar to the one he experienced after Marina had left him in his office a year ago. "Wow, what a journey!" he whispered openly to himself. The girl seemed to be observing or supervising some of the younger kids. Some were upside down on the monkey bars, some were running up the slide and colliding with friends coming down. All were playful, soaking up the last bit of afterschool winter sun before being called home for dinner. But the teenager was just sitting. Watching. And surely thinking through the strange day that had already unfolded in front of her.

"Hi there. I'm Tom," he said feeling like a pedophile as he approached Halle. She glanced up and gave him a suspicious stare before looking away in the direction of the kids. With a gentle smile he said, "I am not here to…I am not some freak trying to befriend kids at a playground. I was asked to come talk to you."

"You from the school? Because that girl hit **me**. I didn't provoke her. I didn't say nothing to her and I definitely didn't hit her back. That's not my way. If I fought everyone who had

263

been mean to me in my life, I would be blue all over instead of black." Halle delivered this unsolicited story without any anger in her voice. She was telling facts as if she was reading a homework assignment.

"Why did she hit you then?"

"I guess she gets some sick satisfaction out of letting the new kid know who's in charge. But that's her problem, not mine. She'll have to live with that insecurity the rest of her life. I'm moving on."

"So you just started a new school?"

"Started in August and she's been targeting me for the last three and half months. I've been avoiding her and her little group pretty well until yesterday." Halle paused for a moment in conflict. "I thought you said you was from the school? Why would you ask if I was new there?"

"I never said I was from the school," Tom said with a calm advantage.

"Then who sent you to talk to me?"

"Something." Tom looked at the girl's expression of uncertainty and quietly said, "I know about the note."

"What note?" Halle said this without the conviction needed to throw Tom off the mark. Her face betrayed the lie and he could see the fear, the confusion in her eyes.

"The note from Hope."

Halle's eyes widened with shock but she said nothing.

Tom continued slowly but deliberately. "I had the same reaction when my instructor came to me and dropped that bomb. You haven't told anyone about it, have you?" a statement not a question.

"What do you mean instructor?" Tom made a quick

observation that she had cleverly moved the conversation past the denial of the note, at least for a moment.

"I received my note on November 11, 2011—11/11/11. Don't think the irony was lost on me. I hadn't told anyone about the note...and really didn't understand it...when a woman came into my office and told me she was there to instruct me. I was shocked as you might expect and thought someone was playing a trick on me. I quickly realized there was no joke and that my life with this gift would be forever changed."

"Gift? I don't understand what you're talking about," Halle calmly proclaimed as she focused her glare back to the playground.

"The gift of Hope."

"I thought you said I received a note not a gift."

Tom smiled. He appreciated the entrapment game she was playing by not stating outright denial but also not admitting anything. "The note is the gift. It's the opportunity to make certain choices for other people that most humans don't get."

"What did your note say?"

"Same as yours, I presume. Ten miracles of life for ten deaths." The girl fidgeted on the merry-go-round making it sway slightly back and forth. "The gift gives you the free will to make 20 choices for other people. Choices that have long-lasting and mostly permanent consequences for those involved. Each choice should somehow validate Hope either for the recipient or someone associated with the recipient."

"How can it validate hope for someone?" Halle's tone and question let Tom know that she was still weighing the reality of the conversation.

"If someone is sick, really sick, they're always Hoping they'll get better. They trust in their treatment and Hope their

265

ailment will go away. Some get that Hope validated by getting better. Some lose the battle and don't. As gifters we have the opportunity to make choices for some of the people and therefore validate their Hope."

"What about the deaths? How can that validate hope for anyone?"

"My instructor probably said it best. We can choose a death that creates a good outcome. A death may bring comfort. It may give Hope to other people who knew and potentially suffered under the deceased. It can provide Hope."

"I don't wanna kill anyone. I'm not going to ruin my life by going to jail. I've seen that play out too often with friends and family."

"It's not like that," Tom said with comforting sincerity. "You don't have to shoot, stab, or beat anyone up. The gift is given with a slight squeeze of the shoulder to the person you make the choice for. The manner of their death, or life for that matter, is not something that you decide or carry out. You just make the decision, the choice, and the rest takes care of itself."

Unsure of how to react openly to what she was hearing, Halle fired back in the defensive.

"This is crazy. How can anyone have that power? This is something only God or fate can possess." Halle was only slightly hinting at the anger stage. Tom was impressed with the control the girl had with her confused emotions. She was much calmer than Tom had been with Marina. "I have no business making these types of choices for other people."

"I felt the same way until I fully understood the reason. By validating Hope, one person or choice at a time, you are slowly but surely making Hope something people can believe in. Someone hears the story of one of your choices—even though you are anonymous—and decides Hope can be powerful for them too. This propagates to help others believe."

266

"Propagates?" interrupted Halle.

"It snowballs. One person believes, then shares their story so the next one believes and so on. It's a means of spreading Hope in a society that can use a lot more of it. The choices are difficult sometimes but in the end they are life-changing for you and obviously for the people you make choices for."

"Why me? And how many other people are out there doing this?"

"Because you have a pure heart, Halle. You and me and my instructor and her instructor...we were all chosen because we have pure hearts. If God had given the gift to people without pure hearts then the choices would be selfish, or based on revenge, or even used to make large geopolitical changes in the world that would only benefit a few. The power would be corrupting if it were given to people whose hearts were not pure."

"How do you know my heart is pure?"

"I know because you wouldn't have been given the gift otherwise."

"So you think this is God giving us this gift?" she said with humble questionability.

With a smile and thoughts going back to his and Marina's conversation, Tom said, "I don't know. Everyone's definition of God is different. My instructor was agnostic—didn't really believe in a God so to speak—yet she had a belief in spirituality that defined the gift as coming from *something*, something divine. Her instructor was a young Muslim boy from Palestine. And his instructor was an elderly Jewish man. It opened my eyes to the reality that there may be one omnipotent God...I mean all of our Gods may be the same supreme being. I struggled with that concept of my faith, but I'm coming around to the idea that it really doesn't matter. It's an answer we may never get so why try to understand who it is? I'm learning to just accept it as *something*. But certainly there is a common thread since the gift has been trusted to very different people with varying beliefs. The common thread is the pureness of heart."

"What if He or *something* is wrong about me? What if my heart's not pure?"

"It took me a long time to trust that my own heart was pure, that my choices were not based too much on emotional attachments. A pure heart doesn't mean you can't hate evil. It just means evil can't corrupt it. I believe, as did my instructor, that as long as the choices are made without revenge or self-promotion, then the person can maintain the pureness of their decisions. It's a bit more complicated than that but it serves as a good foundation when making a decision. Also, if your choice can validate Hope for at least two other people then the choice is more easily justified, especially for the under choices."

"The under choices?"

"The deaths," Tom said calmly. "We call the life miracles the numerator or the over and the deaths the denominator or the under. Like a fraction—10 over10. The deaths were the difficult part for me. I had a real problem justifying death as means of validating Hope. As my journey progressed, the choice of death became clearer for me. As the Palestinian boy proved, you can take the gift and turn it into 20 miracles if your choices validate Hope for someone."

Halle sat silently for a few minutes thinking through the conversation and obviously struggling with the responsibility of the gift. Tom wondered if his more direct approach with Halle was the right way to explain the gift. Somehow, he felt she would comprehend the direct approach better than the slow, in-depth discussion he and Marina had. Tom let the silence linger noticing that her emotional range was now moving towards acceptance.

"So you've completed the gift?" she asked with a submissive

quiet tone.

"No. I am 8 over 8."

"So you're almost finished? What then?"

Tom was a little unprepared for that question. He had thought about life after the gift, understanding that his journey provided a foundation for him to continue helping others whether they were victims or in need of support. Halle asking the question out loud made Tom stumble for a moment to gather his thoughts.

"The gift has given me a renewed belief in Hope. A belief that Hope is validated every day through the actions of so many people who don't, or never did, possess the gift. It's inspired me to continue spreading Hope and looking for Hope in the most unlikely places. That may not make sense to you now but it will when your own journey takes shape."

"Am I one of your choices? I mean, am I one of your overs you're using to save me?"

Tom smiled at the innocence of the statement. "No Halle. You are one of *something's* choices. I guess one of his overs...although I imagine he is not limited to just 10."

Halle smiled at the humor and seemed to understand.

"I think the wisdom in deciding who possesses the gift is something that each of us can only understand individually. It will change you differently than it has changed me," Tom said with a slight shrug, almost as a question to himself. "We all have a little bit of saving in us, but each save is always personal and individual."

They sat in the cold December sunlight on the motionless merry-go-round for 30 minutes or more as Halle asked about rules, restrictions, and other expected questions of curiosity. Maybe it was her youth, maybe it was her own power of belief, but Halle's acceptance of Tom's explanations were concrete already. She was less skeptical at this point than he had been with Marina. Certainly less skeptical than Marina had been at this point with Aarzu.

"Have you told anyone about the gift...that you have the gift?" asked Halle.

"No. My instructor and I talked about that and we believe, as do the previous gifters, that if you tell someone about the gift then it could influence your decisions, even if they mean well. It can take the purity out of the choice even if the person has a pure heart themselves. I desperately wanted to share the gift with my wife. She probably has a purer heart than I do. But in the end, I realized that I would always be seeking her approval with my choices. Then they don't become pure choices without interference. Trust me, it's a burden to carry the secret all alone. But I think ultimately it's for the best."

"That makes sense. Also, I don't want anyone to know that I may have caused someone harm...or helped them. Then people would be asking for favors which might get complicated."

"That's absolutely true. Halle, trust in your own pure heart. I believe *something* has made a good choice in you."

"My life hasn't been great. But I know what I want to do with my life and more importantly, I know what I don't want to do." She sat in pensive thought for a moment. From her expression, Tom knew she was already thinking ahead to some of her possible choices. Coming back to the realization that Tom was still sitting next to her, she turned and faced him with the innocent expression of a normal teenage girl. "Thanks for coming to see me. I was a real mess this morning when I got my note. I thought someone from the school had left it for me. I've been analyzing it all day trying to figure out what it meant. I am glad it came from...well...*something* instead of someone from the school."

"I'm glad you were chosen next. You're a very bright young girl and you made my instruction encounter easy for me. I gotta

270

say, I was a bit nervous. Especially when I saw that you were a teenager. But you're obviously wise beyond your years."

"Can I call you if I have questions or need help?"

"No. It's probably best if we don't see each other again. I don't want to guide you once you start your journey. Then I may unwillingly influence your choices. I think you will do fine if you keep your eyes clear. Remember, no choice is a mistake. It is strictly your choice. I guess whatever or whoever is giving the gift can't make choices based on the human heart. It's divine. It's looking to us to make human choices that It can't make."

"Got it. Tom?"

"Yes Halle?"

"You did good. I'll remember this conversation for when I'm an instructor."

"Thanks. Take care Halle. I know you're going to do great."

Tom walked away from 16-year-old Halle Winford and never spoke with her again. He had expected to get a third note provisioning him to call when her journey became difficult just as Marina had done for him. But the third note never came. Halle must have found early peace with her choices and never allowed doubt or corruption to cloud her purpose. He often wondered with nagging curiosity how Halle fared during and after her journey. He wanted to look her up even if from a distance. But he decided to leave it to fate, or rather *something* to decide if he and Halle should cross paths again. Tom wondered many times throughout the rest of his life how his journey would have been different if the gift had been given to him at such a young and innocent age.

Chapter Forty-Five

Tom got home from Illinois Friday around 6 pm after spending most of the day touring the Frank Lloyd Wright homes in Oak Park and River Forrest. The rest of the weekend was spent with Laura and the kids. He had a short week of work ahead of him since they would be leaving Wednesday to go to Asheville for a pre-Christmas visit with his sister's family. Based on the good reviews from the meetings in Oak Park and the fact that his other projects were either in the final construction phases or the early stages of development, he was comfortable with the timing of the upcoming holiday. Sunday afternoon sitting in front of the television watching the Titans beat up the Baltimore Ravens, Tom began Googling on his computer. He returned to the local newspaper in Camp Hill, PA where the high school football coach was undergoing treatment for advanced prostate cancer. He found a recent article giving an update on the team's progress but it said little about the health of the coach. The only reference was at the end of the article.

> *"...Cedar Cliff High School has won 6 of the last 7 games with the kids being inspired by Coach McMillan who has yet to make it to the sidelines since beginning his treatment for prostate cancer. While he has been able to speak to the team from his home, he has been too ill to make a Friday night game. He hopes to be well enough to appear on the sidelines during the opening round of the district tournament where his team will face the Scranton High Tigers, ranked number 2 in the state. His presence would certainly be a welcome sign for the team and the community who supports him."*

The article was almost two months old. The team had obviously finished their season but he couldn't find any updates on their success in the state playoffs. Although disappointed he didn't get to Pennsylvania in time to provide a miracle to get the coach on the sidelines, Tom was determined to give the coach and his kids an inspirational next season. He looked into flights to Pennsylvania and where Camp Hill was in relation to the larger cities. He planned to visit Coach McMillan on Tuesday after the New Year and provide the coach with miracle #9a – the over. For miracle #9b – the under, Tom was at a loss. He couldn't find any stories that struck a chord with him, so he decided to hold on to 9b for a while and see what presented itself. Certainly #8b, the robber and rapist at the Mapco had been unplanned, but Tom hoped he wouldn't run into that type of situation again. He would prefer to plan ahead for 9b and 10b and avoid risking his life.

After the long holidays, Tom confirmed his plans to travel to Camp Hill. He told Laura he was going to look at a potential client's site and do some reconnaissance before approaching the client for work. It would be a quick trip, out late afternoon Tuesday and back mid afternoon Wednesday. He carried the little white lie to the office as well and disappeared alone Tuesday afternoon. He made it to Camp Hill late Tuesday night after driving two hours from the Philadelphia airport. He settled into a cheap hotel and browsed through the local phone book to look for the address of Bruce McMillan. Coming up empty, Tom decided to inquire about the coach the next day at some of the local haunts. Surely in a town of this size it shouldn't be difficult to find their superhero coach.

In the morning, Tom drove through the old downtown that was desperately hanging on to its quaint town-square layout. He found a diner that still seemed to be the center of the morning rush of a sleepy town. The place was buzzing with blue-collar workers readying for their workday and white-collar professionals meeting with clients. Tom chose a stool at the counter where he could casually interact with the waitresses and find out more about Coach McMillan. He decided to go under the guise of a reporter from a local Tennessee newspaper who wanted to do a story about high school coaches who had made a positive impact on kids. Between the waitress serving the counter and the two guys sitting next to him at the counter, Tom uncovered the coach's address—well at least the street name—without being too intrusive. After breakfast and using his map app for guidance, he drove toward Salaster Street while thinking through his reporter cover. He was concerned about showing up at the coach's door unannounced and expecting an interview. Tom decided he'd stretch the lie a bit further and tell the coach he was in the area this week and felt a face-to-face introduction would be better than a random phone request for an interview from a stranger. If the coach was uncomfortable giving an interview right now, then Tom was screwed. It was a weak guise but it was all he had for the moment. Luck would have to be on his side. Driving down Salaster Street, he approached a house with a speckling of signs in the yard. There was one large sign declaring this the residence of the Coach of the Cedar Cliff Colts. This represented the intertwining of high school football and community at its best where each player and coach had a sign in their yard with their respective position and jersey number. For the residence at 232 Salaster Street, the yard was also filled with signs of prayer and well wishes for an ailing, beloved coach.

Tom parked on the street and approached the front door with a steno pad in hand to better play the part of an old-school reporter. As he knocked on the door, he immediately noticed movement inside through a large picture window just to the left of the main entrance. Maybe his luck was holding and he hadn't traveled all this way just to find an empty house. A frail man gingerly opened the door and peered out at Tom with a genuine smile.

"Coach McMillan?"

"Yes."

"Hi my name is Tom Roddin. I wanted to introduce myself

in person and ask if you would be willing to schedule an interview with me sometime in the near future. I'm a reporter for the Jackson Sun in Jackson Tennessee."

"Hello Tom. Come on in. I would love to hear what brought a reporter all the way from Tennessee to our little borough of Camp Hill."

Coach McMillan moved aside and opened the door wider to let Tom pass. They moved into the living room and the coach motioned at two recliners facing the stone fireplace. He was weak enough to need a cane for support but the fire in his eyes and voice had not given in to the disease yet.

"What sort of story are you writing and how the hell did it lead you to me?" he asked with humble sarcasm.

"I'm doing a story about coaches and other educators who are having a positive influence on the lives of young people, particularly high school kids. I happened across an article where your players and the community were singing your praises about your leadership and how many players having come through your ranks are better for it."

"Well, they'll say anything to get their name in the paper these days," he joked trying to deflect any praise. "I am sure you have plenty of teachers in Tennessee that are deserving of the recognition."

"Yes sir. We do. But the more I researched the more I wanted to make it a national story about adults from all walks of life and all regions of the country. Besides, I thought Pennsylvania could use some positive press in light of the situation at one of your major college institutions." Tom had decided earlier that he didn't want to make reference to the scandal, but in the moment it seemed appropriate to make it clear that he was looking for the good to balance the evil in Pennsylvania. Too often the bad news got more press than the good.

"Well, I'm not sure if I'm the right person to interview but I'll be glad to chat for a bit. I am a bit removed from the kids this season trying to get well again. Cancer seems to have found a way into my life and turned it a bit upside down. But I am fighting and hoping with the prayers and support of my family and the community."

"With all due respect sir, I believe you are exactly the type of person I am looking for. The praise from your players, the parents, the community in general tells me that you've had a significant impact on the lives of many youth. I didn't expect you to do the interview today, unscheduled. My real intent was to meet you and see when you would be available, when you would have time to talk at your convenience. I completely understand if this is not a good time."

"I appreciate your consideration, but actually, now is a pretty good time. I had a treatment Monday and the second day is usually better than the day immediately after. My next treatment is tomorrow, so your timing is good. I'd be glad to talk for a while but I may not last longer than an hour. I seem to get tired very easily these days."

"I understand. Stop me anytime you want to finish. When did you start coaching?"

Tom and Bruce McMillan talked for nearly an hour and a half. They covered topics pertinent to Tom's pretend article and a variety of topics completely unrelated. Tom made indistinguishable notes on his pad to maintain the ruse but generally just listened to the man tell his life story, with infusions of wisdom and humble good deeds. Throughout the conversation Tom realized with each passing minute that this was a man with the utmost integrity, humble almost to a fault, and completely dedicated to being a mentor and counselor to the youth in his small universe. Bruce was very open about his battle with cancer and the fear of leaving this place at such an early age. He desperately missed the sidelines and the practice field and would trade anything to have those pleasures back in his life. Tom also noted the man had a deep faith in Hope, as he talked about beating the disease and moving on with his mission in life. As they talked about the disease and what it had done to his body, Tom began to understand how sick the coach really was. Although the official diagnosis was prostate cancer, the illness had affected his entire urinary tract including the bladder and lower intestines, which caused him unspeakable pain and discomfort. This, on top of the side effects from the chemo, had ravaged his body, turning him to a withered old man despite his young age of 51. In the 90 minutes Tom spent with Bruce he grew to love and respect him…a reaction that Tom had never experienced in such a short time and certainly one he hadn't expected.

When the 'interview' was over Tom stood up and faced Bruce still sitting in his chair. He seemed to be tired but also lost in thought with the last topic of their conversation. It was about Hope and how each man defined Hope. Bruce had said, "There's a difference between hope and desire. Desire is the wish that something will happen and it usually involves a bit of selfishness. Not always in a bad way, but it usually relates to something that is a personal benefit. Hope is far more mystical. It is a faith, a belief that some outcome will come about despite the odds against it. I usually see hope as more of good outcome. A miracle if you will, whereas desire can be either good or bad. I always feel that with hope, with miracles, there's always one on the way."

"I agree completely," Tom said with a conviction that the coach would never truly understand. "Hope for me removes fear from a situation. Not completely, I guess, but it lowers the fear factor enough to move forward. Even if Hope doesn't fulfill itself, it provides a mechanism to manage fear in a way that doesn't overwhelm the situation itself. Too much focus on the fear distracts a person from believing in and focusing on a positive outcome. We certainly need more Hope in the world. It's part of my story. I want to show some strong elements of good in our society in order to validate Hope for anyone willing to believe in it."

In an effort to shake Bruce out of his thoughts, Tom reached down and gently squeezed the sick man's shoulder. "Thanks for your time this afternoon. You are an inspiration to so many people and now you can add me to that long list."

"Oh, well thank you Tom," coach stammered as he came out of his thoughts. He rose from his chair with the help of the cane and extended a hand to Tom. "It's been a pleasure talking to you. I look forward to your article."

"It may be a few more months before I publish it, but I will definitely send you a copy. Bruce, I have Hope that you will get better soon. You will be yelling at the boys from the sidelines before you know it."

Chapter Forty-Six

The remainder of Tom's week was as satisfying as he could remember in a long time. His visit with Coach McMillan, coupled with his encounter with Halle, had reaffirmed his belief in the gift and how powerful its message was. As he neared the end of the journey he thought more and more about his post-gift life. He recognized how the gift had changed him and also how it had not. It hadn't corrupted his pure heart. It hadn't created an unfamiliar desire for power and it certainly hadn't affected his ability to do things, act on things with a slant toward the selfish. He was still Tom…but with a deeper perspective on religious tolerance, human abuse, and the need to seek out and recognize the smallest slivers of good in the world. He wholeheartedly believed he had validated Hope for a small subset of people and that that Hope—one individual at a time— could spread to potentially infinite dimensions. It was his goal to continue helping people believe in Hope even if he didn't have the influence to make choices for others.

He picked up the phone in his office and dialed the number of Martha Chalmer, Sophie's mom.

"Hello?"

"Hi Martha, this is Tom Roddin. I met you and Sophie in the hospital last month."

"Oh yes. The stab wound guy," she joked. "How are you recovering?"

"I am fully healed and 100% again. Thanks for asking."

"Good. Glad to hear you're ok."

"I wanted to check in on Sophie and see how her latest check up went. I was hoping we could have another celebratory sundae."

"That's nice of you to call. Sophie went back to the doctor just before Christmas with some pains in her lower back. They had to delay her monthly scan—the one a month after we met you—so they finally did it when we went in with the back pain. Unfortunately..." Martha paused for a moment apparently choking back some tears that Tom immediately felt over the phone. "...they found some spots at the bottom of her spine where they believe the cancer has metastasized."

"I am so sorry," Tom replied. "How did Sophie deal with the news?"

"Like an angel as always. She's probably stronger than we are."

"Is she back getting treatment yet?"

"The doctors are unwilling to expose her to additional chemo this soon. Radiation is out of the question due to the location of the masses although the doctors said this type of mass probably wouldn't respond well to radiation anyway. They're putting on the table the possibility of an operation but there are mixed opinions about the risk versus the reward. It's a very complicated procedure."

"Is she at home? In pain? Or have they been able to relieve the pain for her?"

"She was home during the week of Christmas, but had to go back to the hospital last week. The pain gets worse every day and the hospital is the only place they can administer the morphine to manage it. So, she'll be there until they decide what to do about her treatment." Martha had recovered her cracking voice but Tom could sense the exhaustion in her soul from the hundreds of hours of worrying about the life of her child.

280

"Martha, would it be ok if I went to see Sophie in the hospital? I would certainly understand if you objected or if Sophie might not want strange company." Tom made this last statement in an effort to give Martha an out without having to admit that she didn't want a strange man visiting her child in the hospital.

"Sophie would love to see you and Larry and I have no objection. It's strange that you called." Martha paused for a brief moment. "Sophie has talked about you ever since the day we had ice cream together. I don't know what you said or did but you've made an impression on her. We kept telling her that we probably wouldn't see or hear from you again, but she insisted that 'He'll call. You'll see. He's my guardian angel'. Please don't take offense, but we kept hoping she would forget about you so she wouldn't be disappointed. Yet, here you are, reappearing again just like you promised. I think she holds you in some sort of revered regard, Mr. Roddin. Like I said, you certainly made an impression on her."

Tom was without words and the silence became awkward before he found the courage and words to speak. "Well, to be honest, it was a very brief introduction we had but her spirit in the midst of all her trials really made an impression on me. I've been thinking about her ever since and have Hoped that her remission was permanent. I have no doubt she is fighting like hell despite the new prognosis."

"Her courage and acceptance of the situation are far beyond her years. I just wish she could be a worry-free kid again."

"Please tell her I said hello and that I'll be coming to see her in a few days. I have some other commitments tonight and tomorrow but I'll be by Friday to see her. She's a special person, Martha. Whether she knows it or not she will have an effect on many people including ones she doesn't even know yet."

Chapter Forty-Seven

When Friday came, Tom left work early to make a run to the hospital. His first stop was to his old friend, Lester Howe, who had been admitted two days earlier after breaking a hip during a fall. Lester had been wandering around his own neighborhood apparently disoriented and had fallen on the front stoop of a neighbor's house as he tried to pry the front door open. Thinking he was at his own house and the door was just stuck, Lester was forcing the lock open when the startled owner quickly opened the door sending Lester reeling onto the threshold, head in the house and legs flailing on the porch.

As he entered the room of his famous hockey-playing friend, Tom was shocked at the sight of the once physical specimen. Lester was thin, frail almost and had more tubes coming in and out of him than he could count. He walked to the bed and reached out to take Lester's hand. The man gave a sudden scream and stared at Tom through clouded eyes.

"Who are you? And what the hell are you doing in my room trying to hold my hand? Are you some kinda faggot or something?"

"It's me Lester. It's Tom, Tom Roddin. I just came in to check on you…to see how you're doing."

"Tom who? What are you doing in my house?"

"Trust me Lester. We've been friends a long time. And you're in the hospital, not your house."

"Bullshit! Get the hell out of here before I…Colleen, where's my shotgun? Someone's broken into the house and trying to rape us!"

Tom knew Lester was talking to the ghost of his long-deceased wife. He had no idea Lester's condition had deteriorated so quickly. He had visited him in late November after the Mapco incident giving Lester the opportunity to scold his young friend. "See Tom. You're always trying to be a hero. Look where that got you." Tom knew Lester's comments were dripping with sarcasm. Lester was the type of guy who would stick up for the afflicted and the weak no matter what the consequences. During that visit Lester was already showing signs of significant deterioration. His memory wasn't as sharp as it was a few months earlier but he had certainly recognized Tom as a friend and not as a rapist. He had known for a year that this might need to be one of his choices. He hoped the gift would be completed before Lester got to this stage, relieving Tom of a difficult choice. But based on the last visit, Tom began to surrender to the idea of giving Lester his wish. Standing there in the hospital, Tom knew what had to be done. Despite his reluctance to use an under on a friend, Lester's current state of mind coupled with Tom's now pure belief in and understanding of the gift helped ease the choice for him. Before Lester's ranting attracted the attention of the nurses, Tom calmly leaned over Lester, placing his hand on his friend's left shoulder and gently squeezed while whispering in his ear, "Time to take you out old friend. I love you and say hello to Colleen."

With that, Tom slowly backed away as Lester relaxed himself in the bed. Tom gave his friend one last smile and walked out of the room. Halfway down the hall he heard the sudden buzzing of alarms and the clamor of feet as several nurses hurried towards Lester Howe's room.

Tom walked the crosswalk between the main hospital and the Monroe Carell Jr. Children's Hospital wing at Vanderbilt. As he walked, he tried to switch gears and focus on Sophie and her plight. Letting go of his close friend so quickly and without much debate was difficult. But for Sophie, his choice would be rewarding enough to counter the life he just took. Tom reached the girl's hallway and stopped outside her room to steady himself. With a deep breath of stale hospital air, he entered the room with a big smile and a warm heart.

"Hey there Sophie!" he said with as much excitement as he could muster.

"Hello there Tom," Sophie returned. Her sly little smile was part glad to see him and part testing his patience by calling him by his first name.

"It's Mr. Roddin to you young lady," he stated with a serious face that he couldn't hold long enough.

"Yes sir, Tom," Sophie laughed.

"How you doing Soph? Your mom tells me you're having some pains in your back. You managing ok?"

"As best I can. It hurts, I can't deny that. These little spots just don't want to go away."

"They must have a sweet tooth since they like to stick to you."

"Whatever! They're a pain…get it pain, hurt. I am so funny." Sophie giggled but with less enthusiasm than she had a month ago.

"Do you understand what the doctors are going to do next?"

"Not yet. They seem to be arguing about the best way to attack the little buggers. They think I'm not listening or understanding them when they talk to my parents. But I get that this is serious. I know that I could die."

"We all could die Sophie. We just have to keep Hoping that the best outcome can happen for any of us. Hope is a powerful thing. Don't lose it."

"I know. I still have hope. Somehow it keeps me from being sad, makes me feel safe. My hope makes me think about today and not worry about tomorrow."

Tom almost started crying when he heard this sweet little girl utter those words. Her thoughts were more grown up than anything he had heard from adults in similar situations. He wondered if somehow Sophie and Coach McMillan were long-time friends. "You're so brave Sophie. I think your Hope will save you quicker than the doctors' medicines."

"Tom?"

"Sophie?"

"I like you. I know we don't know each other well but since the first time I met you I felt like you got me. You have a protective way about you that I like. It's comforting. So, I feel like I can tell you something and you'll understand."

"Tell me what Sophie?" asked Tom with a slow uncomfortable drawl, worrying about her next confession.

"I'm not afraid of dying Tom. I don't mean that just to be brave. I really mean it. I'm not afraid of it. If my cancer is going to kill me then I'm ready for it. What I am afraid of is having to battle my sickness and pain for a long, long time. I'm not saying I wish I were dead. No way. I want to beat this disease and I hope I do. But if it comes down to me dying, then I am ok with that. I just don't want to be sick and deformed forever."

Tom was unable to respond. He looked at Sophie for what must have been several minutes trying to find the words of comfort. Before he recovered, she said, "I could never tell my parents this, they'd think I was giving up. But I know you understand what I'm saying. I don't want it, but I'm ok with it if that is the choice."

Tom reached over and grasped her hand. "You're going to be ok Sophie. I'm going to help you Hope."

<u>**Chapter Forty-Eight**</u>

Just then his phone lit up with a text from Laura.

Anna hurt, just arrived at the Vanderbilt hospital. Call or come immediately!

As he read the text, Sophie could see the concern on his face.

"You ok?" she asked.

"I have to go check on something Sophie. But I'll be back in a little while and I'll show you how strong Hope is."

Tom rushed out of the room and asked the nearest nurse which way the ER was. As he reached the ER waiting room he asked the clerk at the admittance desk if a young girl and her mother had arrived.

"What's the name, sir?"

"Roddin. Anna Roddin."

"Yes sir. Are you a relative?"

"I'm her father," he said with a little irritability.

"They're down the hall in room 214."

Tom ran the length of the hallway to 214 and turned to find Laura against the far wall while a team of 4 or 5 doctors and nurses attended to Anna. Laura was crying and Anna was unconscious on the bed. The hospital staff was poking and prodding Anna with a variety of medical devices in a surreal dance of movements that were oddly in sync with music generated by the life support machines.

Tom went to Laura and hugged her tightly. "What happened?"

"Anna was attacked on her way home from school. She, Isabella, and Catherine wanted to go to Catherine's house to start their science fair project. I thought it would be fine." Laura was crying hysterically now and speaking between quick gasps of air. "You know Catherine only lives two blocks from the school. They've done it a million times. Someone approached the girls and starting asking them strange questions. They did exactly what they were supposed to do. They walked straight into the yard of the nearest house to get a neighbor to protect them."

"The man ran after the girls and happened to grab Anna. They all screamed and apparently Anna kicked the man over and over but couldn't get away. He dragged her toward his car even though she was still fighting. The girls said he stopped on the sidewalk unable to control Anna and started hitting her. By the time the neighbor came out to help, the man was hitting Anna with a baton or something and she was just lying there. He tried to run away but the neighbor tackled him. She's non-responsive Tom. Oh my God! How could this happen to a little girl."

Tom hugged her again and asked, "Where is the attacker now?"

"He's in police custody or maybe here at the hospital. The neighbor nearly beat him to death."

"What did they say about Anna when they first brought her here?"

"Catherine's mom came and got me and I rode in the ambulance with Anna. I don't know...they were trying to get her to respond to questions."

Tom turned and looked at the team working on Anna and listened intently to see if he understood their language. The one thing he did understand was the steady tone of the monitor that indicated a flat line on the screen. Much to their objections, one of the nurses led them out of the room as the team began prepping the paddles to reverse the monitor's assumption.

After 20 agonizing minutes of waiting and wondering, a doctor emerged from Anna's room and approached Tom and Laura.

"We've stabilized Anna but she's still unconscious. Consider it a comatose state but one that is probably more medically induced rather than due to her injuries. We believe we can bring her back to consciousness but are not sure it will be to her benefit just yet. She suffered severe head trauma from the beating and we want the swelling in her brain to go down before considering other options."

"What other options?" asked Tom quickly focusing on the dangers she might be facing.

"If the swelling doesn't come down on its own then we may need to do surgery to take the pressure off the brain and minimize the potential for further damage."

"Further damage?" asked Laura acute to the doctor's choice of words.

"As I said, she's suffered serious trauma to the head. As of now we're unsure whether any of the damage will have a permanent effect on her brain. Once the swelling goes down, she may have no lasting effects. But we just don't know for sure at this time. All of her body's systems and organs are working properly, but the swelling is a concern. The next 12 to 24 hours will be telling. She's stable now and we're waiting for test results that will help us determine the best course for her."

"So there's a possibility that she may have permanent brain damage to some degree or another?" asked Laura in disbelief.

"There is that possibility but it's too early to tell now. She momentarily quit breathing earlier but we were able to revive her. The brief lack of oxygen was not long enough to cause any damage to her brain function but the damage done by the beating may have long-term effects that we are unsure of now. I know this sounds frightening, but really the next 12 hours will tell us more and we can assess the best course of action."

Laura and Tom were both in such a state of shock that neither had the mindset to thank the doctor for bringing Anna back to life before he turned and walked away. They walked into her room and stood over her bed thinking through the innocence of their own child and the fragile life now being held in the balance by a wait-and-see period of time. It was 5:30 in the evening and the hospital was busy with preparations for a shift change. People were coming and going through the hallways and the waiting room as if it were just another day. For Tom and Laura, this was not another day. It was a day where they faced the most frightening scenario a parent could ever imagine.

Around 7:00 p.m. Laura checked in with Molly to make sure Brady was home safely and taken care of. She spoke to him briefly updating his sister's condition and reassuring him that everything would be ok. "We'll be staying at the hospital tonight and Molly will be with you at the house."

"Tell her I love her momma."

"I will sweetie. Everything's going to be ok. I'll call you first thing in the morning with any news."

She reluctantly hung up the phone wishing she could put her protective arms around her healthy child. Disoriented, she wandered to the waiting area to find Tom.

"Are you ok?" she asked. Tom had an intensely angered look on his face that she rarely saw.

"I just don't understand. How could someone do this to a little girl? How sick do you have to be to beat a person half your size to the point of death?"

"She's not dead Tom. She's hurt, yes, but she's still with us."

"The police came by a while ago and told me the guy is still in the hospital and will probably stay the night. When the doctors release him, they'll book him and charge him with aggravated assault, attempted kidnapping, and a few other things that I didn't understand or care about. They said he'll never see the light of day again, but I'm not sure I believe them. I asked if they knew why he beat her? They had no answer since he was still unconscious. Apparently he's not in much better shape than Anna. Why didn't he run away when things went bad? Why did he stand there and beat her in broad daylight knowing that he wouldn't get away? I just don't understand the minds of people who have this kind of violence in them."

"I don't know honey." Laura slowed her breathing and speech trying to counter the fierce mood that had fallen over Tom. She was always the calm, positive one when it came to dealing with traumatic issues in their lives. Tom was cool-headed and collected with friends and co-workers, but when it came to issues in the family, his reactions were not always calming. "He'll be punished but that is not our concern right now. We need to be strong for Anna and make sure she gets better."

"God Laura, what if she has permanent damage? What if…"

"She's stable and there's a good chance the swelling will go down and there'll be no damage at all. We'll know more in the morning. There's nothing we can do now except Hope."

Tom was crouched over his lap in a sitting position, wringing his hands in an attempt to release the anger from his body. His face was contorted in an odd dichotomy of grief and hatred. Half his face was ready to kill, the other half seemed to be crying. Inside, his mind was racing toward a quick conclusion about the remaining numerators and denominators of the gift. His promise to Sophie had long left his now-troubled thoughts.

Laura saw the struggle within him and wondered how his thoughts and actions might be biased by the gift. Did he still possess the gift or had his journey already ended? She noticed the fire of revenge in his eyes and worried what actions he may take before thinking through the long-term perspective he needed to be truly comforted. She sat beside him and reached for his hand.

"Tom, when I was 14, I was babysitting for the neighbors who were at a party that was probably going to last late into the night. I had put Selma, their four-year-old daughter, to bed and was watching something stupid on TV when there was a knock on the door. Normally, I would never have answered the knock, but I recognized the car in the driveway as a close friend of the parents, so I opened the door. Stan Michie came in and apologized for frightening me. He'd just left the same party as the parents and was coming by to borrow some tools from Mr. Patterson. I'd only met Stan Michie once or twice in passing at their house and really knew nothing about him. But he was a friend of my neighbors, in his late 30's or early 40's, and seemed like nice man, so I let him in to get the tools. I didn't even think about why he left the party so early or why he decided to come by when they weren't there. None of the normal questions or safety alerts went off in my head as a 14-year-old that now seem obvious as an adult. So, he went to the laundry room and started shuffling around in the drawers and cabinets. A few minutes later, he came out with a screwdriver, pliers, and a large wrench, which I now know is called a pipe wrench. I remember the day I found out what the name of that tool was…I still can't look at one without a sudden urge to vomit. He walked into the den, sat on the couch, and nonchalantly asked what I was watching. Thinking he was just being friendly but getting a little uncomfortable, I told him I was watching *Overboard.* Five minutes and a few strange questions later he had managed to move towards my end of the couch and was sitting next to me with little room to spare. It all happened so fast, that I didn't have time to react. At 14, a protest was more awkward than just sitting there hoping nothing strange was going to happen."

Tom was stiff in his chair with an intense look on his face as Laura continued the story.

"I don't even remember what he was saying while he was sliding down the couch to get closer. I have played it back in my mind a million times and I still don't remember anything suspicious or unusual about his movement until he was actually right next to me. It was only then I knew something was not right but I didn't know how to diffuse the situation that was developing. He casually put his arm on the back of the couch…around me but not touching me yet…and asked if I had ever kissed a boy. Never looking away from the TV I said, 'No.' He said, 'Well I can teach you how so the boys will really like you when you're ready.' I immediately stood up and said, 'I don't think that's a good idea. I'm going to get some water. Did you get the tools you needed?' He quickly jumped up and followed me to the kitchen where he pressed himself against me, pinning my hips against the counter. I was terrified! I had no idea what was going on or what was about to happen. He just stood there for a minute and stared at my face thinking thoughts that I can only now as an adult begin to imagine."

"Jesus Laura…I am so sorry. You don't have to continue if…" said Tom sympathetically.

"No. Let me finish. There was a loud noise back by the bedrooms that startled both of us and loosened his focus on me. Just then Selma came running into the kitchen crying and scared because she thought she heard thunder. He immediately backed away and turned towards Selma to say hello. She didn't even acknowledge him and jumped into my arms burying her head into my shoulder for comfort. I have never in my life so loved a hug like the one Selma gave me that night. Even with the adoration and love I have for our own kids, I've never felt so much protection and relief from any other hug. Stan Michie turned toward the front entrance and calmly announced that it was time for him to leave. I carefully followed him to the door keeping plenty of distance between us so he didn't get the impression that I was 'chasing' him. At the front door, he turned to me and said in a steely voice, 'I think it is better for you and your safety not to tell anyone I was here. I trust Selma will not remember enough to tell her parents since she is so young and probably half asleep. Who would believe her anyway?' He was hardly off the porch before I locked the door and took Selma to her room. I remember lying down with her trying to give her more comfort than she was unknowingly giving me. She eventually fell asleep and I cried in petrified silence until her parents came home." These last words trailed off into a soft voice as Laura was staring off into her memory.

Tom sat in silence unsure of what to say and why Laura was telling him this story now, after so many years. He could understand her intentions to bury this experience deep down where no one, including herself, could find it. But burying things was not a habit Laura usually employed. She was more the type to expose it even if only to one friend or relative, analyze it, then move on. Tom assumed she had never brought it up with him because she had talked to someone long before they met to get it over with and out of her system.

Startled from her own thoughts, Laura calmly said, "I have never told anyone about that experience. It was so surreal and started and ended so quickly that I still wonder if it really happened. I mean, I know it did, but it almost seems like it happened in another lifetime."

Tom was shocked to hear that she had not fully digested the experience by letting it out before now. "I can't believe you've been keeping that secret all these years. Were you really that afraid of him that you kept yourself from telling someone about it?"

"Not afraid, not really embarrassed or guilty. I guess I was just determined enough to never let it happen again that I just pushed it away. I probably would have felt differently had something more happened that night. But given the relatively safe outcome, I just internalized it."

"Did you ever see the guy again?"

Laura looked directly at Tom and held his eyes with a focus that virtually paralyzed his ability to look away. "Tom, a few months later I was given an opportunity to make some choices...for other people...that had consequences beyond what I had ever imagined. Choices that challenged me and ultimately changed me. When I say change, I mean validated a belief in myself and clarified some spiritual aspects that I had long questioned. It solidified my belief that yes there is *something* that intervenes in our lives in a silent but very strong, definitive way."

"Laura, what do you mean by...choices?" Tom asked with a slight hint of suspicion and fear of the answer.

"I saw Stan Michie one more time in my life. It was a year and half after the incident. I didn't speak to him or even make eye contact. But I think he knew I saw him. By that time I had lost my hatred of Mr. Michie...it had turned to pity. I could have easily made a choice to get revenge, but there was something unsatisfying about the thought. I came to realize that revenge doesn't justify choices. Revenge may strike back to ease the pain of one person, but our choices, yours and mine, serve the purpose of many, not just one."

Tom sat in stunned silence at the revelation he was having. How could this be? His wife was telling him things that she knew only he would understand. Things that were perfectly aligned with the gift and his own struggles with justifying the use of the gift. Here she was telling him she understood what he had been feeling for the past 14 months. "Laura...do you know about choices given to certain chosen people?"

"Yes Tom. I do."

"You know about the gift of Hope?"

"Yes. The gift was presented to me when I was 15. Those choices changed the way I approach life."

"How long have you known about me having the gift?"

"I realized it, to my own astonishment, last spring when you were struggling with Barry and his outrageous behavior in the firm."

"And you didn't say anything to me?"

"No. I couldn't. I was shocked when it all came together for me. For starters, I couldn't believe that two people who knew each other – much less who were married – could ever possess the gift, even if it was at very different times. The close proximity of two gift givers utterly confused me when I tried to comprehend the reason or randomness of the chances. I can't imagine that has happened often. Secondly, I didn't want you to allow me influence over your choices. This is your journey. I had my journey and you needed to make your own independent choices in order to preserve the integrity of the individual human decisions the gift is based on. My instructor told me that sharing the knowledge of the gift would ultimately make the choices a group decision. She believed this would compromise the true intention of the gift—to have individual human emotions from pure-hearted people make choices for the Brahman."

"Brahman?"

"Yes. She was a practicing Hindu. The Brahman is like a God but without any human-like personality or form. Anyway, in her opinion the gift gave the Brahman or *something* divine intervention with a human element that it could not exercise because it was not inherently human."

Tom was amazed that the integrity of the gift had not been compromised over the years by individual bias. Even more amazing was the confirmation that the gift had been present in the world for at least 26 years. Most likely it had been around much longer since he doubted Laura's instructor was the first gifter.

"My instructor, or rather her instructor, had a similar view of keeping the gift a secret," said Tom. "She told me when the decision became influenced by too many people it led to corruption."

"I agree. For the choices to remain pure they must be made individually. So I didn't say anything because I knew you would want to discuss your choices if for no other reason than to help justify them. Given our differences in religious philosophies, I didn't think it would be fair for me to bias your decisions with my beliefs or justifications. Tom, you have a pure heart. I have no doubt of that. But I've noticed how you've struggled with justifying some of your decisions. It hurt me to watch and I wanted to wrap you in my arms, tell you that I knew, and comfort you. But I just couldn't. Not then. I have only told you now because I assume you are at the end of your journey and I can see the revenge factor in your eyes with Anna's attacker. I am not going to counsel you, the choice is yours, but I wanted to share my story to give you a perspective from a typical victim. The gift is precious and I don't want to see you regret using it in an act of revenge that will only save your own pain."

"Do you not think using the gift on this animal could keep him from hurting others?"

"I can't answer that for you. As I said, I don't want to get involved with the decision or debate the gift's use with you…it wouldn't be fair to the purpose. I just wanted you to hear a related story. I don't want to know how, when, or to whom the gift has been used. I will never ask you about your choices, including the choice before you now. In return, I hope that you will never ask me about the choices I made as a 15-year-old girl."

"You're a much stronger person than I am Laura. You have such clarity in life about what is right and wrong and what to be indifferent about. Even at 15, I think you were much better equipped to handle the gift than I am as an adult." Tom's eyes welled up for reasons he couldn't even pinpoint…love and fear for his daughter's life, relief that his journey was almost over and yet a longing to keep the gift forever, his love of the person sitting next to him sharing something so intimate that no other couple could ever experience. All the emotions came together in an overwhelming blend of purity. "I love you dearly Laura. I've never wavered in that love, since the first time I met you. And now with this secret between us...I can't thank you enough for finding me and letting me into your life."

"Tom, you are the most remarkable man I know with an amazing ability to love. There is no other person that I would trust more with the gift of Hope than you."

They sat together in silence for a while before Tom stood up and said, "There's someone I have to go see."

He wandered back over to the children's cancer wing to see Sophie. When he got to her room he saw Martha and Larry sitting quietly with Sophie sleeping peacefully in the bed. As he walked in he noticed both parents had been crying and were obviously distraught. As they turned to acknowledge his presence, he looked squarely at Sophie's face and realized the color had completely gone from her complexion. She was hooked up to a ventilator and was breathing steadily with the help of the machine.

"Is Sophie ok?" Tom asked quietly.

Martha was unable to speak and began sobbing heavily. Larry turned to Tom and said, "She's had a setback. It appears that her previous treatments coupled with the new masses and the morphine have taken a toll on her. She's had what the doctors are comparing to a stroke. Her brain isn't getting enough oxygen so she's losing some normal motor functions. They believe she'll have trouble with muscle control in her hands and arms as well as speech problems. But, at least she's alive. They want to keep her in a comatose state for another 24 hours to let the blood flow to her brain stabilize."

"How...how could it have happened so suddenly? I was just here talking to her a few hours ago."

"It was unexpected but the doctors were concerned about this happening. It's why they were reluctant to perform any surgery earlier. They just weren't sure if her body could handle it. Apparently, it couldn't handle the surgery or the new diagnosis. The stroke hit around 5:00 and she slipped into a coma shortly afterward. The threat of her dying is mostly over, but there will certainly be life-altering permanent effects." Larry was being upbeat but Tom could tell her life might not be worth the life that lay in front of her.

Larry couldn't speak anymore and began crying silently as he turned to look helplessly at his alive but altered daughter. Tom put his arm around Larry and touched Martha's arm.

"I am so sorry. Sophie has more courage than anyone I've ever met. She told me earlier..." Tom hesitated for a moment recalling their last words together. "She told me she loved the life you had given her and that all the masses in the world couldn't take that away from her. If you don't mind, I'd like to come back in a little bit and sit with her briefly."

Martha and Larry nodded their approval but couldn't find any words to part with. Tom stumbled back to the ER and found the hallway where two policemen were drinking coffee while guarding a particular room. Not wanting to draw suspicion, he sat down in the nearby waiting room where he could watch the guarded room and observe their diligence in keeping people out or, more importantly, someone in. A flood of emotions hit Tom and he began weeping uncontrollably. He had been seconds away from making an over choice for Sophie so she could live a normal healthy life free from pain and worry. Now, he was faced with an impossible decision with his last two choices. 10a and 10b. Could he protect Anna without the choice of being selfish? Would he be betraying Sophie if he didn't give her the choice as he promised? Could she even be saved at this point given her condition? His mind fell back to his friend Adam who had ALS. The gift was able to stop the progression of his disease but was unable to reverse any of the existing symptoms. Using the gift on Sophie may only bring her back to a conscious state but wouldn't necessarily restore her health. And then there was Anna's attacker. Did he deserve a choice to ensure he didn't harm anyone else or was that thought based on revenge for Anna? Tom cried and anguished over the situation for what seemed like an eternity. There was no good answer to his questions; yet, deep in his heart he knew what he had to do. Gathering his emotions, he glanced down the hallway as the guards left their posts and left the attacker's room temporarily vulnerable. With firm resolution, Tom got up from his chair and walked down the hallway.

Chapter Forty-Nine

As he entered the room he could only hear the steady pulse of the machines providing life and stability to the figure in the bed. The room was empty except for the patient and the lights were low enough to give the face a sense of life. He stood over the bed, gently reached his hand to the patient's shoulder, and leaned toward the ear.

"You are a divine princess among mere mortals sweet child. Rest in peace and greet our maker with the same innocence that you possessed here on earth."

With a gentle squeeze, he kissed Sophie's forehead, dropping a tear on her hair. He was remembering her wishes and her bravery in facing a situation like this. *I just don't want to be sick and deformed forever.* "I'm so sorry I couldn't come sooner, Sophie," he whispered with a quivering voice. "You deserved to see the better side of Hope. May your parents find comfort in your passing, knowing that you will not have to fight for the rest of your life."

He walked back to the ER wing where Anna was safe from her attacker and sat next to her bed. Tom was still distraught over the decision to relieve Sophie of a life that would be tangled in permanent frustration and physical limitations. She would have been stripped of the quality of life that a child so much deserves. He had been too late in making his choice for Sophie. He was certain she was beyond the help that even the gift could properly provide.

He looked at his own child, examining every line in her face. Despite having no expression, he could visualize the way Anna's lips would move to create a smile. He could picture the contortion her muscles would make when she was embarrassed by her parents. He could see the movement it would take for her to give him that look of undying love. The look only a child can give their own parent when all things were right in the world. The look she would give her older brother. The look Anna would someday give her husband. The look she would unconditionally give her own children. Sitting there looking into the life of his child, her future, he realized that Hope for Anna could be validated for more than just himself. Physically, she was hurt, but without the same threat of permanent damage that Sophie's body faced. Tom raised his hand and placed it on Anna's shoulder. With a slight squeeze, he whispered, "Wake up my sweet little angel. It's time to meet Hope."

AFTERWORD

Dear Coach – I Hope this letter finds you healthy and happily back in the meeting room with your players and soon to be on the sidelines making a difference. Thanks for our talk…you have inspired me in ways I cannot explain. I have included a copy of the column that finally got published. Thanks for validating Hope for so many in this world.

Yours,

Tom Roddin

The Jackson Sun – March 23, 2013

From my humble existence as an architect, father, and husband, I was viewing life through the rose-colored lenses of an upbringing where good and evil go hand in hand without much concern for the cause of either. Everything in the world would work according to a plan pre-destined for the human race. While I sympathized with tragedy, I always shrugged it off as a distant necessary evil that was a part of our existence. The good showed itself in random kind acts from a minority of do-gooders. Thanks to a new and unexpected friendship, I experienced an awakening nearly 16 months ago that set me on a path to seek out Hope even in the faintest of light. What I found is a testament to the human spirit and an idea that Hope is validated in the smallest of acts from people whose lives, jobs, and experiences create miracles every day.

For every tragic death from an illness, there are three miraculous stories of survival where the odds have been beaten. Stories where the caregivers along with the patients have willed their Hope to create an inexplicable outcome. This has never been more evident than with the children I met who faced incredibly difficult roads for recovery from potentially terminal illnesses. Despite the pain, surgeries, and general loss of childhood, they continued to believe in Hope and fight against tremendously bad odds. Hope seemed to give them strength of survival that was inspiring to all who cared for and loved them. Not all Hope is validated by successful outcomes. But in its least common denominator, faith in Hope lessens the fear of the battle in seemingly desperate circumstances.

I have found the validation of Hope in those who are suffering at the hands of other humans. It sometimes comes in the unfortunate form of death...when an abuser is removed from the lives of those they abuse, leaving no holes or grief. I am not talking about murder on the part of the abused, but rather luck or chance where the abuser has run into natural or self-inflicted elimination. Hope for relief from emotional and physical pain that has been validated by a seemingly natural elimination process. While any death is a tragedy, I have seen the relief and the lifting of spirit when someone is freed from the bondage of fear that an abuser can inflict.

Also, I have witnessed the validation of Hope from those who have continuously used their position of authority and influence for good. Yes, I said power and good in the same sentence. These are the teachers, coaches, nurses, general caregivers, CEOs, managers, and parents who provide nurturing and guidance to those they come in contact with despite their position's charter to be 'in charge'. As a side effect, or rather side job to their normal responsibilities, they take the extra time and effort to mentor, support, and change the lives of those around them. One 'friend' in particular is the football coach of the Cedar Cliff Colts in Pennsylvania. Parents and the community have entrusted Coach McMillan for over 20 years to improve the football skills of young men. In addition to the success he has found at his real job, Coach McMillan provides a service that is neither paid for nor recognized by any trophy or title...he creates men. He taught young men to hold themselves to a standard based on a self-defined moral creed combined with a long-lost belief in traditional chivalry.

Talking to the players who have passed under his tutelage, 'Coach', as he is affectionately referred to, has been the biggest positive influence in their lives, sometimes more than their own fathers. He and many other ordinary people in 'power' have provided Hope in extraordinary ways and have validated that Hope through belief, trust, and counsel.

This journey, as I like to call my quest to discover the contagious element of Hope, has opened my eyes to the miracles that occur every day if we are willing to see them. It has inspired me to look for opportunities to validate Hope in my own life and in the lives of others. With every validation of Hope comes another believer that Hope can be validated for them. It can roll and roll and roll on in exponential fashion like a trending topic on Twitter. The difference is its longevity. Encourage it to move forward through your own actions.

Grant Fletcher Lives in Nashville, Tennessee with his family. Author information and ordering can be found at www.grantwfletcher.com. (don't forget the W. or you'll get a stunt man in Hollywood!)

Thanks to all who helped shape this book with honest critiques of the early versions…you have drastically improved the final product. Hope you've enjoyed the journey as much I enjoyed creating it.

Made in the USA
Coppell, TX
26 March 2022

75569974R00184